Bedtime Erotica

Lexy
Harper

Bedtime Erotica

Please practise safe sex.

All characters in this publication are fictitious and any resemblance to real persons, living or dead, is purely coincidental.

The author and publisher specifically disclaim any responsibility for any liability, loss or risk, which is incurred as a consequence, directly or indirectly, of the use and application of any of the contents of this book.

The text of this publication or any part thereof may not be reproduced or transmitted in any form or by any means, electronic or mechanical, including photocopying, recording, storage in an information retrieval system, or otherwise, without the written permission of the publisher or author, except for brief quotes used in reviews.

First published in Great Britain 2008

Copyright © 2005 Lexy Harper
All Rights Reserved.
www.lexyharper.com

Published by Ebonique Publishing, London.
ISBN-13: 978-0-9556986-1-3

CONTENTS

To people everywhere who love a good *fucking* story.

ANOTHER WOMAN

*V*alerie Roberts tested a single grain of basmati rice between two fingers to ensure it had softened sufficiently. It had. Smiling, she lifted the cover of the saucepan and checked the chicken korma curry simmering gently on the adjacent hob, then pulled her apron off before turning both knobs on the electric cooker off, leaving the latent heat to finish cooking the meal.

Suddenly, without warning, she was grabbed from behind and held against a hard body.

"Don't scream," a man's voice whispered threateningly in her ear as his hands came up and grasped her breasts through her denim dress.

"My husband is coming home any minute now," she warned, trying to keep the panic out of her voice.

"I will fuck you before he gets here."

"Please, there is money in the house and my jewellery. Just take those and go!"

"I don't want money or jewellery, I want *pussy*."

He spun her around in his arms and she screamed as she came face-to-face with a man wearing a black ski-mask.

"I'm going to fuck you right here in the kitchen."

He pushed her against the refrigerator, pulled the zipper on the front of her dress down and looked at her for a moment.

"Your husband is a *very* lucky man."

Cupping her naked breasts, he bent his head and took a nipple into his mouth. She moaned as he started sucking it firmly. Her breasts were very sensitive; she couldn't help the pleasure that coiled around her insides.

"You're a hot one, aren't you? I bet your husband doesn't fuck you enough. Don't worry, I'll make up for the neglect."

He moved to her other breast and against her will she found herself cupping his head as he sucked hard on her nipple. He slid his hand upwards between her legs and she tensed as his fingers touched her naked pussy.

"You *really* are a hot one. No underwear—I think you've been waiting here for me to come and fuck you."

"No!" she denied. "I'm waiting for my husband to come home. He doesn't like me to wear underwear."

"Lucky for me then!"

She tried to keep her legs pressed together but his mouth on her breast was so tormenting she found herself opening her legs wide as he pushed two fingers inside her and thrust them slowly back and forth.

"Stroke my cock for me," he commanded.

"No!"

Abruptly, he stopped touching her, unzipped his pants and pulled his semi-erect cock out. "Suck it."

"No."

"I *said*, 'suck it'. Don't make me have to force you!"

He pushed her to her knees and placed the head of his erection against her lips. She had no choice but to open her mouth.

"Open wider, I want you to take this whole cock into your mouth."

She complied, letting him slip it all the way into her throat. He held her head and fed his cock to her with gentle thrusts. He was hard in seconds.

"You're very good. My cock hasn't been sucked like this in years. You have a nice deep throat, I think I might have to kill your husband so I can have you all to myself."

She started to struggle but he held her head firmly as he continued thrusting, building the tempo slowly as he became more aroused.

Suddenly he pulled himself away and lifted her to her feet. "I'm going to fuck you now."

"Please use a condom," she begged, thoughts of STDs and AIDS filling her head.

"No, I want to feel your pussy walls against my naked cock. I want to plant my seed inside you. I want to make you pregnant...leave you with a permanent reminder of me fucking you," he breathed against her ear as he placed her on top of the small kitchen table.

She lay back and closed her eyes, knowing she couldn't stop the inevitable. Positioning himself against her, his hands on her ass, he entered her in one smooth, deep stroke. She moaned as he filled her, but automatically her hips started moving in time with his. He fucked her deeply, his thrusts steadily gaining momentum. Minutes later as she came, she felt him shoot his sperm deep inside her. He collapsed weakly onto her as he tried to catch his breath. She put her arms around him and held him against her tenderly. He had fucked her so wonderfully.

"How was it for you, sweetheart?" Her husband Henry stood up, pulled off the ski-mask and leaned down to kiss her.

"It was the best so far, honey. I really enjoyed it."

"So did I," he said before kissing her again. "I only wish you'd at least consider the other proposal."

All lingering pleasure evaporated instantly. Henry had been begging her to let another woman make love to her while he watched but she had refused. She didn't want another woman's hands on her body and she didn't seem able to make him understand. She loved him and hadn't looked at another man since they were married three years ago. She simply didn't feel the need to make love to anyone else.

"Honey, you know I would do anything for you but please don't ask me to do that," she implored once again.

"I think you would enjoy it much more than you think but I'll leave it up to you." Henry held her head and kissed her again, softly.

"Are you hungry?" she asked, quickly changing the topic as he broke the kiss.

The unresolved issue had been ongoing for two years and the last thing she wanted was for it to take up any more of her valuable time.

"I'm starving!" Henry admitted. He was always ravenous after sex.

Valerie got off the table and zipped up her dress. She washed her hands, wiped the table top and dished up the food in two large serving bowls. They sat down to eat the meal at the same table in the kitchen instead of the larger one in the dining room which they used for guests or special occasions.

"This is delicious," Henry complimented as he took another helping of the korma. He didn't like anything too spicy but she had learned over the years to use subtle herbs to give her food a distinctive flavour.

"Thanks, sweetheart."

***

Saturday morning Henry leaned over the bed and kissed the side of Valerie's face. She turned in her sleep and the duvet shifted to reveal her naked breasts. He covered one with his hand and stroked the sleepy nipple. He watched as it awakened and stood out stiffly. When it had distended fully he bent and sucked on the hard bud. Valerie cupped his head and held him against her, moaning softly as he pulled quite strongly on her flesh. After a minute or so, he reluctantly straightened. "I have to leave now or I'll be late. I should be back by five if I don't get caught in traffic."

"Have a good day at the office, baby." Thankful that she didn't have to work as well, Valerie snuggled back into the cosy pillow, her nipple tingling pleasantly.

She nodded off again but woke half an hour later feeling refreshed. She jumped out of bed energetically and headed for the shower. It was a beautiful day, much too beautiful to waste lying in bed.

As she let the warm water cascade over her body, she cupped her breasts and tweaked her nipples. The memory of Henry's insistently pulling lips warmed her insides. She almost couldn't wait until he got home later. They usually spent all Saturday making love. It was such a pity that he had to work overtime on *their* day.

She debated stroking her clit and having a quick release but decided against it, she wanted to be extra horny for him later.

To buff her skin to the high shine Henry adored, she used a soft exfoliating scrub, lathered with a generous dollop of her favourite body wash. But as she rubbed it against her nipples and then between her legs she almost changed her mind again about masturbating as the abrasive texture made her desire more intense. Reluctantly she rinsed the body buffer and hung it back on the silver shower rack, then turned the faucet to its highest setting and let the water pummel her skin for a couple of minutes.

When she stepped out of the shower she felt stingingly alive. Smiling contentedly, she reached for her towelling bath robe.

Just then, she heard the sound of the doorbell. Quickly pulling on a light satin wrap, she ran down the stairs and squinted through the peephole in the door.

A tall, very handsome Black man in blue workman overalls stood on the doorstep, waiting patiently.

What the hell did he want?

Valerie secured the night chain, cracked the door open and asked puzzled, "May I help you?"

"Good morning, madam. Your husband reported a leaky bathroom faucet."

"Do you have any identification on you?"

He pulled out his company card and handed it over to her. She compared the likeness, confirming that he was the person in the photograph before she slipped the chain off and ushered him inside.

"My husband didn't tell me you were coming today." She knew her voice sounded cold but she couldn't help it, she'd just decided to spend the day pampering herself.

"We had a last minute cancellation," the plumber explained. "When I called him he said that it was okay to come today since you would be at home. Is there a problem?"

"It's alright. It's just that I was about to go for a massage and get my nails done."

"I'll be as quick as I can," he promised as his eyes lowered to the outline of her breasts. Her nipples peaked involuntarily and she wished that she'd gotten dressed before answering the door. "Where is the bathroom?"

"I'll show you." Pulling the belt on her robe a bit tighter, she preceded him up the stairs, then pushed the door open and stood aside to let him through.

"The cold water tap is leaking," she informed him, pointing to the faucet that was steadily dripping.

"Yes, I can see that." His voice was filled with secret amusement.

Macho bastard, she thought. He was probably surprised that she knew the difference between the cold and the hot tap.

"Would you like a cup of tea or coffee before you start?" She was in no mood to make him a cup of anything after his sarcastic comment but she felt obliged to offer.

"No. I'm fine, thanks." He smiled sexily at her but she didn't return it. He was really rather good looking. His fit body filled his work clothes in all the right places and Valerie didn't doubt that women all over London would probably pay extra for him to see to *all* their plumbing needs with his 'special' pipe.

"I'll leave you to it then." She quickly walked to her bedroom, slipped inside and locked the door.

She took her time applying lotion to her skin. Normally she preferred to do it while her skin was slightly damp to seal in the moisture but the plumber had come at the most inconvenient time. Smoothing on another thin layer of the fragrant rich lotion over her body, she slowly rubbed it in until it disappeared completely leaving her skin kissably soft. Walking to her underwear drawer, she pulled out a half-cup bra and its matching, miniscule thong that Henry usually took great pleasure in peeling off her. About to step into the panties, she spun around at the distinct sound of the bedroom door knob turning. She watched, the breath catching in her throat, as the plumber tried to open the door again without success.

"What do you want?" she shouted at him through the door.

There was no response but suddenly she heard the sound of a key in the lock.

Oh my God! How did he get a key?

The door pushed inwards. She screamed and covered her exposed breasts as he stepped into the room—naked and fully erect! His tall body looked even better naked than it had done in his overalls. It was obvious that he worked out regularly; his muscles were sculpted, honed to perfection.

"GET OUT OF HERE!" she screamed indignantly but he just smiled and continued walking towards her. She ran around the bed, her chest heaving. He kept coming and just as he was about to grab her she jumped onto the bed. Suddenly he exploded into action like a sleek panther, catching her before she could scramble off it. He trapped her under his large body, his hard cock nestled between the cheeks of her ass.

"Your husband told me he wouldn't be home until late this afternoon, so we've got plenty of time," he breathed into her ear. "I don't know how a man could leave a woman as beautiful as you at home alone. If you were my wife—"

"I'm *not*, so get off me!" She struggled against him but he held her securely. He was too heavy for her to shift and he used his superior weight to keep her in place.

"Shhh! All I was saying is: if you were my wife I would want to spend my day off making love to you not doing overtime." He ran his hand along the side of her thigh and upwards to her breasts. "Now, let's have some fun."

He grabbed her hands and tied them together with the

sash from her bathrobe before tying the end to the bed. He left a little slack but not enough for her to turn over if she wanted to.

"Please untie me. I'll do as you say," she begged.

"No, I don't want you scratching my face. You look like a tigress to me."

He eased his weight off her slowly. And she immediately tried to kick out at him, but he had anticipated the movement and held her legs against the bed.

"Do you want me to tie your legs as well?" he threatened.

She quickly shook her head, her mind filled with an image of being left tied naked to the bed and never being rescued.

"Then behave yourself!" he commanded.

He pulled her hips upwards, fondled her ass before he knelt behind her and tongued her clit. She jumped in surprise at the first flick of his tongue, but as he continued she tilted her pelvis to push her pussy back at his mouth. He opened her nether lips and pushed his surprisingly long tongue inside her. She worked herself onto it as he pushed it deeper, rotating her hips faster and faster as her pleasure built. When he reached out and tweaked her nipples firmly, she came.

Sitting up quickly, he plunged inside her and pummelled her with fast, even strokes and minutes later he came too.

But he wasn't finished with her yet.

As soon as he got his wind back she felt him part the cheeks of her ass. She instantly pressed her body into the mattress and tightened her butt muscles.

"Please!" she begged, knowing that he wanted to have anal sex with her.

"Your husband doesn't fuck this pretty ass of yours?"

"No."

"He is a very silly man letting this lovely ass go to waste."

His breathing quickened as he rubbed his hands over the firm flesh and then gave them two quick slaps that made her jump. "Now raise yourself and let me get at this ass."

When she didn't move, he gave her two more slaps, hard enough this time to sting her flesh. Her eyes watered at the impact and reluctantly she raised her hips off the bed.

"That's it." He pulled her upwards until she was kneeling on the bed with her head buried in the pillows. He separated the cheeks of her ass once again, leaned forward and tongued her asshole. She squirmed at the intensity of the sensation and tried to move forward but he held her firmly against his mouth. He circled the sensitive rim with his tongue repeatedly and soon she was moaning softly as she relaxed involuntarily. Suddenly he straightened. "I'm going to fuck your ass now!"

"No!"

"Yes! I *need* to fuck this tight ass of yours."

She closed her eyes tightly and prepared for the pain as he positioned his stiff cock against her anus. Then, to her intense relief, he moved it downwards and quickly plunged it into her pussy. He leaned over her, his body snug against hers, and fucked her until she climaxed again. Seconds later, he followed.

For a few minutes he let his weight rest against her, the room filled with the sound of their breathing and perfumed with the carnal smell of sex. Finally he rolled off her and reached up to untie her hands. The loose knot came apart at the first touch of his fingers. Pulling her against him, he asked in amusement, "Were you scared?"

He laughed as she punched his upper arm without answering. Then he sobered and apologized, "I'm sorry if I scared you. Honey, you know I would never do that to you. I know you'd hate it."

"You sounded serious this time."

She'd actually been a little worried. It was the first time Henry had made the threat when she was tied up and she had felt vulnerable. She didn't even allow him to finger-fuck her ass but she knew he'd had anal sex with previous partners and enjoyed it. She had told him that she didn't want to try it when he had brought the subject up and he hadn't persisted. Sometimes though, when they role-played he would, as he had done today, pretend that he was going to take her anally.

"It would be very painful if I tried to force you against your will, and you should know by now that I love you too much to knowingly do anything to hurt you." He kissed her and she felt reassured. He was a caring, gentle husband, that's why when he had started these little role-plays she hadn't objected. Their sex life had always been good but the little games had improved it dramatically.

"I love you, too." Suddenly she remembered the tap she had deliberately left dripping. "Did you turn the tap off?"

"Yes, I did." He snuggled his body closer to hers and closed his eyes.

Moments later she listened to the even sound of his breathing as he slept with his arms wrapped around her. She was glad he hadn't brought up 'the other woman' fantasy as he usually did every time they role-played. Because she had finally decided that she would agree to it. There was probably no harm in it. She loved the feel of Henry's hard body against hers and it would be strange to have a woman's softer body touch hers, but it was his ultimate fantasy. She would make it come true for his birthday in two weeks' time.

The following Monday she made enquiries and was sent the portfolios of the two women who appealed to her the most—the dental nurse would probably have the cleaner mouth, but the struggling writer seemed so much more fun.

***

She and Henry sat on the sofa sipping champagne, three-quarters of his birthday cake still on the table in front of them.

"Thanks for the digital camera, sweetheart. Now I can take beautiful pictures of you."

Henry kissed her as he opened the top buttons of her dress and reached inside her bra to fondle her breast. When her nipple became pebble hard he pushed the lace aside and covered it with his mouth. Waves of pleasure swept through her. He knew how much she loved it when he pulled her breast out of her bra and sucked on it. It reminded her of the days of heavy petting, and the first stolen pleasures of her young boyfriend suckling while they sat on her bed with the bedroom door left open as per her parents' instruction. They had never been caught because she had kept her ears open for any sounds, even if her eyes had instinctively closed as his young lips had tugged greedily on her flesh. She'd had many wonderful orgasms as he'd sucked on her nipples. Those had been days of pure bliss.

The doorbell rang shattering the silence of the room. Henry released her nipple, his eyebrows creasing in annoyance. "*Who* is that now?"

Valerie shrugged. "I don't know. Are you expecting anyone?"

"No."

"Maybe it's your brother come to wish you happy birthday," she suggested.

"Damn!" Henry got off the sofa, reached down and hid his erection strategically before walking to the door and pulling it open without first checking to see who was outside.

"Happy birthday, Henry! I'm Samantha." The slim

woman at the door had smooth dark skin and was almost six foot tall in her high heels. She opened her fake fur coat to reveal an incredibly sexy body, covered in liquid latex. "I believe you have a wife who needs fucking."

Henry's jaw dropped as he turned to look at Valerie.

"This is the other part of your birthday present, darling." She smiled and came over to kiss him.

Henry took the woman's coat and hung it in the small custom-built cloakroom under the staircase and they all hurried upstairs to the bedroom. He undressed Valerie as Samantha ripped the latex off her magnificent body in one quick, obviously practised action. She had the hard slim body of a medium-distance runner. Her breasts were small but beautifully shaped with erect nipples and areolas that were much darker than her taut breasts. Her ass was small, almost flat, but like the rest of her body it was sexy and toned. She stood looking at Valerie for a few moments, her eyes taking in the heavy breasts, the slim waist and the curvy hips. Then she turned Valerie around and admired the full cheeks of her backside before she faced her forward again.

As the woman pushed Valerie back against the bed, Henry took out his camera and started filming.

The woman cupped Valerie's jaw but instead of kissing her right away she looked deep into his wife's eyes.

Valerie wanted to tear her gaze away but there was something hypnotic in the other woman's eyes. Samantha rubbed her thumb gently against Valerie's lips. When they parted obediently Samantha leaned down and kissed her softly. The kiss was intensely erotic, light but amazingly arousing. Samantha didn't seem in a hurry to break the kiss and it went on and on. Finally, she slowly lifted her head and looked into Valerie's eyes again as she cupped her breasts. She pressed the nipples firmly, painfully, between her fingers and Valerie felt an immediate rush of heat to her pussy.

Samantha broke eye contact and dipped her head. Valerie arched her back and offered her breasts to her. Instead of taking one of the hard tips in her mouth Samantha laid her face against Valerie's erect nipples and rubbed her cheeks against them.

When she finally took a nipple into her mouth Valerie moaned as she pulled quite strongly on the hard peak. The firm sucking was unlike the soft almost playful rubbing of her face. The contrast made Valerie's stomach cramp in arousal. She reached for the woman's breasts, more for something to do than a conscious desire to pleasure her. Samantha's round breasts were amazingly firm but Valerie had seen them when the woman had pulled the latex off and knew they weren't implants. She ran her hands over their taut contours and felt the nipples respond. Valerie continued to tweak the aroused buds and Samantha immediately started sucking harder on her nipple. The firmer Valerie tweaked, the harder Samantha sucked until Valerie unbelievably felt herself cum. She hadn't cum while someone was just sucking on her breasts since she was about fifteen, but at that time it was the only thing she'd allowed her boyfriend to do—incredible!

Samantha slid down her body and looked at her pussy, opening the wet folds and examining her almost like she had never seen a vagina before. Then, like she had done with her breasts she rubbed her face over Valerie's entire pubic area before she pushed her nose against Valerie's clit, slid her tongue inside her and tasted her.

The sight of Samantha's naked, shaved pussy as she tongued his wife was too much for Henry, he put the camera down and reached down to finger her clit.

Samantha gave a little scream and jumped off the bed

immediately. She turned around and faced him angrily. "No Henry, *you* can't touch me! I am here to fuck your wife only, I don't sleep with men."

Henry had never said anything about wanting a ménage à trois so Valerie hadn't asked for a woman who would sleep with them both, assuming that he would be too busy trying to catch the special moments on film for posterity to have time to join in.

"I'm sorry." Henry smiled at Samantha in apology. "Go back to what you were doing, I'll keep watching."

Henry didn't mind *just* watching, it was even more fun than he'd imagined. He had only tried to finger Samantha because her wet pussy had looked a bit lonely. He picked up his camera and took up his position again.

Samantha climbed back onto the bed and Valerie surprised herself by sitting up and covering one of the woman's erect nipples with her mouth. It felt just like Henry's, except bigger and she sucked it hard just like Samantha had done hers. Samantha reached down and rubbed her fingers expertly around the tip of Valerie's clit. She gasped and let go of Samantha's nipple.

Samantha immediately went back to Valerie's clit, pushing the hood back and putting her mouth on the exposed nub of flesh. She applied just the right amount of tormenting pressure to it, tonguing it in a way that had Valerie gasping for breath. The sensation was so intense that Valerie reached her hand out for Henry's. He grasped it in his and took pictures one-handed. As Samantha continued relentlessly, Valerie pulled Henry's hand to her mouth and bit it. Finally her whole body stiffened. Raising her hips high off the bed, she came against Samantha's mouth.

Samantha seemed bent on continuing but Valerie pulled her head away. Her clit felt like it was on fire and the merest touch raised the hairs on her body. Not deterred, Samantha moved up the bed and sucked on one of Valerie's nipples, but gentler this time, just hard enough to send little waves of pleasure shooting from breast to groin as she pushed two fingers in Valerie's pussy. Valerie reached down to fondle Samantha's clit and almost pulled her hand back in surprise. Not only was Samantha's clit pierced, it felt hard, quite unlike her own. Valerie moulded it between her fingers in amazement. Samantha moaned and sucked harder on her breast as Valerie continued to mould her stiff clit. Suddenly the woman rolled on top of Valerie, positioned her clit against hers as she kissed her and tweaked her nipples. Samantha then started a serious clit-rubbing that shocked Valerie. She was even more amazed to feel her clit harden too and try to compete with the woman's larger one. Within minutes they both came.

Samantha kissed her lingeringly, then slid off her and lay on her back panting.

Henry opened his fly and used his left hand to placate his aching cock with awkward, but gratifyingly soothing strokes. As the two women came almost simultaneously, he pulled his wife closer to the edge of the bed and thrust himself to a quick orgasm.

Valerie moved up onto the bed to make room for Henry and the three of them lay there for several minutes, sated.

"I take it my services were satisfactory?" Samantha asked as she sat up and looked down at them both.

"You were sensational!" Henry smiled as he too sat up and openly admired her slim body. "A wonderful birthday gift, though it would have been the *perfect* birthday gift if I could have fucked you too."

"Sorry, can't oblige even if it is your birthday. Don't *do* men."

"That's alright. I'll have my lovely wife all to myself later."

"Right, I must go. I need to write another 1500 words to stay on schedule." Samantha got off the bed and Valerie followed suit.

"Honey, let me see Samantha out and I'll be right back." She pulled on a robe and followed the naked woman down the stairs.

"What are you going to wear?" Valerie asked as she remembered that the woman hadn't worn anything except for the latex.

"My coat, of course!" Samantha pulled the leopard-print coat from the cloakroom with a flourish, swung it around her shoulders and quickly buttoned it.

"I hope the police don't stop you on the way home!" Valerie laughed. "Did you drive over or do I have to call you a cab?"

"I drove. My car is parked in the driveway."

Valerie gave her the money they had agreed on, plus a generous tip for her stellar clit tonguing and nipple sucking performance.

"If I didn't need the money this one would have definitely been on the house. I really enjoyed sucking on those luscious nipples and that juicy clit of yours." Samantha winked at her. Valerie couldn't tell if the woman was serious or it was a practised line she gave to all her clients. "Here's my card, call me *any* time."

"Thank you." Valerie took it politely though she doubted that she would need the woman's services again.

"Now, I need one more suck."

Before the words registered properly in Valerie's head, Samantha had pushed the robe aside, bent her head and was sucking hard on Valerie's nipple.

Henry must be wondering where I am, Valerie thought minutes later but instead of freeing herself and going back to her husband, she cupped the back of the woman's head encouragingly. The woman wrapped her arm around Valerie and nibbled and then pulled on her nipple repeatedly. The sensation was so wonderful, Valerie wished it would go on indefinitely.

When Samantha straightened again she looked into Valerie's aroused eyes and said, "Call me."

"Drive safely." Valerie opened the door and Samantha kissed her softly on the lips before she walked briskly to the red Ford Focus parked behind Henry's silver Lexus.

"I told you that you'd enjoy it."

Valerie spun around guiltily. Henry was standing at the bottom of the stairs wearing only his boxer shorts.

"You were right. It was fun!" She walked up to him and put her arms around him. "Now, let's go and have some *real* birthday loving."

He held her hand and raced up the stairs ahead of her. They jumped onto the bed and it groaned under the impact. Henry rolled on top of her and looked down at her. Something lurked in his eyes that she had never seen there before but she recognized it instantly—jealousy.

"I love you." She pulled his head down and kissed him.

"I love you too." Henry slowly peeled his lips off hers, opened her robe and looked at her breasts. "Samantha really liked your breasts. I thought she'd never stop sucking on them."

"Henry, it was your fantasy, not mine," she reminded him. " I did it for you."

"Yes, I know. But I didn't expect you to enjoy it half as much as you did. I noticed that you came when she was *just* sucking on your breasts. *I* never made you do that. And I still can't believe you bit my hand when she was eating your pussy, she must have an incredible tongue."

"Henry, let's not do this. She is gone and that is the end of that. It's your birthday, let's enjoy the rest of it."

"Okay." He rubbed his face across her breasts, the way Samantha had done, but it felt different as his stubble cut into her tender skin.

Henry please don't do this, she begged silently. She didn't want him to imitate the woman's actions so that she could compare their techniques. She'd never had any complaints about his performance before, why was he suddenly changing? When he took her nipple into his mouth he sucked on it really hard, it hurt and she gasped his name. Samantha had just been sucking the same nipple. She pulled his head away to guide it to the other side, but before she had a chance to do so, he raised his head.

"What?" He looked down at her angrily. "Am I not doing it right?"

"I was just moving your lips to the other side," she explained.

"Why? Is this her side now?" he demanded, his voice cold.

"Of course not!" she denied instantly. "My nipple's just a little sore."

"Well if *she* can suck it, so can I!" He dipped his head and sucked on the same nipple again.

What had happened to her loving, considerate husband?

But Valerie understood how he felt. She knew if she ever found out that Henry had been unfaithful to her with another man she would leave him without hesitation. If it was another woman there would be a slim chance that she'd forgive him. It wasn't that she was dead set against homosexuality, it was simply that she felt she couldn't compete with a man.

Gritting her teeth as he continued to suck on her sore nipple, she thought of faking an orgasm. She dismissed the idea after less than a second's thought; he would see right through it. So she did the one thing guaranteed to distract and arouse him, she reached down and slipped the tip of her finger into his anus. She didn't like playing around assholes and would usually only do it if he'd just had a shower but desperate times called for desperate measures.

Immediately, he lifted his head from her breast and groaned his pleasure. She continued, not pushing her finger any deeper but increasing the thrusting motion of her hand. His cock hardened almost to the point of bursting against her.

When he'd had enough he put his hand over hers and she pulled her fingertip free. He kissed her as she reached down and slipped the head of his cock inside her. He pressed it up into her slowly and she held him tightly against her as he made the smallest, deeply-invasive motions with his hips, his pubic bone lightly brushing against her clit. It wasn't too long before she shuddered into her release.

As soon as her last contraction died, he abruptly stopped moving. He lay on top of her, his still-rigid cock deep inside her and yet she felt like he was miles away. She pushed against him gently and when he eased his weight up, she turned around and got on all-fours. If she had ever considered anal sex, this would have been the time to try it, but for her it was out of the question. Yet he needed something to allay his sudden moodiness. So, she did the next best thing—his favourite position.

Henry immediately slipped his cock inside her slick entrance. She tilted her hips back to the maximum and put serious effort into her gyrations as he thrust solidly into her.

When he came he groaned her name loudly and slammed his hips against her behind. She lowered herself slowly, keeping him inside her, until she was resting on the bed. He lay against her, his breathing harsh in her ears. She reached around and pulled his head down onto hers. They stayed this way until his flaccid cock slipped out of her.

He moved to the side and lay on the bed beside her, smiling sleepily at her. "Thanks for a wonderful birthday, honey."

"It was my pleasure."

He kissed her and pulled her closer to him. She laid her head on his shoulder and breathed in his crisp masculine scent. They were asleep within minutes.

***

"Valerie?"

She didn't recognize the female voice at the other end of the telephone line.

"Yes," she answered hesitantly.

"It's Samantha."

There was a brief awkward silence, then politeness forced Valerie to say, "Hi Samantha, how are you?"

"I'm fine but missing that sweet clit of yours. I haven't taken any bookings since I tasted your pussy, baby. It has me whipped. I need to eat it again."

"Samantha, I can't get involved with you. It would hurt Henry."

"You told me he was the one who wanted to see another woman fuck you."

"Yes, but—"

"I'll come over again and he can watch if he wants to. I don't mind."

"No! I'm not sure he wants to see his fantasy acted out again. He thinks that I enjoyed it far too much."

"You did, didn't you?" Samantha's voice dripped with smug satisfaction. "Does he make you cum the way I did?"

"He is my husband and I love him." Valerie didn't try to deny that the woman had made her cum faster and harder than she had done in a long time.

"I could give you everything he does."

"Samantha, leave us alone, please!" Valerie begged.

"I will, if you promise to meet me tomorrow during your lunch—"

"I don't think so." Valerie didn't let her finish.

"Please, Valerie, just let me tongue your clit one more time…that's all I'm asking."

Valerie felt a shiver run down her spine as she thought of the way Samantha's tongue had gently abraded her clit until she had almost screamed.

"Okay, just once and that's it."

"That's all I'm asking."

Valerie put the phone down with a bang. She had pushed Samantha's card deep into the bottom of her bag after retrieving it from the bin where she had purposefully thrown it the day after Henry's birthday. At first, she had thought it wise to get rid of any permanent reminder of the night, but then she remembered the way Henry had acted. Sadly, she'd realized that their happy marriage might never be the same again. If she and Henry were to split up she wouldn't mind having Samantha around to see to her needs. Of course, not if she had to pay for it. She had thought of Samantha a lot in the five days since and had been relieved that the pleasure the woman had given her was gradually fading from her memory, or so she'd thought—Samantha's voice on the phone had brought it right back.

The next day at 12.45 Valerie paid the driver and alighted from the taxi. She took half a dozen steps towards

Samantha's gate, hesitated and then turned back. The taxi driver pulled away at precisely the same moment and she cursed under her breath. She turned her head at the sound of the front door opening.

Samantha was standing at the top of the short flight of stairs, dressed in a red silk robe, waiting for her with a broad smile on her face. Valerie's stomach felt suddenly empty as it somersaulted in anticipation. She quickly covered the short distance.

Samantha shut the door as Valerie stepped inside, held her head and kissed her passionately. When she finally lifted her head she started taking Valerie's clothes off. She was naked in seconds. Samantha slipped her robe off her shoulders and grabbed Valerie's hand. "We haven't got much time."

The bedroom was elegantly designed but Valerie scarcely had time to admire it before Samantha pushed her on to the four-poster bed, dipped her head and started eating her pussy.

"God yes! Eat my pussy, honey." She had bitten back the words the last time because Henry had been in the room but now it was just the two of them and they spilled out of her. "Yes-s! Just like that! Just like fucking that!"

Damn! She had almost forgotten just how good Samantha was with her tongue! Grasping handfuls of sheet, she arched off the bed. Samantha continued to sweetly torture her clit and moments later Valerie had her first orgasm. This time Samantha didn't stop, not even when Valerie tried to pull her up by her hair. She clamped her mouth on Valerie's clit and pulled a second even more intense orgasm out of her. Again Samantha didn't give her a chance to draw breath, as Valerie's pussy clenched Samantha pushed two fingers in her and finger-fucked her hard.

Valerie couldn't believe it as she felt herself peaking again, but just as she was about to cum Samantha pulled her fingers out.

"I want to fuck you with a dildo. Is that okay?"

Valerie nodded, her pussy felt empty, it needed to be filled—Samantha's fingers had brought her close, something bigger would be even better.

Samantha quickly grabbed a dildo and strapped a leather harness over her hips. She pulled a condom over the dildo and noticed Valerie's look of surprise. "I'm just making it more comfortable for you, honey."

The choice of a dildo slightly longer and fatter than Henry's cock was deliberate. Samantha fingered Valerie's clit as she slowly pushed it inside her. When it was buried to the hilt, she leaned down and sucked on Valerie's breasts as she started a smooth, rhythmic thrusting. Valerie reached for Samantha's hard breasts and tweaked the nipples firmly. Samantha increased the tempo until she was slamming the dildo into her.

"Yes, honey, fuck me! Fuck me hard!"

Valerie almost never cursed, she didn't believe that foul language was necessary, but just like earlier when Samantha had been eating her pussy, the word 'fuck' seemed to be the only one suitable to convey her message. Henry always teased her about being a lady in bed—if he could hear her now! She opened her legs wider and let Samantha force the fat dildo harder and faster inside her, surprised that she was enjoying the slight discomfort of it filling her pussy with each stroke. When Valerie felt herself cumming she pulled Samantha closer, sucked hard on her breast and took Samantha with her. Again Samantha didn't pause. She turned Valerie over and plunged the dildo into her from behind.

"Fuck me, honey. Fuck me! FUCK ME!" Valerie screamed, mindless with pleasure.

"I'm fucking you, honey." Samantha rolled the nipples of Valerie's swinging breasts as she pummelled her with fast, hard strokes until she came again.

Then Samantha un-strapped the harness and rubbed her large clit against Valerie's and made them both cum again. Finally she wrapped her lips around Valerie's nipple and sucked it in the same arousing way she had done before. Valerie didn't cum this time but she let Samantha carry on the sweet sensation for long moments before she reluctantly pulled her up and kissed her, indicating she was ready to leave.

She got back to the office an hour and a half late and gave her female manager a lame excuse about being stuck in traffic. The woman looked at her over-bright eyes, gave her a knowing look but didn't comment.

***

The following Saturday morning Valerie was reading the newspaper, sipping a cup of Darjeeling tea when she heard the postman slip the letters through the letter box. She quickly placed the cup back in the saucer, hurried to the door and threw it open.

"Ryan, come back here a minute!" she shouted to the mailman who was already about twenty metres away.

He walked back to the door and stood looking at her expectantly, his heavy bag over his broad shoulder. He obviously still had a lot of deliveries to make but with Henry out of the house, she had to make her move.

"My husband's gone to work. Do you want to come in for a while?"

"Are you sure he's not going to come back anytime soon? If I get caught I'll lose my job." She could see that he was torn between duty and pleasure.

"I promise you he will be gone until evening." She smiled encouragingly.

"Okay."

As soon as he walked through the door, Ryan dropped his bag, grabbed her and kissed her hard, without finesse.

"Oh, Mrs Roberts, I wanted to fuck you for a long time." His eager hands grabbed her breasts.

"Do you want to do your deliveries first and come back?" She teased.

"No, I want to push my cock inside you right now." He opened the zip of his dark blue trousers, pulled his cock out and massaged it.

"Aren't you going to undress first?" she asked. His clothes would get all rumpled.

"I can't wait that long."

He grabbed her and spun her around before pushing her over the back of the sofa, throwing her skirt up over her head. He didn't even bother to pull her panties down; he just slipped the crotch aside and pushed his stiff cock into her.

"You have a tight pussy, Mrs Roberts."

"Call me Valerie, please. It's ridiculous for you to call me Mrs Roberts when you have your big, hard cock buried inside my pussy."

"Okay, Mrs Roberts."

She let him finish, regretting the urge to let the horny teenager fuck her. He was selfish and if she hadn't been wet already he would have pushed his large cock into her dry pussy and possibly hurt her. He had lots of energy and kept going for ages. Finally, as he was about to cum he pulled out of her and pumped sperm all over the back of her legs.

"Sorry, Mrs Roberts, I didn't have a condom and didn't

think you would want me to cum inside you."

"It's okay, Ryan. I'll clean the mess up later."

"When can I fuck you again, Mrs Roberts?" he asked eagerly as he stuffed his still-hard cock back into his fly.

"Well, Ryan, my husband fucks me far better than you did. I won't be repeating this experience."

"You didn't like the young, horny postman?" Henry asked as he wiped the last of his spunk off her leg.

"He was too horny for me!" Valerie laughed and put her arms around him. "Now show him how it's done."

Henry swung her up and marched to the staircase. He put her feet on the first step and she ran ahead of him to their bedroom. He stripped off his postman's outfit as she undressed. When they were both naked, they smiled at each other and climbed onto the bed.

Henry's eyes widened as she positioned herself doggy-style but he wasted no time in getting behind her and slipping inside her again. As they moved against each other Valerie thought of the last time she'd been in this same position. Samantha's dildo had penetrated her more deeply and had been just a bit more satisfying than Henry's cock. She pushed the thought out of her head and concentrated on the sweet gentle way he filled her. Within minutes she felt the tell-tale tremors start deep in her womb and soon both she and Henry moaned as they came almost together.

Later that evening the phone rang as she was preparing a fruit salad. Henry was asleep and not wanting the sound to awaken him, she raced to answer it. "Hello!"

"It's me."

Valerie's heart sank for a moment and then started beating at an erratic rate. "Samantha, we agreed that it would be only *once*."

"Come on Valerie, be a big girl. Henry can't make you

feel as good as I can. Plus, I've got bigger dildos that I could fuck you with if you want; Henry can only offer you the same size."

"Henry's cock is adequate, thank you very much," Valerie retorted, annoyed at the woman's arrogance.

"Why settle for adequate when you can have spectacular?" Samantha taunted.

"Samantha, I can't do this to Henry. Don't call me back." Valerie slammed the phone down and went back to the kitchen.

She wished that she hadn't let Samantha use the dildo, the oral sex was already enough to make her want to sleep with the woman again but the way she fucked her with the dildo using her slim hips to drive it hard into her pussy had been just as incredible. Even when Henry role-played he still treated her fairly gently. She had never thought that she would like it a bit rough and although the larger size had made her sore afterwards she had loved the way the dildo had gently grazed her vaginal walls every time it was forced inwards. The idea of an even bigger dido doing the same made her feel weak. She had to stop thinking about this nonsense—she was a married woman!

***

Three weeks later Valerie logged off her computer, tidied her desk and popped her head around her boss's office door.

"Bye, Lisa."

"Enjoy your afternoon off, Valerie."

"Thanks. See you tomorrow."

Valerie grabbed her coat and took the lift to the ground floor. She hailed an empty taxi and within minutes she was standing outside Samantha's flat, pressing the buzzer. Samantha came to the door rubbing her tired-looking eyes. She must have been sitting at her computer, writing. Her whole face lit up when she saw Valerie. Smiling broadly, she ushered Valerie inside and closed the door.

"God, I missed you so much," she groaned as she wrapped her arms around Valerie and kissed her hungrily.

"I missed you too, honey."

Samantha's hand eagerly reached to unbutton Valerie's blouse.

"I've got the afternoon off."

"Perfect." Samantha slowed down her manic movements and instead tried to tease Valerie by going agonizingly slow. Impatiently Valerie pulled the cup of her bra aside and offered her breast to Samantha. Samantha bent her head but rather than suck it hungrily in her usual fashion, she gently tongued it.

"Suck it hard." In desperation Valerie grabbed a handful of the woman's hair and pressed her nipple against her mouth.

Samantha chuckled but she pulled it into her mouth obligingly. Valerie's legs almost gave out as a cramping sensation raced down to her groin and upper thighs. Samantha continued for a few minutes. When she raised her head she rolled the wet black pearl between her fingertips. "I need a shower. You can join me if you want to. Then we can get down to some *real good* fucking."

"I'll join you." Valerie quickly undressed and they raced to the bathroom.

The shower cubicle was small, but easily big enough for the two of them. Yet they pressed themselves together, as they kissed and caressed, as though there was only room for one person. Valerie completely forgot to grab a shower cap, she hardly noticed when, the hairstyle she had spent almost half an hour in front of the mirror in the morning to carefully create, became limp and then plastered itself to her scalp. When Samantha turned off the shower they stumbled out of the cubicle like drunken sailors off a ship and grabbed a towel. They used it between them to get most of the moisture off but when they clambered up onto the high bed they were both still damp.

Samantha slid her smooth dark body onto Valerie's and looked deeply into her eyes as she had done the very first time. Again Valerie felt the strange hypnotic pull. They locked gazes for an inordinate amount of time before Samantha lowered her head and gave Valerie a long drugging kiss, then moved down to her breasts and rubbed her face against them. Suddenly Valerie heard the faint sound of crying. She looked down and her breasts were wet. Gently she pulled Samantha's head up and saw the tears in her eyes.

"What's the matter?" she asked puzzled, hoping that the other woman hadn't recently received bad news.

"I missed you so much, Val. I thought I'd never see you again. I can't sleep at night. I spend hours in front of the computer screen and I can't write a thing. You have messed up my entire life and you don't even care."

"Samantha, I do care about you but I love Henry."

"I am not asking you to leave him. I just need to hear the sound of your voice, I need to hold you, to touch you when I can. I need to know that even if we are apart you think of me sometimes."

"Samantha, I do think of you and honestly other than Henry there is no one else I'd rather be with. But he loves me, I can't hurt him just to be with you."

"I love you too, you know."

Valerie was shocked by Samantha's declaration; she'd thought their connection was physical not emotional.

"No, I didn't," she admitted honestly.

To her horror Samantha's face crumbled and the tears

started rolling down her face again. Valerie rolled over, covered Samantha's lighter body with hers and wiped her tears away.

"I do think about you. I promise to come and see you whenever I can and I'll try and call you from the office more often, but not from home. OK?"

"Okay." Samantha finally smiled.

Valerie moved down and pulled the tip of one of Samantha's hard breasts into her mouth as she reached for the woman's unusual clit. It stiffened at her touch and Valerie felt an immediate desire to tongue it. She didn't even need to part Samantha's pussy lips; the hard clit pushed itself upwards and parted them of its own accord. She covered the tip with her lips and Samantha moaned.

"That's it! Keep your mouth right there," Samantha commanded as she gripped Valerie's head and rubbed herself against her mouth. As Samantha increased the tempo of her hips, Valerie covered the woman's hard breasts with her hands and tweaked her nipples. Samantha screamed her name and came instantly.

Valerie moved up the bed and snuggled into Samantha's embrace. Up until this point *she* had been the one who came seeking pleasure, she had never thought that Samantha needed her in any way. Truthfully, she had thought that the woman had simply been trying to outdo Henry and had been determined not to develop any deep feelings. Now that Samantha had laid her soul bare it was going to be much harder for Valerie to keep her emotional detachment.

This was going to be, in three words, a fucking mess.

"It's my turn now." Samantha raised her head, kissed Valerie and then slid down to her breasts. "I missed these."

She rubbed her face against them before she pulled one erect bud into her mouth and sucked it hard. Minutes later she moved onto the other one and Valerie felt her orgasm build inside her until it exploded in waves of heat. Samantha gave her nipple one last hard suck and moved southwards.

"I especially missed this." Samantha buried her face between Valerie's legs and inhaled her delicate fragrance. Even before she uncovered the tip of Valerie's clit it was quivering in anticipation. As soon as she tongued it softly Valerie grabbed handfuls of sheet and arched her body in ecstasy.

"Oh fuck! Yes, eat my pussy, honey. Yes, baby, tongue my fucking clit just—like—that!"

Damn! Double damn!

Henry had started it all. She had never wanted to sleep with another woman, the desire had never been in her. Now she couldn't get enough of Samantha's tongue on her clit. The woman was a pussy connoisseur and knew exactly how and when to make Valerie cum.

Samantha was becoming an addiction, sooner or later Valerie might have to choose between her husband and the woman who had given her more multiple orgasms than anyone else had ever done. But today wasn't the day to think about it. Today she would just lie back and let Samantha use her magic tongue on her clit and then fuck her with that sweet big dildo again.

***

Another Woman is a warning to couples who try to live out their sexual fantasies. Sometimes they add spice to a flagging relationship but they can also ruin it completely. Men often fantasize about lesbians and assume that it is safer to have other women make love to their partners rather than other men. I say the risk is about equal. If your woman loves her pussy licked, don't even take the chance—women claim that **women** *are better at eating pussy.*

*****

DOUBLE THE TROUBLE

*A*lyson jumped off the number 25 bus and ran the short distance to the Engineering department. It was only the first Friday of her final year and already she was falling back into her old habit of getting to the classroom with only seconds to spare.

As usual, the only unoccupied tables were those in the front row; most of the guys liked to sit at the back of the room. She pulled her rucksack off her back and sank tiredly into the nearest chair, trying hard not to show how much running up the two flights of stairs had taken out of her.

Five minutes later she wished she'd taken her bloody time—the lecturer was late. She pulled a textbook out of her neatly-packed bag and resumed reading from where she'd left off the previous evening. Immediately she felt someone's eyes on her. She tried to ignore it but the weight of the person's gaze was almost physical. She turned her head and looked around. There were very few familiar faces, most of her colleagues had achieved their Bachelors' degrees and left the university. She still had another year to complete her four-year Master's course.

She had almost done a comprehensive sweep of the room

when her eyes encountered those of a bespectacled young man sitting obliquely opposite her. Mr. *Delicious* Nicholson. She didn't know his first name but they had shared a Mathematics lecturer in her first year. It had been an extremely large class, the only one that combined the Civil, Electrical, Electronic and Mechanical Engineering departments. Spectacles did nothing to detract from his dark good looks and she had been dying to find an excuse to talk to him. The opportunity had never presented itself. Then he had disappeared and she'd thought, *oh well, that one got away.*

He smiled and she waved nonchalantly back. He got to his feet and headed in her direction. She watched his long stride quickly eat up the short distance between them and almost licked her lips. His shoulders looked even broader than the last time she'd seen him a year ago.

God, he was as smooth and fine as Belgian chocolate!

"Hi Alyson, I didn't expect to see you here."

He knew her name?

"I'm doing the MEng," she explained.

"Oh!"

The surprise in his voice pissed her off slightly—he probably thought she'd had to repeat a year. "What are *you* still doing here?" He should have also graduated last year.

"I did a year in industry last year—worked for BT. Now they're sponsoring me for my final year."

"Well done!" She was impressed, the scheme the company ran was for a *very* select few.

"It was a necessity," he replied modestly. "Every employer is looking for work experience now. I recently read that almost a quarter of last year's graduates are still unemployed. I am glad I took up their offer, but it's going to be tough getting back into study mode again."

"All you've got to do is stay on top of the work," she advised.

"That's easier said—" he broke off as a postgraduate student entered the room, stood in front of the whiteboard and waited patiently until the din in the classroom had reduced by several decibels.

"Professor Moore's had a family emergency, he won't be in today. You can stay here if you choose, but please keep the noise down." He turned and walked out the room, the majority of the class on his heels.

Alyson closed the book and gathered the equipment she had laid out on the table in preparation for the lecture. She stood up and hooked her rucksack over her left arm. "Good start to the year!"

"Do you want to grab a coffee?" he asked.

"Sure." There was still another forty-five minutes before her next lecture. "By the way, what's your first name?"

"Sorry, I should have introduced myself. I'm Darren."

"How did you know mine?"

"I made a few enquiries when I first saw you in Maths class."

"Really?" she asked in surprise. He was by far the best-looking brother on campus. She hadn't thought he knew she existed.

"Yes, but you were always surrounded by those three musketeers!"

She laughed at his description of her three Nigerian friends Ade, Segun and Ula. She had hung out with them since the first year but they had all graduated last year. Ade and Ula had returned to Nigeria and Segun was now living in the US. He had graduated with first class honours and had immediately been headhunted by the American company, AT&T.

As he paid the cashier for her tea and his coffee, Alyson looked around for an empty table. The canteen was surprisingly full for the time of day but she spotted one just near a window and walked quickly over to it before it was claimed.

"Is it sweet enough for you?" she asked as she watched him open a third packet of brown sugar and pour it into his coffee.

"I like my coffee like I like my women—black and sweet." He winked suggestively at her and she couldn't help but laugh. "Now, back to our previous conversation—were those guys your *bodyguards*? I mean, a body as sexy as yours does need some protection, but damn, those guys were on the job twenty-four seven!"

"We weren't always together!" she protested.

"It seemed that way to me."

"What if I said that I'd been checking you out too?" she asked boldly.

"Seriously?"

"I've got eyes too, you know. But you seemed a little arrogant so I didn't want to make the first move."

"Me arrogant? You hurt my feelings." He feigned a hurt look that was as unconvincing as the words he uttered. "But tell me, exactly which part of my body were you checking out?"

"You think I'd tell you? You are already too full of yourself!"

"Why not? I could tell you which part of your body I've been checking out."

"Okay, go ahead then," she dared him.

"Let me tell you *later*." The way he said the word 'later' sent a shiver down her spine—it was full of hidden promise. "What time's your last lecture?"

"One o'clock," she replied.

"Mine's eleven. I'll wait for you in the library."

"Okay." She looked at her watch. "I'd better go before I'm late for my next class. See you later."

"I'll be waiting." He winked at her.

She smiled and shook her head at him as she turned to leave. She knew that he was watching her butt as she walked away so she put a little more sway into the movement of her hips. She liked her behind, it was the most prominent thing on her 5'4" frame and she loved the havoc it wrecked.

When Gareth, her last boyfriend, had complained that her ass was getting too big she knew he'd just been looking for an excuse to leave. How can an ass be too big? It simply wasn't possible! She'd told him if he couldn't handle her big ass then he wasn't man enough for her. He'd told her to 'fuck off' and stormed out of her flat, taking his small dick with him. He had the kind of small dick that hadn't quite reached her itch. It had given her many nights of frustration. No great loss.

Still, a small dick was better than no dick and she hadn't so much as smelled one in the last two months. She'd been too busy working as a part-time cashier at Debenhams, doing all the hours available to build a little nest egg to see her through the next year of university. But now she was ready to climb a wall…or Darren! He looked as solid as a wall but should be much more fun to climb over and under.

Her step lighter, she made her way back to the Engineering department. Suddenly university life took on a new dimension; he would be useful when she needed a distraction from studying. She couldn't wait for her last lecture to be over.

***

When she walked into the library at five minutes past two

he was sitting at a table only metres away from the door, she couldn't have missed him if she tried. He saw her as soon as she entered and got up to meet her half-way.

"Do you want to eat something first?" he asked, his eyes devouring her.

The kind of *eating* she had in mind didn't involve anything cooked, but he might be hungry.

"Only, if you want to," she answered.

"We could order Chinese or Pizza, *later.*" That word again, and another little shiver down her spine.

She supposed she should be a little coy and pretend to be offended that he thought she was easy. But what would be the point? She'd thought that she'd never see him again and now here he was—all 6'2" of him. She wasn't going to waste time dating him for a couple of weeks only to end up in bed with him anyway. Plus, if they'd both wanted each other for three years *that* could be considered dating time.

Twenty minutes later they were in the smelly elevator on their way to her seventh floor flat. She automatically took off her shoes and placed them on the worn mat by the front door and was pleased when he followed suit. She liked to walk around bare footed and there was no telling what could be dragged in on shoe soles. As he straightened up after bending to take off his trainers, she realized for the first time just how small her home was.

"Have a seat." She motioned to her had-seen-better-days sofa. "I'll grab us a couple of beers from the fridge."

Opening her small fridge she took out two chilled bottles of Budweiser and checked their best before dates.

Loads of time left—nice one, small-cock Gareth!

She used the opener-cum-fridge-magnet to pop them open before wiping the tops with a clean paper towel. She could have pretended to be a *lady* and grabbed a glass for herself but she thought, *nah!* It wouldn't hurt to give Darren a sneak preview of her fellatio technique with the bottle, if time permitted.

Bottle of beer in each hand, she walked back to the sofa where Darren was sitting looking through her modest collection of CDs. Jaheim's *Ready, Willing and Able* started playing softly as she approached him.

Damn, he was reading her fucking mind!

"There you go." She handed him a bottle.

"Thanks."

She looked at the fingers of his right hand as he took it from her. The nails were clean and neatly trimmed.

Nice pussy-fucking fingers!

"Cheers!" He hit the bottom of his bottle against hers and she almost dropped it—she'd been so engrossed in imagining those long fingers doing all sorts of nasty things to her.

"I see you are a big Whitney fan." He pointed to the five albums by her favourite singer and the three soundtracks from the movies in which she'd had major roles.

"She's still my girl," she admitted. "I know she's not doing too well at the moment, but I'm keeping my fingers crossed for her."

"You better start crossing your toes as well!"

"I'm an optimist." She sat down next to him, her thigh brazenly brushing his. "Anyway, why are we talking about Whitney? I can bet you fifty pounds *she* isn't talking about us!"

"What do you want to talk about, then?" He took a drag of his beer and her eyes followed the motion of his Adam's apple as he swallowed the liquid.

"Let's talk about you. How many current girlfriends? If none, why not?"

"You are not going to believe me if I say none, are you?"

"Not likely. But if you gave me a really good explanation, I _might_."

"I was seeing someone from college but she went back to Martinique."

"Really?"

"Yes," he confirmed. "She was an overseas student—she got a 2:1 in Law and went back home."

"Why do I _not_ believe you?"

"You must have seen her around campus. She was tall and had long, thin dreadlocks."

"_Caroline_ was your girlfriend?" Alyson asked him in surprise.

"Yes."

She had met _Miss Thing_ on a few occasions but they had hardly been friends. They had taken an instant dislike to each other, as good-looking women often do. Then one day at lunch with a mutual friend, Caroline had turned her nose up at the lovely piece of fried chicken on Alyson's plate and they had gotten into a heated argument on the topic of killing animals for human gratification. Just before they had stabbed each other with their forks, the mutual friend had intervened.

Caroline had the body of a supermodel, one of those lucky women who were born thin. She had legs for weeks (days were far too short), slim rounded arms and a long graceful neck. When she'd pranced around campus, with her thin dreadlocks brushing the top of her neat, firm backside, all eyes had followed her and _girlfriend_ had known it.

Alyson was a classic T & A—_tits and ass_, in case you didn't know. Her full breasts were firm and round, she only needed a bra because her impudent nipples were known to show themselves at the oddest moments like two naughty raisins. Her behind would have inspired the finest painters of the past to capture their full magnificence in oil, they resembled dark brown marble and were just as smooth to the touch. Her waist was ridiculously small in comparison to the fullness of her breasts and the voluptuousness of her ass. She and Caroline were opposite ends of the beauty spectrum but both had the ability to bring men to their knees. Usually they each attracted a different kind of man.

"So, if Caroline's your type what do you want with me?" she asked him, puzzled. How does a brother go from a tall, dreadlocked, vegetarian earth-mother type to a short, straightened-hair, meat-eating sister in less than three months?

"I don't have a type—I just love beautiful women."

Good answer!

"But we are nothing alike," she persisted.

"You are both young, intelligent Black women."

"But men generally tend to prefer light-skinned *or* dark-skinned women."

A lot of brothers thought Alyson was too dark.

"Not me, I love every shade of Black. *And* they do say—the blacker the berry the sweeter the juice."

Great answer!

Now she was going to have to prove just how much sweeter she was than that fried-chicken-ain't-finger-licking bitch. She was not going to be outdone by some salad-eating giraffe!

She took a nice long swig of her beer and almost immediately felt its effects. She didn't have a head for liquor—half a pint of lager and she was *nice*, a full pint and she was anybody's.

Darren put his arm around her shoulders and she nestled closer to him as they listened to Jaheim's distinctive voice.

He finished his beer and placed the empty bottle beside his chair.

"Do you want another one?" She looked up and found his eyes fixed on her full lips.

"No. I want you." He bent his head and covered them with his. At first his lips were soft and playful as if he was waiting for some encouragement from her. She parted hers and his arms tightened around her as he plunged his tongue into her mouth.

As they exchanged deep, drugging kisses, he undid the buttons of her shirt and slid it off her shoulders. Then they fell back onto the sofa, the weight of his body pressing her into the soft leather. His fingers tweaked her nipples through the lace of her bra and she felt the answering tingle between her thighs. The lace was abrasive, the sensation almost too much to bear. When his lips left hers to cover a tormented, hardened blackberry as he pulled the lace aside, it wasn't a moment too soon.

The rhythmic sucking motion of his mouth intensified the cramping in her groin. Reaching down, she ran her hand along the length of his cock and couldn't wait another second to have it in her bare hands. She quickly undid the buttons of his jeans, reached inside the elasticized waist of his boxer shorts and pulled it out. It jerked and pulsed as she ran her hand up and down its length. It was soft to the touch but as hard as a rock—velvet-covered steel.

She opened her legs a bit wider and pushed her groin upwards as he ran his hands up her outer thighs. He cupped her butt and the firm, full contours overflowed his big hands. Slipping the damp gusset of her thong aside, he rubbed his thumb lightly against her clit, then slid a finger into her dripping entrance and slowly finger-fucked her. The sensation of his mouth on her breast and his long finger inside her was maddening but it wasn't nearly enough. She raised her hips higher and met the forward thrust of his finger hungrily. Responding to her silent demand he pushed another finger alongside the first and quickened the tempo of his wrist.

In the meantime she gathered the drops of moisture oozing from the head of his cock and used them to run her hand over his throbbing length with greater ease. She tightened her hand and felt the tell-tale signs of his impeding eruption. In turn, his fingers thrust into her with even greater frenzy. She felt herself climbing and climbing....

But it wasn't what she wanted!

"I want you inside me," she moaned.

"I didn't bring any condoms," he confessed, looking as though he wanted to kick himself.

"What did you think you were coming here to do?" she asked indignantly. "Hold hands?"

If she wasn't so horny or he wasn't so *fine*, she would have thrown him out of her flat for his stupidity.

"I was hoping for some kisses and maybe if I was lucky a feel or two," he admitted honestly.

Ah! He had mistaken her for someone who didn't fuck on the first date! Such a sweetheart! Instantly she forgave him. It had been a while since any man had made *that* mistake.

"Well today is your fucking lucky day. Come on, I have some in my bedroom."

Darren got off the sofa, pushed his jeans down his long legs and kicked them aside. Alyson unzipped her skirt and ran ahead of him into her small bedroom. She grabbed a pack of condoms from the top drawer of her bedside table just as Darren came up behind her, his erection pressing into the small of her back.

Expertly, he undid the front clasp of her bra and her swollen breasts burst free. She handed him a condom, pulled the duvet off and climbed onto her single bed. Before she'd had a chance to turn over onto her back, Darren pulled her up against him, his cock unerringly finding her slick entrance. She groaned at the burning sensation as he pushed it slowly inside her. It filled her completely as she worked herself back against it, matching the rhythm of his hips as he pressed forward. One of his hands left her hip to stroke her swollen clit and she clutched handfuls of the cool blue cotton sheet to stop from crying out. It was *so-o-o* delicious!

Suddenly Darren grabbed her hips, pulled her hard against him and held her still. She had to bite her lip to stifle a groan as she felt him go deeper in her than any cock had gone before. Damn! She'd thought he was all inside already.

"Are you okay?" Darren asked as his hips started a tantalizing motion. All she could do was nod her head weakly as she lowered it to the bed, needing the support of something tangible as every nerve-ending in her body was stimulated. It was the most incredible feeling she'd ever experienced.

The change in position gave Darren even deeper access and as he thrust forward once more, she came. No, 'came' was too mild a word—she 'arrived in style'. Her skin felt too tight for her body, her inner walls gripped Darren tightly, milking him as he shot his load. Moments later he collapsed onto her, his body slick with perspiration, her pussy clenching around his deflating cock.

When he made to slide his body off hers she whispered, "Don't move."

He was heavy, but he felt wonderful pressed against her. Gradually their breathing quieted. When he tried to roll off her again, she didn't stop him.

"Damn girl, what have you got in that pussy?" Darren's voice sounded bemused as he smiled down at her.

"Dynamite," she replied saucily.

"You're damn right! It's wet, but so fucking tight!"

"Well, for your big cock any pussy would be tight."

"This boy isn't so big." He reached down and playfully slapped it against her thigh.

She looked down in surprise. It was erect again and she had definitely underestimated the length when she'd been wanking him earlier. He didn't wear those size eleven or twelve trainers for nothing!

***

Two weeks later, Darrell turned to greet his brother as he heard the sound of the key turning in the front door lock. His eyes nearly popped out of his head when the door opened and a cutie preceded his twin into the room. His eyes flew to his brother's in confusion but Darren gave him a warning look.

What was Darren playing at? They never let women know there were *two* of them.

"Alyson, this is my brother Darrell."

"Hi Alyson, it's a pleasure to meet you." Recovering quickly, Darrell came around the chair to take her hand.

Alyson was stunned at just how identical they were. Unlike Darren, he wore contact lens and used his sexy eyes to full effect.

"I'm pleased to meet you, too, Darrell." She really was.

He was still holding her hand as Darren headed for the carpeted staircase, throwing over his shoulder, "Alyson, I'll be down in a second, I just need to grab my laptop."

"Darren didn't tell me how beautiful you were," Darrell lied easily—he didn't even know his brother had a new girlfriend.

He kept hold of her hand, stroking her palm softly, suggestively. Alyson didn't mind but she wondered if Darren would object when he came back downstairs. But all he did when he re-entered the room, with the strap of his laptop case diagonally across his body, was grab her free hand and head for the front door, saying to his brother, "See you later, El."

"OK. And Alyson…," she turned to look at him at the sound of her name. Darrell winked at her, "…I hope to see you again real soon."

"Bye, Darrell."

Darren opened the latch on the gate and let her precede him through it.

"Why didn't you tell me that you have an identical twin brother?" she demanded.

"Well, at first…" He paused and looked down at her as if he was trying to decide whether or not to reveal a secret.

"Go on," she urged, intrigued.

"Well, at first it was because Darrell and I pretend to be one person…and share girlfriends."

"What?" She'd heard of it happening but she hadn't really believed it. "Women fall for that shit?"

"They do. We have only been found out by one girl so far. Two years ago we went to a cousin's wedding and the girl turned out to be a close family friend of the bride's. We were caught fair and square!"

"It still doesn't explain why you didn't tell me that you had a twin brother."

"Because you would have wanted to meet him and once he'd met you he would have wanted to sleep with you. I didn't want to share you."

"Why not?"

"I like you far too much."

"Are you telling me you've shared *all* your girlfriends with Darrell?"

"Yes."

Even Miss Prissy Caroline? If girlfriend ever found out they were both dead men!

"So why does everyone get special treatment except *me?*" she asked indignantly.

Darren laughed and hugged her closer as they walked to West Ham Tube Station. He thought she was joking; she was as serious as a hole in the head! She had to find a way of making it happen. It could be *double the trouble* if they started fighting over her but if they worked together, like she hoped they would, it would be double the pleasure!

***

Later that day Darrell sat watching *Boyz N the Hood* while he waited for his brother. It was one of his favourite movies but tonight it couldn't hold his interest. He'd never expected his twin to hide anything from him and it worried him.

Darrell was the more extrovert of the two. He was the firstborn and the first to do almost anything. He'd lost his virginity at fifteen; Darren hadn't lost his until he was almost seventeen. Even then it was *he* who had set it up so Darren could sleep with the girl he'd been seeing at the time. He knew Darren wasn't as comfortable as he was with their arrangement but surely it was one of the perks of being identical. They had shared a womb, as far as Darrell was concerned that gave them the right to share everything else.

At quarter to eleven Darren walked in and went straight to the kitchen. His head was buried in the refrigerator by the time Darrell got there.

"What was that, bro?" Darrell demanded.

"What was what?" Darren stalled for time as he poured himself some ice-cold milk.

"Why didn't you tell me about Alyson?"

"It's new."

"But you're fucking her, aren't you?" Darrell asked angrily.

"So?"

"I thought it was share and share alike, baby brother."

"Not this time."

"What? Are you in love with her or something?"

"El, I like this girl."

"Are you going to let some pussy come between us?" Darrell asked, shocked.

"We aren't teenagers anymore. It's time we stop this nonsense!"

"Okay, all I'm asking is that you just let me *hit* it one time and that's it."

"No!" Darren downed the milk in one gulp and walked out the room.

Darrell knew from experience he couldn't convince his brother to change his mind. That night he tossed and turned on his king-sized bed. He had to hand it to Darren, he did choose some fine-looking women. He remembered Alyson's butt and he felt his cock harden. He wanted to smack himself against that ass of hers and he was going to find a way of doing so if it was the last thing he did!

He spent the next two months trying to subtly get information out of his brother, but Darren knew exactly what he was up to and ignored his questions. He searched Darren's room regularly but couldn't find a trace of Alyson's details.

Then, just when he'd been about to give up he noticed an envelope on Darren's writing desk. It was already opened, and inside there were two tickets for an Angie Le Mar show at Theatre Royal, Stratford. *But* more importantly it had

Alyson's full name and address written on the outside.

Bingo! All he needed was time and fucking opportunity!

The following Monday he returned home exhausted from a long, tough day. Four computers had been infected by a virus and he'd had to work single-handedly to stop it spreading and affecting all the other machines on the network since both his manager and his other work colleague had called in sick. Darrell suspected that they had overindulged on alcohol or sex—the older married man had been fucking the young gay man almost from his first day of employment, his need for his subordinate so insatiable he had thrown caution to the wind. Only a week after the gay man had started working for the company Darrell had seen the younger man enter but not exit his manager's office, yet minutes later when Darrell had popped in to inform his boss that he was on his way to repair a faulty computer, his colleague was nowhere in sight. With only one way out of the room, barring the sheer drop from the window, there was only one logical explanation—the younger man was under the desk, tying the manager's shoelaces *or* his cock in a knot. And even if Darrell had been willing to entertain the thought that his colleague had turned Spiderman, jumped through the window and used a web to lower himself to the pavement outside, his manager's perspiring face had given the game away.

Darrell had first assumed that the older very 'macho' man was simply using the younger man to polish his knob as and when he felt the urge, since his boss hadn't appeared to have a gay bone in his body. Until he had returned to the office late one evening after realizing that he had left his wallet, containing over one hundred pounds in cash and his credit cards, in his desk drawer. Though he knew it was unlikely that the cleaner, who *never* cleaned his desk, would search his drawers, he had made the hour and a half return journey, just in case. As he switched on the office lights he noticed the band of light coming from under his manager's door. Thinking that his manager, who always insisted that they do their bit for the Planet by switching off the lights at night, had forgotten his own instruction, Darrell had collected his wallet and pushed the door open to turn off the lights. And immediately wished he had said, *fuck the Planet* and left the lights burning all night. If the men had been both dark- or light-skinned, all Darrell quick glance would have a registered was a strange two-headed being, but the older man's light complexion contrasted sharply with the ebony-skinned younger man's and the image of their entwined bodies burned itself into Darrell's retina before he'd hastily closed the door again. The next day they had all pretended that the incident hadn't occurred, but Darrell had known that the obscene bonus he received the following quarter had more to do with his manager's appreciation for his discretion than his job performance.

He opened the fridge and took out the leftovers from the Sunday dinner he and Darren had cooked the previous day. He sliced off three thick slabs of roast chicken breast and put them onto a plate with four baked potato chunks. Quickly warming the meal in the microwave, he took it up to his room and made short work of it; he had been too busy to have anything but cups of sweetened coffee all day. His eyes were gritty from staring at computer screens, so he took out his extended-wear contact lens before he stepped into the shower.

Half an hour later, he was lying in bed when he heard faint sounds coming from the room next to his. He had assumed that Darren wasn't home, that he'd be at Alyson's as usual. Surprised, he got off the bed.

He tapped on his brother's door and popped his head round it. "Aren't you going to Alyson's tonight?"

"No. I've got three assignments to hand in by Friday."

"Do you need any help?" Darrell knew his brother would refuse but he felt compelled to ask anyway.

"I've got it under control, thanks."

"Okay then. I'm going over to see Nicky."

Nicky was a former girlfriend who couldn't get enough of Darrell's dick even though they had split up over three years ago. He had finally let her go seven months ago when Darren had told him that she seemed too highly-strung, if not a little mentally unstable, and warned him if he didn't stop toying with her it would end badly.

"I thought you were done with her." Darren didn't hide his anger.

"Sorry bro, I feel like *pussy* tonight." Darrell avoided his brother's eyes as he backed out the room and closed the door. He rushed back to his room, dressed hurriedly and left the house.

***

At ten-thirty Alyson heard a tap on her front door. She ignored it as she turned the page of the textbook on her lap. It was probably her drunk of a neighbour wanting to borrow some milk or sugar, as usual. The person tapped again, louder this time. Reluctantly, she pushed the duvet back and got off the bed. Looking through the peephole, she saw Darren and quickly unlocked the door, smiling as she stood back to let him in.

It was probably intuition, because there was no other way of her knowing, but as he came through the door and wrapped his arms around her, she knew it was *Darrell*. And the same intuition told her that Darren didn't know about his brother's visit.

"God, I wanted you so badly I couldn't concentrate. I had to come over and do a little *something-something* to get it out of my system."

He lifted her bodily, walked to her bedroom and tossed her unto the bed. Then he pulled his keys, mobile phone and two condoms out of his pockets and put them on her dresser before starting to rip his clothes off. Belatedly, he remembered his glasses as they got stuck when he tried to pull his T-shirt off.

That was the confirmation Alyson needed: Darren wouldn't have forgotten to take his glasses off; he had the same model of Nokia phone, but his was *blue* and he had already left a supply of condoms in her top drawer, *he* would have known that he didn't have to bring any when he came over.

She watched Darrell undress—he was slightly bulkier than Darren, his muscles more sharply defined. He pulled off his boxers and his penis reared up in front of him like an angry cobra, ready to strike her. Arrogantly, he handed her a condom. She ripped it open and rolled it in place.

He pushed her back against the bed and climbed onto it, his legs straddling her hips as he reached for the hem of her nightshirt. She was naked underneath and his eyes widened as they travelled the curvy length of her body.

Lowering his head, he kissed her, plunging his tongue deep into her mouth as he grabbed her breasts and squeezed them hard. Her period was due and her nipples were sore, when he rolled them firmly between his thumbs and forefingers she pulled her lips away and gasped. He kissed her neck, then lowered his head and took a nipple between his teeth. She grabbed his hair but it was so short she couldn't get a grip. Finally she pushed her hand between them and rescued her tortured nipple.

He placed his hands on her thighs and pushed her legs back until her knees were either side of her ears. He paused for a minute to admire the plump, pouting lips of her pussy squashed between her upper thighs before he plunged his head forward and tasted her. As far as he was concerned foreplay was for wimps, a waste of fucking time, literally, but he'd go down on a woman or do whatever it took to get her wet enough for him to get inside her. Thankfully, Alyson was nice and wet, already.

Grabbing his penis firmly in one hand, he pushed the head just inside her opening. He let it soak in her juices for a minute and then pulled it out completely. Then did it again and again, teasing her.

He slid his hands upwards and held on to her ankles. When she tried to make him go deeper he held her down securely and stilled any movement. Suddenly, without warning, he pushed forward, right up inside her with one quick motion and she screamed in pain. He didn't pull back. Instead he tried to penetrate her more fully, grinding himself against her while pushing her legs even further back.

Darrell couldn't believe that *finally* he was fucking her. Her skin was smooth and baby-soft with no visible sign of hair except for the curly bush covering her pubic area. He ran his hands repeatedly over the firm contours of her body. He'd never felt such incredible smoothness before. Darren was such a lucky bastard!

He concentrated fiercely not wanting to cum too quickly. It may be his first and only chance and he wanted to make it last as long as possible. But her pussy was clinging and tight, he couldn't last much longer in this position. Grasping her by the waist, he turned onto his back, taking her with him. Her breasts bounced up and down as she rode him, her leg muscles taut as she lifted herself a couple of inches and rotated her hips back onto him. He watched his glistening condom-covered penis disappear and reappear. It was an awesome sight.

He had deliberately chosen this position—no woman had ever made him cum while she was on top; he liked to be in control. He put his hands on her breasts and pulled until she was close enough for him to take a nipple into his mouth. Instantly the speed of her gyrating hips increased and she ground herself against him. He pushed her breasts together and repeatedly flicked his tongue from one nipple to the other. Suddenly her body stiffened and she came with a soft moan.

His cock was pulverized by her vaginal muscles as she went through the throes of her climax. He gritted his teeth to stop himself from shooting his load. Incredible! It was the first time he'd come close to cumming with a woman on top of him!

He turned her onto her belly and she went willingly, her body like putty in his hands. He'd known that she had a big butt but it was bigger than he'd imagined. Moulding the flesh between his hands, he separated and squeezed the firm mounds back together alternatively, revealing and concealing her tightly puckered asshole. Then he ran his forefinger along the wet folds of her pussy, moistening it before running it up the crack of her ass. Lightly, he rimmed her asshole with his fingertip. When he felt her relax, he pressed more firmly against it, trying to gain entry.

"No!" She tightened her butt cheeks, threatening to break his finger if he persisted.

Fuck! The ass was off-limits! Annoyed at being thwarted, he pulled her into a kneeling position and plunged his cock into her dripping pussy with one quick, smooth motion and was rewarded with her muffled moan. The sight of her ample ass as it tapered into her small waist was too much for him, he lasted only a few strokes before he came with a loud, shuddering groan.

It was heaven to have her ass pressed up against him as he lay on top of her trying to catch his breath. He could have stayed there all night but reluctantly he kissed her shoulder, got off the bed and went into the bathroom.

His cock was still hard when he walked back into the room and started dressing. "I've got to go, babes."

She turned over and watched him quickly pull on the T-shirt and jeans he'd hastily discarded less than half an hour ago. He picked up his glasses, keys and mobile phone and leaned over to kiss her.

"See you tomorrow."

As he turned to go she said, "Darrell."

He tensed, but didn't turn around. Had she said Darren or Darrell?

"Yes, you heard me correctly, *Darrell*. I know it's you. Next time slow the fuck down—you're not running a race. Okay?"

He turned around to face her and she was lying there naked, watching him. He reached for his belt but she shook her head. "Bye, Darrell."

He beat a hasty retreat; Darren might change his mind and come over. Damn! If she was his woman he'd be in that tight box every single night! It had been everything that he'd thought it would be and more. And once was definitely not enough, she needed to be fucked hard and regularly. He wasn't sure his baby brother was up to the job.

As he walked to his car which he'd parked four corners away, he smiled broadly. When he got home, he quickly parked in the driveway, took off his glasses and slipped into the house as quietly as possible. He didn't want to meet

Darren on the way; he couldn't wipe the silly grin off his face and the last thing he wanted was for Darren to become suspicious.

He fell asleep with the smile still on his face.

***

Alyson lay on the bed for ten minutes after he'd left before she got up and went to the bathroom. She'd already had her evening shower so she used a wet flannel to wipe herself off. The lips of her vagina were puffy and tender. With Darrell she knew she'd been fucked! He was impatient and aggressive—the sex had been manic.

She switched the bathroom light off and made her way back to her bedroom. Picking up her textbook off the carpet where it had fallen when Darrell had swept it off the bed, she resumed reading, her mind clear and receptive like it always was after sex. Her girl friends complained that all they wanted to do after sex was curl up and sleep. Sex, like exercise, left her energized.

***

After only one night on his own Darren missed having Alyson's butt pressed into his groin as they slept spoon fashion. The next evening they went straight over to her flat after his last lecture. She curled up in bed with a textbook while he used her small dining table as a writing desk. When she put her head down to study, she didn't play around and to his surprise he got more work done at her place than he would have at his.

At eleven thirty, as planned, he logged off his laptop. A minute later Alyson came out of her bedroom and stretched sexily.

"Are you ready for bed?" she asked him with a wink.

"Are you ready for me?" He covered the short distance and pulled her against him.

"Any time, big boy!" She pressed closer and rubbed herself against him as he bent to kiss her.

He propelled her backwards to the bed and pushed her onto it. Impatiently she pulled his T-shirt off as he slipped out of his jogging bottoms. Like her he hadn't put on any underwear after his earlier shower and his cock was already at half-mast. He pushed her T-shirt up and cupped her breasts as he kissed her again. His cock pulsed against her as it hardened. Pulling her lips away from his, she teased his small sensitive nipples with her tongue. He was rock hard in seconds. He quickly moved down to her breasts, sucked on them both before travelling downwards and tonguing her clit.

She was surprised how eager she was for his cock—you would have never guessed that she'd had his twin banging her only the night before. She reached over, grabbed a condom from the drawer and ripped it open. She kissed the soft velvety head of his cock before she rolled the condom over it, then lay back and opened her legs as he positioned himself against her entrance.

He pressed inside her and her whole body jerked as a sliver of pain ran through her. "Ouch!"

The sound surprised them both: Darren stilled his forward motion and looked down at her in shock; she hadn't realized that she was still sore until this very minute!

"You okay?" It was probably her imagination but there seemed to be a hint of suspicion lurking in his eyes as they searched hers. Shit! She hoped he didn't know that Darrell had left the house the previous night.

"I'm fine, baby." She smiled and he relaxed. "I had just forgotten you have an extra large screwdriver."

"It's only been out of your toolbox *one* night! What would have happened if I'd stayed away the entire week?"

He laughed as he bent to kiss her again, taking his time as he slid deeper inside her.

Soon she was matching the rhythm of his slim hips as he did his unique combination of a forward, backward and sideways motion. Damn, he knew how to move his fucking waist!

When she felt herself nearing her climax she bent her head, sucked on his left nipple and took him along with her.

She felt the tension in his arms as he supported his weight on them and she pulled him tighter against her, letting him relax as his jerking cock pumped his seed into the condom. She was still trying to convince him that she loved the way his body pressed hers into the mattress; *he* believed he was too heavy for her.

All too soon he slid off her and went to discard the condom. When he came back he kissed her and pulled her back against him. Within minutes he was asleep, his arm around her waist, her naked butt pressed against his sleeping cock. She listened to the quiet sound of his breathing and her mind flashed back to the previous night. He and Darrell might be identical but they certainly had very different temperaments. Her pleasure was important to Darren; any pleasure she'd received from Darrell had only been a by-product of him pleasing himself. Darren was steady and dependable; Darrell edgy and unpredictable. She could never date someone like Darrell but having him around added to the excitement of dating Darren. Darren with about five percent of Darrell would be the ideal package!

***

Though Darren didn't move into Alyson's flat, he spent every night there. Sometimes he would go home first to check his mail, shower or get some clean clothes and then go to her flat. At other times, after lectures the two of them would catch the bus or walk to her flat, if the weather was good.

Darrell became angrier and angrier with his brother with each passing day. He had always given his twin a chance to fuck any of the women he dated, and even though Darren had refused many times, at least *he* had given him the choice. He couldn't understand why Darren was being so selfish with Alyson.

Darrell had thought that once he'd fucked her he would have gotten her out his system, but instead the need to fuck her again was becoming an obsession. All he could think of was her smooth skin, her big ass, her tight pussy and the way she had screamed when he had first pushed his cock inside her. She was more than enough woman for both of them and he was sure that she wanted him to fuck her again. But he didn't want to mess with Darren because even though *he* was slightly heavier and bulkier from having the free time to go to the gym more regularly—his brother was cool and deadly. When they were younger *he* always picked the fights and Darren always beat him. The last time they'd had a fight was playing one-on-one basketball in their backyard when they were fifteen years old. They had disagreed on a point and he had punched Darren and split his lip. Darren had jumped on him and it had taken a scream from their mother to get Darren off him.

His brother always had his back while they were growing up and other boys thought twice about taking on either of them. Darrell knew Darren loved him—he just couldn't understand why he was being so fucking possessive!

***

Three weeks later Darren and Alyson walked through the front door and found Darrell watching the highlights of an Arsenal v Manchester United football match. Arsenal had gained a surprise victory, winning the penalty goal shoot-out.

"Hi, Darrell." Alyson hoped her voice gave nothing away.

Darrell raised a hand in greeting but his eyes never left the screen.

"We're going upstairs." Darren's voice was cool, almost as if he was talking to a stranger.

Once again Darrell raised his hand in acknowledgment but kept his eyes glued to the TV screen.

"Did you two have a quarrel?" Alyson asked as soon as they were out of earshot.

"Ignore him—he's just tripping."

Darrell had been a bit distant lately but he was going to have to get over it. Darren knew the way Darrell treated women and there was no way that he was going to let him get his hands on Alyson. He knew that some women liked the rough way Darrell handled them because once when he'd made love to one of Darrell's girlfriends she'd kept screaming, "Harder, harder. Come on, Darrell, fuck me harder!"

When he'd let Darrell fuck Caroline, he'd noticed the dark smudges on her breasts, arms and legs the next day. Like a fool he'd asked her where she'd got the bruises, thinking that she had hurt herself in some kind of freaky accident. Her reply had shocked him, "You were rough with me last night. If I didn't know better I would have thought you were high or drunk."

He'd apologized to her and later he'd warned Darrell if he did something like that again it would be the end of their little arrangement. Darrell had confessed that he couldn't have helped himself. He'd said that he had tried to be gentle but she must bruise easily.

"Are you two quarrelling because of me?" Alyson asked,

trying to sound as casual as possible. The last thing she needed was for the brothers to start arguing and Darrell to confess that *he* had fucked her.

Darren didn't answer and she knew she'd hit the nail right on the head.

"I don't want to come between you guys."

"Don't worry, he'll get over it."

"Are you sure? I don't mind, you know."

"You don't mind *what*?" Darren turned to look at her, one eyebrow raised in inquiry.

"I don't mind if you want him to make love to me. I'll do it, but I want you to be there as well."

She could see it wasn't the response Darren had expected. He looked shocked for a moment, then he smiled. "Are you sure?"

"Yes."

"Thanks, Alyson." He kissed her gratefully. "We have never fallen out for this long before and it worries me. I'll go and talk to him."

Alyson undressed quickly, slipped under the duvet and waited, knowing that Darrell wouldn't need persuasion. Minutes later they both walked through the bedroom door, smiling broadly. She sat up, deliberately letting the duvet fall away from her breasts before she cupped them and rolled her nipples into hard peaks. They both watched her as they ripped their clothes off and within seconds they joined her on the bed, Darren on her left and Darrell on her right. In unison they leaned forward and each closed their lips around an erect nipple.

Bliss! Pure fucking bliss!

She didn't die but she was as close to heaven as she could get while on earth. She had fantasized about that moment a thousand times but the reality was so much better than the fantasy. She reached down, took a hardening penis in each hand and ran her fingers up and down their *identical* smooth lengths. Darren kissed her, she knew it was him—his kisses were softer, more sensual than Darrell's. His brother kissed the side of her neck and left a wet trail with his tongue as he travelled back down to her breast. His teeth nipped and teased her tender flesh as he reached lower, found her clit and massaged it firmly between his fingers.

Darren in the meantime had again taken her other nipple in his mouth and was pulling on it with that firm, sucking motion that she loved. She felt his fingers run up her inner thigh and when he felt the moisture that Darrell's touch was producing, he breached her entrance with two long fingers. Alyson's moans grew louder and louder as they worked in harmony and before she knew it, she was exploding!

Darrell sat up, reached for a condom and rolled it onto his engorged penis. Without hesitation, he reached down and pulled Darren's fingers out of her pussy and pushed his cock in their place. He pummelled her pussy almost as hard as he'd done before and came within minutes. As soon as he pulled himself out of her, Darren took his place, filling her as deeply as his brother had done. He gyrated his waist and his cock found every corner of her pussy. She held on to his strong shoulders and synchronized her movements with his, almost forgetting that Darrell was in the room with them.

"Come on, bro. What's taking you so long?" Darrell was hard and ready to go again.

"You had your turn." Darren ignored his brother and kept up his rhythmic strokes.

"But *you* fuck her all the time!" Darrell protested.

He reached between them and tried to pull his brother's cock out of her but Darren slapped his hand away. Darrell, undeterred found her asshole with his fingers and maybe because she was so relaxed he managed to get a finger inside her.

"Okay then, let me fuck her up the ass."

"No!" Alyson wasn't too lost in sensation to voice her objection.

"Please!" Darrell pushed his finger a little deeper and groaned at her tightness .

"Darrell she said *no*." Darren's reply brooked no nonsense.

Sensing the storm that was quickly brewing, Alyson acted to diffuse the situation. "Come here, Darrell."

She knew he just needed to stick his cock in a hole—*any* hole. He climbed onto the bed, leaned over her and held on to the top of the headboard. Wrapping her lips around his cock, she placed her hand on the shaft to regulate his movement, she could deep-throat but he was wild!

Darren's mouth returned to her nipple and Darrell's hand groped between them to fondle her free breast. Darren's hips quickened tempo and she felt the tremors start deep in her womb. She took Darrell's cock more deeply in her throat. He, of course, immediately grabbed her head and tried to go even deeper. The next instant he came again, his loud cry drowning out the other moans in the room as they too reached the point of no return.

Later, she lay sandwiched tightly between them on Darren's king-sized bed and purred like a cat with a bowl of double cream. She'd had this fantasy since she was nineteen years old and had seen a pair of *fine* identical brothers on an Oprah Winfrey show. Finally, it had come true and had been everything that she'd dreamed. In fact, it had been even better than the fanta-fucking-c!

Darrell's finger in her asshole had created the weirdest sensation—it was painful and arousing in equal measure.

She had always considered anal sex out of the question—
something for gay men with no pussy at their disposal—but
hmmm that finger might have awakened her to the possibility.
It would be bliss to have them both at once, Darren at the
back and Darrell in front. Yes, definitely Darren at the
back—no way was she going to let Darrell fuck her up the
butt—he was so wild he was likely to rip her another asshole!

She smiled as she joined the sleeping twins in
slumberland—it could be the beginning of a beautiful
relationship.

***

Twins have always fascinated me so naturally **Double the
Trouble** *was my first erotic short story. Sleeping with two men is my
biggest fantasy, sleeping with identical twins would completely blow my
mind! The idea of two pairs of hands all over my body, a pair of lips on
each nipple...oh, stop!*

*****

Do As I Say

*E*ighteen-year-old Tonya Phillips ran up the carpeted stairs and into her bedroom. She wanted to freshen up before she met her boyfriend Eric later. Usually they went straight to his house after college but today he was off to the pub to celebrate his friend Peter's eighteenth birthday. He had promised to be home by six o'clock, so she'd decided to make use of the free time by coming home and having a quick shower.

She was just about to open her wardrobe to select a suitable outfit when she thought she heard a faint thump coming from the room next to hers. She held her breath and listened—there it was again!

Her heart started beating faster. No one should be home, her father should be at his surgery and her mother at the Women's Group meeting at church.

She cautiously tip-toed to her parents' bedroom and peeped through the half-opened door. She nearly screamed aloud at the sight reflected in the mirror! Her best friend Karen was bent over the stool in front of her mother's dressing table, her long single plait extensions cascading over her head, her body naked except for her cheerleading skirt which was bunched up around her waist—and Tonya's father was *taking* her from behind.

Tonya stood paralysed in shock and watched as her father pummelled her petite friend with fast, hard strokes. Karen's mouth was open and her loud moans filled the room. Her father's feet were planted firmly on the mushroom-coloured bedroom carpet and with each stroke he was travelling almost half a foot backwards before plunging forward into Karen again.

Just as she began to wonder if her father had somehow forced her friend to have sex with him, Karen screamed, "Slap my ass, Nathan!"

Her father brought his large hand sharply down on the plump cheeks of Karen's backside and the sound reverberated around the room.

"*I'm gonna cum!*" Tonya hardly recognized the husky, pleasure-filled voice as that of her close friend's, although she had known her for almost eleven years.

The words had an immediate effect on Tonya's forty-one-year-old father. He pulled Karen's legs further apart, grabbed her small, firm breasts and increased the speed of his strokes, until the movement of his hips was little more than a blur. Then he stiffened and called her name, his body arching backwards from the waist as he ground his pelvis against her ass.

Finally Tonya felt the strength return to her legs. She ran back to her room, grabbed her bag and sped out of the house as if she was being chased by demons. She continued to run as fast as she could until she got to the nearby park and sank weakly onto a wooden bench.

Her father was such a hypocrite! Every year since she was fourteen he had made an appointment for her with a female gynaecologist, who attended the same church as they did, to ensure that she was still intact. He had threatened to throw her out of the house if he ever found out that she was having sex. He always gave her long speeches on chastity, purity and the dangers of pre-marital sex.

How long has he been screwing Karen?

She and Karen were inseparable friends, Karen had even taught her to kiss when they were sixteen. Although Karen's parents weren't as strict as hers, Tonya had assumed that, like her, Karen was still a virgin. They had done everything together until two years ago when Karen had started cheerleading. Tonya's father had forbidden her to try out, saying the uniforms were too revealing and no daughter of his was going to kick her legs up in the air and show her underwear to an auditorium full of spectators.

The bastard had let Karen kick her legs in the air and show him her underwear, though!

Every Friday after their last class she and Karen went to the Girls' locker-room to change out of their school uniforms. Tonya would usually put on a T-shirt and a skirt or a pair of jeans, Karen would change into her cheerleading uniform. They would part at the school's large double doors. Tonya would leave the building and Karen would head to the auditorium for practice. Today had been no different from any other Friday. Karen had even kissed Tonya's cheek as they had parted.

Tonya sat on the park bench for almost two hours, lost in thought. She'd been betrayed by two of the most important people in her life. Worse was that she couldn't turn to her mother, the person she would have gone to in such a crisis. She was angry that she had locked her feelings away inside her for years, tormenting herself, thinking her natural sexual urges were disgusting. Twice when she had awoken in the morning her panties wet from the erotic dream she'd had the night before, she had felt she was no better than the common prostitute her father warned her she'd become if she had sex before marriage. It had worried her so much that she had tried to think clean, pure thoughts just before she went to bed so that the dreams didn't reoccur.

She'd been dating Eric for over a year and she hadn't even let him kiss her properly because her father had warned her that heavy petting led to sex, and sex to destruction. She had only started going to Eric's house about two months ago when she was finally convinced that he wouldn't get carried away and rape her when she refused to sleep with him. Girls were lining up around the block to take Eric away from her because they knew what a goody-two-shoes she was. It was a small wonder that he had stuck with her for so long!

She glanced at her wristwatch and jumped up; it was ten minutes to six. She ran all the way to Eric's house as tears threatened to overwhelm her. Thankfully, he had returned from the pub. As soon as he opened the door she rushed into his arms and held him tightly. For the first time she let her body mould itself to the hard planes of his and she was surprised how good it felt.

Eric at the age of nineteen was every girl's fantasy: his short, curly, jet-black hair; broad shoulders; 6'4" athletic body and last but by no means least—his sexy dark eyes had gotten him more than his share of girls. In fact, he had probably bedded more girls than some of his classmates had had hot dinners. He usually avoided good girls and any girl who hadn't freed up her pussy within a month of him dating her was unceremoniously dumped. Not that there were many girls who won't give it up to the most handsome young man for miles. Something about Tonya made him more patient than he had ever been in his life. He had fallen for her so hard he was planning to marry her as soon as she finished her A' Levels at the end of the school year. His parents had agreed to the marriage and to release his trust fund early provided he went to university as planned after they were married.

His jet-setting parents had left on Wednesday for their annual two-month-long holiday in Barbados, so he and Tonya were alone in the house. He kept his arm around her as they made their way up to his bedroom, where they usually listened to the latest pop songs on his newly acquired hi-fi system and exchanged chaste kisses.

He'd had three beers before leaving the pub and though he wasn't drunk, he felt hornier than usual. As soon as Tonya sat on the side of his bed, he sat beside her and bent to kiss her softly.

He couldn't believe it when she opened her mouth and allowed his tongue to touch hers before she sucked on it, the way Karen had showed her. He had been trying unsuccessfully to make her French-kiss him for months! Then he remembered the way she had pressed herself against him when she had first come through the door—usually she kept a respectable distance between them. He sensed a new dimension to their petting this week and wanted to explore it to the fullest. As he kissed her he lightly stroked her breasts through her sweater. When she didn't protest, he slipped his hand under the soft cashmere and touched her right breast. She didn't stop him! Instead, she pressed her hardening nipple against his palm. Breaking the kiss, he quickly slipped the sweater over her head and pushed her gently back against the bed.

He'd no idea she had such full breasts, they were twice the size he'd imagined them to be. Her baggy tops had concealed them well. He covered her body with his and kissed her deeply as his hands came up between them to cup her rounded breasts. He raised his head and watched her nipples harden and become visible through the white cotton of her bra as his fingers tweaked and aroused them. Easing one of the cups aside, he saw her naked breast for the first time. It was so beautiful. He paused briefly to admire the contrast of her dark areola to the lighter skin of her breast before he dipped his head and flicked at the swollen peak with his tongue. She gasped in shock but made no attempt to stop him. Instead, moaning softly, she waited for him to do it again. He flicked at it several times, expecting her to suddenly sit up and push him away but she didn't. Encouraged, he pulled it into his mouth and sucked on it.

Still feeling like he was dreaming, he continued, the sound of her moans filling his ears. They grew louder as he sucked on her with greater enthusiasm, opening his mouth to pull the entire tip hard into it. She gripped his head tightly and held him to her breast. After a while he freed the other breast and covered it with his mouth, using his fingers to keep the other fully peaked. He continued to suck and fondle her breasts, moving from one to the other until she was writhing against him, pressing her groin against his hard body.

Time passed endlessly. He couldn't believe how much he was enjoying just sucking on her beautiful breasts. He had never spent this much time on any girl's breasts before but all he'd wanted to do as soon as he'd bared her breast earlier was latch on to her dark nipple.

The alarm on his mobile phone went off. It was six forty-five—time for Tonya to leave. He pulled the cups back in place and kissed her one more time.

Reluctantly Tonya allowed him to pull her to her feet. She had been so close to a feeling that she'd never experienced in her life that she resented having to leave. She kissed Eric goodbye and hurried home. Her father insisted on them sitting down at seven o'clock each evening and eating one meal together as a family, she didn't dare be late.

She slipped quietly through the front door, hoping to avoid her pompous father before she got to her room but he looked up from reading his newspaper, a beer in hand. He had forbidden her to touch alcohol but freely partook of it himself. He was always telling her, *do as I say and not as I do.*

"Young lady, you barely made it home on time. Go up to your room and wash up quickly."

"Yes, Daddy."

She rushed up the stairs to her bedroom and changed her damp panties for a fresh pair, then looked at her reflection in the mirror. Her eyes looked sleepy and glazed, so she quickly splashed some cold water on her face.

She got to the table just as her parents were about to sit down.

"Let's say Grace." Her father reached for her hand as he bowed his head. His large right hand enfolded hers and she remembered that it was the same hand he'd used to slap Karen's bottom. She almost let it go.

She looked across at her mother's serene face and knew that she was blissfully unaware of her husband's deviant behaviour. Her mother was one of those women who let the man rule the home—she did nothing until he gave approval. She worshipped the ground her husband, the respected doctor, walked on.

During the meal Tonya listened to their conversation but made no contribution of her own. She was too busy reliving the feel of Eric's mouth on her breasts. They felt unusually heavy and she prayed that her aroused nipples didn't show through her sweater. The crotch of her panties felt wet again. She couldn't wait for the meal to end so that she could escape to her room.

Her mother had baked apple pie, Tonya's favourite dessert but she refused a slice and asked to be excused.

Helena Phillips looked at her daughter in surprise. "Are you feeling alright, dearest? You look a little flushed." Then turning to her husband whose opinion she thought was vital in every matter, she asked, "Doesn't she, darling?"

Before her father could examine her too closely, Tonya mumbled untruthfully, "I'm trying to lose weight." And rushed out of the room.

She locked her bedroom door, although neither parent was likely to disturb her, undressed and slipped under her duvet wearing just her matching white Marks & Spencer underwear. Cupping her breasts, she tweaked the nipples, trying to imitate Eric's actions. Her response was not the same—her nipples hardened but there was no answering tingle between her thighs. She reached into her panties and touched her wet, slippery vagina. She found the bud of her clitoris, hidden under tight pubic curls, and ran her hand repeatedly over it. The pleasurable sensation increased as she continued to fondle herself but it was not enough. In desperation she slipped a finger inside, breaching the narrow opening of her virgin channel. Minutes passed and although waves of pleasure washed over her, she still couldn't get the same feeling Eric had aroused earlier. She alternatively rubbed her clitoris and fingered herself but to no avail. Finally, her hand became tired. Resigned, she gave up trying to achieve her first orgasm but she was so frustrated it wasn't until the wee hours of the morning that she finally dropped off to sleep.

The next morning as soon as her mother left for work, Tonya had a quick shower, dressed and rushed over to Eric's house. He opened the door, fresh from the shower himself, dressed in a green T-shirt and faded blue jeans. She took his hand and led him straight up to his bedroom. Then excused herself and went into the adjoining bathroom, returning less than two minutes later, her face flushed.

Eric was sitting on the bed flicking through the channels, looking for a decent movie. She walked over and stood in front of him, her eyes bright. He opened his denim-clad legs and pulled her close to his muscular body. Although he was sitting, he barely had to raise his head to take her full, sexy lips in his. She pressed her 5'2" slender frame into his and he felt her soft round breasts squash against his upper chest.

He slipped his hand under her T-shirt and encountered firm, warm flesh; she had taken her bra off in his bathroom. Pushing her T-shirt up, he placed a hand over each breast, making slow circular motions over her hardening nipples. His eyes met her glazed, dark gaze before he raised his head and tongued one of her erect nipples, while he rolled the other into a tight peak between his thumb and forefinger. Her hands came up to grip his head and press his mouth against her aching flesh. Taking a nipple between his lips, he suckled and her ragged moans filled the room.

He ran his free hand under her short skirt and up her smooth outer thighs and got a huge shock. She had taken her panties off too! He moved his hands inwards and tangled his fingers in her curling pubic hair. Then separating the folds of her pussy, he ran his fingers along the slick inner lips gathering the moisture that liberally oozed from her passage. Sliding his damp fingers upwards, he gently massaged her clitoris using a rubbing action that made her start to instinctively thrust her hips backwards and forwards.

Eric's fingers felt so much more arousing than hers had done the previous evening. She reached down, pulled the hem of her skirt up to her waist and opened her legs wider to give him freer access.

The sight of her glistening pussy was too much for Eric. He slid off the bed, grasped her hips and positioned her until her streaming pussy was close enough to his waiting mouth. He alternately sucked vigorously and gently flicked at her engorged clitoris with his tongue.

"God, that's so good!" She grabbed his head and pressed it into her crotch.

He plunged the tip of his tongue into her tightness and felt the tremors start to run through her body. When she came he was surprised by the abundant flow of fragrant juice that ran out of her. Her legs threatened to buckle but he kept her upright by grasping her hips while he savoured every last drop. Satisfied that he had caught it all, he lowered himself unto the floor and rolled, taking her with him. He slid his body upwards until his lips were levelled with her bared chest. He still couldn't get over the size of her breasts. Before yesterday she'd never allowed him to touch them, *not* even through her clothes.

"I never knew your breasts were so big," he said cupping the weight of one and teasing the small nipple.

"I hate them, that's why I always wear big tops,"

"They are beautiful." His lips covered a dark tip, pulled on it briefly and then released it. "Your nipples are so juicy I can't stop sucking them."

"I love it when you suck on them, it makes me wet. Last night when I left here I was so hot I tried to masturbate but I couldn't get it right. I even pushed a finger up inside me but I couldn't get off. I'm so glad I came over today so that you could make me cum."

Eric laughed at the way she'd phrased her words. "It was my pleasure to make you cum and I think that it's my duty to make you cum again."

He pulled her T-shirt off, took one of her small tight nipples into his mouth and sucked on it the way that had driven her wild minutes before. Slipping his right hand between their bodies, he fondled the swollen lips of her slippery pussy. He circled her entrance with his middle finger and then slowly pressed it into her opening. The warm folds enclosed it in a tight embrace. He pushed it a bit further and the breath caught in her throat.

"Is it too painful?" he asked, his words muffled against her breast. She was torn between the pleasure of his suckling mouth and the bitter-sweet pain of his blunt forefinger stretching her vaginal passage. She didn't want him to stop doing either. Wordlessly, she shook her head and he pushed his finger a little deeper, simultaneously pressing his thumb against her clitoris.

Soon he was withdrawing and plunging almost half the length of his long finger into her, the slick wetness aiding the motion. He went faster and deeper as she raised her hips off the floor to meet his thrusts. Suddenly her body stiffened, her back arched off the carpet, her pussy walls clenching his finger tighter for a second. Then her whole body went limp as another orgasm ripped through her. He picked her up and climbed onto the bed with her.

After Tonya had left last night Eric had gone over to Linda's. They had fucked all night and finally satisfied, he had slipped out the back door of her parents' house just before dawn. He wasn't sure just how far Tonya wanted to go with this petting but he was horny again. He gently eased open the first button of his jeans, and then the next one— grateful that he was wearing his button-fly Levi jeans and not the zipped ones he usually wore; he was so hard he might have hurt himself trying to unzip them. He slipped his hand into his Y-fronts and his eager cock leapt onto his waiting palm, begging for some attention. He wrapped his fingers around it and stroked his hand backwards and forwards a few times but his heart wasn't really in it, his cock longed to be buried in Tonya's tight folds.

He sat up, pulled his T-shirt off and slipped his jeans down his legs. Tonya opened her eyes as he lay back down beside her. He put his arm around her and kissed her softly. Her lips parted and the kiss became more passionate. He touched her upper thigh and she instinctively parted her legs to accommodate his seeking fingers. She was so wet he managed to get his finger into her with little trouble. After a few thrusts, he placed a second finger alongside the first. Her body stiffened and then relaxed as he brought his left hand up to fondle her breast as he plunged his tongue further into her mouth.

As she relaxed he rotated his fingers slowly, not deepening his thrusts but widening her passage bit by bit. Her hips followed the motion of his rotating fingers, her tongue sucking on his urgently and her nipple as hard as a pebble between his fingers. Soon she was lost in the pleasure his fingers were creating and her juices drenched them when she came.

"Can I put *just* the head of my cock inside you?" he begged. "I promise I won't hurt you and I'll stop any time you want me to."

She nodded but he could see that she was torn between desire and fear. He kissed her softly and reassured her, "Relax, you can trust me."

At first Tonya was amazed at the softness of his cock as he placed the head against her but her body jerked when he pressed it harder against her and tried to breach her entrance. She pulled her lips away from his to gasp his name.

"Just the head, sweets—that's *all* I want to put inside

you," he whispered softly, gently stroking the damp hair back from her forehead.

"Okay."

He dipped his head and took her right nipple and sucked fiercely as he placed his thumb firmly against her swollen clit and massaged it. The pressure on her clit made her unconsciously press her opening onto his waiting cock as her arousal mounted, and gradually the head slipped just inside her. He withdrew a fraction of an inch and then sank back almost the same distance carefully, and then again and again. Her squeezing tightness was incredible. He put his hand on the shaft of his cock to stop it going any further as she pressed herself harder against it. She was so aroused, if he wanted to, he could thrust his aching cock straight into her pussy and rip through her hymen, but he had made a promise. She would be very upset afterwards. And he wanted their first time to be as pleasurable for her as it was for him. Unenthusiastically, he pulled his tormented cock free and started wanking it.

She looked down and the breath caught in her throat at the size and the beauty of his erection. She reached out and touched it. Putting his hand over hers, he showed her how to pleasure him and soon he was shooting his load all over her hand.

They lay back together for a few minutes in silence.

"My father makes me go for an examination every year to make sure that I am not having sex," Tonya blurted out suddenly, a blush darkening her cheekbones.

"*What?*" Eric sat up and looked down at her. He knew her father was very strict. The first time he had gone to take Tonya to the cinema her father had given him an extensive lecture about fornication, but this was beyond anything he'd imagined. "You are not serious!"

"Honestly!" Tonya's blush deepened. "I love you and I wanted us to make love a long time ago but I was too scared to disobey him."

"Well, we only have to wait another four months until we get married."

"I can't wait to feel you inside me." Eric's cock jumped at her inflammatory words.

"*I* can't wait to be inside you." He pulled the nipple nearest to him into his mouth and gave it a hard suck.

"The gynaecologist only checks my vagina not my ass." The sight of Eric's cock had awakened something primal in Tonya. "Maybe we could have anal sex."

He almost couldn't believe that he'd heard her correctly.

"Are you sure? It will be very painful." He felt compelled to warn her, although it would be his ultimate fantasy come true.

"Yes. I want you inside me."

Last year at her parents' anniversary party she had overheard an older cousin telling her boyfriend that she liked it when he fucked her up the ass. Whenever Tonya remembered the words they sent a shiver through her.

Eric needed no further persuasion. He undid the single fastening on her wrap skirt and threw the garment across the room. Her pussy felt swollen as he ran his forefinger along the streaming outer lips. Gathering some of the moisture on the tip of his finger, he pressed it against her tightly closed anus. It resisted at first but he patiently teased it with a circular motion until she relaxed and the tip slipped inside her. Her anal muscles gripped his finger as tightly as her pussy had done but it softened as he patiently kept up the slow thrusting motion. Soon he gathered some more moisture on a second finger and slipped that alongside the first. Within minutes both fingers were passing the rim of her asshole with little difficulty.

He slipped off the bed and pulled her to the edge of it, so that her legs hung over the side. Then he knelt behind her, separated the cheeks of her ass and tongued her asshole for long moments, feeling her relax more and more. When she had relaxed enough for the tip of his tongue to just push through the rim, he straightened and pushed the two fingers back inside her and vigorously finger-fucked her ass.

Finally, he rubbed his cock across the lips of her pussy, getting it wet with her juices before he held her small cheeks apart and placed the bursting tip against her anal muscles and pressed inwards. She made a faint sobbing noise and instinctively tried to move forward as she felt the tip penetrate her bowels, but the bed prevented her. Slowly he lodged the bulbous head of his cock in her ass and within a few minutes it had sunk about two inches inside her.

He was so caught up in the spectacle of seeing his cock disappear slowly inside her that he didn't realized she was softly whispering his name over and over again. He leaned over, kissed the side of her face and asked, worriedly, "Are you okay?"

She nodded but didn't answer—the pleasure-pain was almost too much for her to bear.

"Do you want me to stop?" He would if she wanted him to.

"No!" She couldn't wait to feel the full length of him inside her.

He reached beneath her to stimulate her clitoris with one hand and her breast with the other. Immediately he felt her relax even more. His hips pressed forward, sinking his cock an inch deeper. He continued to mould her clitoris and her nipple between thumb and forefinger, deliberately keeping the pressure firm, making her lose control. She started to back up against him, taking more and more of his cock into her tightness. Soon he was buried inside her. Her anus pulsed around his embedded cock, squeezing him, driving him to the brink of insanity. He barely managed to withdraw his cock and plunge it back again a couple of times before he spilled his seed deep inside her.

Despite his ejaculation his cock was still rock hard. He urged her up onto the bed and started his thrusting movements again with greater ease and speed as his sperm provided a lubricating medium.

The discomfort of him stretching the tight lining of her rectum was forgotten as Tonya's pleasure climbed to fever pitch. She ground herself back against him, taking him as deeply as possible.

Eric had never had anal sex before. Although many of his friends had boasted that they had tried it, so far none of the girls he'd slept with had let him take them anally. The fact that it was his virginal girlfriend who was giving him his first piece of ass made it even more special. He felt her convulse under him as her orgasm ripped through her. Immediately, he joined her, once again flooding her bowels with his spunk.

Slowly he pulled free and lay down beside her. She turned and smiled at him, her eyes limpid with pleasure. Her breasts were mere inches from his face. He put his arm around her and positioned her until a nipple was close enough to his mouth. He pulled it between his lips and sucked on it. Moments later when they fell asleep he was still pulling on it, like a nursing baby.

They woke two hours later, famished. He made them a 'monster' sandwich each before they had a bath together. Her ass was too sore for another round so he ate her pussy and made her cum one more time before she left at four that afternoon, half an hour before her mother was due home from work.

***

The next Monday when her father dropped Tonya off at school, Karen was waiting at the school gate with her usual, "Good morning, Mr. Phillips."

Her father replied casually, "Good morning, Karen."

In the past Tonya would have been too busy grabbing her bag and her lunch from the backseat to notice the way her father looked hungrily at her friend. Today, because she had deliberately kept her things in her lap and alighted as soon as her father stopped the car, she was able to observe their reactions to each other. As she watched the interchange more closely she realized she'd completely missed an obvious clue: Karen had only started waiting for her by the gates at the beginning of this term. Before, they had met in the classroom just before the start of the first lesson.

Karen didn't wait at the gate for *her*, as she had thought, she waited to see her father!

And Tonya hadn't understood why lately he had insisted on giving her a lift to school every day. In the past he had given her a lift only on the rare occasion that he had no early bookings at his surgery. Up until the end of last term she had taken the bus to school or occasionally had gotten a lift from her mother. She had assumed the daily lift to school was another of her father's ways of ensuring that she stayed on the straight and narrow. Making sure that she didn't play truant, by dropping her at the school gate and waiting until she and Karen walked into the building before driving off.

He probably sat there and watched Karen's ass bounce in her short skirts. The dirty bastard!

Tonya felt repulsed. Karen had been coming to their house since she was eight years old. She was like his daughter. How *could* he sleep with her?

At lunchtime as they sat in the cafeteria Tonya looked into Karen's heavy-lidded eyes. They stared unflinchingly back from her heart-shaped face. She seemed the same as before, totally unchanged. There was no outward sign to indicate that she was being fucked by an older, married man and her best friend's father to boot!

Tonya wondered if her friend could tell that she had let Eric fuck her ass on the weekend. Her parents hadn't seemed to notice that she was no longer their pure virginal daughter. She didn't feel any different. Though every time she remembered the way he had made her cum several times that day, she couldn't help the smile that parted her lips.

Her father still sprouted the same *tripe* at the dinner table each evening but she barely listened to his words. Instead, she counted down the days to when she would see Eric and have his big cock buried deep inside her again.

On Wednesday night in desperation she tried using her finger but it wasn't a fat enough substitute for Eric's thick cock. She tried a candle but the lifeless object didn't feel anything like Eric's pulsating length. She pulled it out and threw it onto the bedroom floor in annoyance. Nothing came close to Eric's sweet cock.

On Friday she kissed Karen at the school's exit and walked purposefully away. But as soon as she rounded the corner she hid in a nearby hedge. A minute later Karen came running out the building, heading in the direction of Tonya's house.

She's going to be fucked by my father again. Tonya's mouth tightened in anger as she ran back to the auditorium. Keeping her voice casual, she asked one of the cheerleaders for Karen.

"Karen hasn't been to practice since the end of last term,"

the girl informed her, confirming Tonya's suspicions.

As she left the building Tonya had a sudden clear flashback of an incident that had puzzled her at the time. When she and her mother had returned home from picking up her father's gifts the Saturday before last Christmas, she had gone upstairs to hide hers in her wardrobe. She'd been surprised to find Karen lying on her bed, looking flushed, an unfamiliar musky smell in the air. Karen had jumped off the bed and kissed Tonya, saying she'd been waiting for almost two hours and had to go home immediately because her mother was expecting her. Bladder full from the large soft drink she'd had with her earlier meal at Burger King, Tonya had rushed to the main bathroom. She had heard the sound of the shower even as she had turned the door knob and found the door locked. As she had run down to use the smaller washroom downstairs she had wondered why her father was having a shower in the middle of the day when he'd had one at six that morning as was his custom. That had to be when the whole thing started—exactly two and a half months ago!

Tonya walked the short distance to the Boys' school where Eric was waiting. His eyes lit up when he saw her. He looked as eager as she felt to get down to some lovely ass-fucking. He put his arm around her, kissed her cheek and they walked hurriedly in the direction of his parents' house.

The day was slightly muggy and he offered her a drink when they got indoors. She opted for a beer much to his surprise—he had never seen her drink alcohol before. They quickly downed two cans of beer in the kitchen before she ran ahead of him to his bedroom.

They started undressing each other as soon as they got there and within seconds they were both naked. He bent his head to kiss her and she wrapped her arms around his neck, automatically clasping her legs around his waist when he lifted her up in his arms. He took a nipple in his mouth, the coldness of his tongue tantalizing her sensitive flesh as she reached down and stroked his already erect penis. He walked over to the bed and they fell on it together, his body beneath hers. He transferred his mouth to her other breast as she feverishly ran her hand up and down the length of his cock, caressing the soft tip repeatedly.

"I want to taste you," she murmured and kissed her way down his body. Eric watched as she put her mouth daintily around his bursting erection. She barely took a little more than the tip inside her mouth but applied a firm motion, like she was sucking a lollipop, that made his toes curl. He sat up without breaking the contact and pulled her legs over to him.

He opened her firm thighs, placed his lips right on her meaty little clitoris and instantly he felt her take him more deeply into her mouth. Her pussy was already dripping. He moistened two fingers and probed her asshole as he continued to suck on her clit. He quickly got one finger inside and slowly worked the other one in. Soon she was begging him to replace his fingers with his cock. She had been waiting for it all week and couldn't wait another second!

He turned her over, positioned her doggy-style on the bed and pressed his cock against her back passage. At first she was as tight as the previous week but slowly his cock sank inwards as she relaxed and opened around him. Soon she was rotating her hips and banging her ass back against him, taking all of his wonderful, full length. They'd both been full of anticipation all week, in less than no time they came together.

They collapsed on to the bed, his deflating cock still squeezed by her tight rectum but within minutes he was hard again. He took her lying on the bed, his mouth sucking urgently on the breast that was in reach now that the top half of her body was resting against the bed. When he felt his climax near he reached down and moulded her clitoris between his fingers and took her with him again.

All too soon his alarm went off reminding them that it was time for her to go home. She quickly used a soapy washcloth to wipe the traces of their recent activities off her body and ran all the way home.

The next morning, as she had done the previous Saturday, Tonya arrived at his house just after eight in the morning. He barely pushed the door closed behind her before she reached inside his boxers for his cock. Within minutes they were both naked, her head buried in his parents' living room sofa, as he fucked her ass doggy style. Her asshole was nice and relaxed from the previous evening's fucking and he was soon pumping away with vigour, burying himself to the hairs in her backside, his hands on her breasts rolling her nipples between his fingers. Less than ten minutes after she had walked through the front door they were both cumming.

He grabbed two cans of beer and they headed up to his bedroom. He took a mouthful of the ice-cold liquid and immediately pulled on one of her nipples. She gasped and he repeated the action on the other side. Her nipples stood out from the centre of her breasts like little black pebbles.

Whispering that he'd be right back, he hurried to the bathroom to quickly soap and rinse his cock. He came back, lifted her into his arms, swung her around and held her in place for a standing 69. She was so light he held her with one arm, reached for his beer can and took another mouthful. She moaned and sucked harder on his cock as his chilled lips met her heated flesh. He continued until the can of beer was empty and she was begging for his cock again.

He sat back on the bed, resting on his bent arms—his

rock-hard cock shooting upwards like an obelisk. She climbed onto the bed, crouched over him and slowly sank onto his waiting cock, her face a picture of concentration as she took more and more of it inside her. Finally, with about two inches to go, she stopped—she couldn't go any further. But she started moving up and down his cock, taking a tiny bit more inside her each time. Her heavy breasts bounced with each movement. The sight of them and her glistening pussy was too much for him. He sat up and pulled a nipple into his mouth and reached down to finger her clit. Immediately, her actions became more frenzied and soon the whole shaft of his cock was pressed inside her posterior passage. Seconds later she came, sending him over the edge as well. Gingerly, she pulled herself off and collapsed on top of him. He put his arm around her and held her against him. They lay together for a while, not saying anything, just enjoying the residual tremors of pleasure.

Then she propped herself up on her elbow and looked down at him. "I enjoy your cock in my ass but when I cum my pussy feels empty."

"Next time I'll stick my finger as deep as I can inside you when you are about to cum."

"No. Next time I want you in my pussy."

"You want my cock *all* the way inside you?" Eric looked into her eyes as he asked the question—he wanted to make sure that he was clear about what she was asking.

"Yes," she replied, without hesitation.

"Are you sure about this?" Eric was enjoying her sweet ass. He could get pussy from several other girls, yet as she'd said the words his cock had hardened again.

"I'm sure," she confirmed.

"Okay, let me get a condom." Grabbing the handle of his rucksack, he pulled it closer and took a packet of condoms from one of the outer pockets. He had already taken a risk of getting her pregnant by putting the head of his cock inside her, he couldn't take another chance.

He quickly tore the packet open and rolled the condom over his stiff cock as she lay back, her legs open. He pushed a finger inside her slick wetness. It slipped in easily, but he had a bit more trouble getting the second one inside her. He sucked on her nipples alternatively as he continued to finger-fuck her. Soon the room was filled with the squishing sound of his fingers going in and out of her tight, wet pussy.

"I want you inside me *now*," Tonya demanded impatiently as she stilled the movement of his hand.

"Okay, baby."

He climbed on top of her and kissed her as she reached down and positioned his cock against her opening. With a few deft movements of his hips he got the head inside her and then pressed inwards until he came to the obstruction.

"Are you sure about this?" Eric asked one more time, although he would die if she said no.

She nodded and he covered her mouth with his, plunging his tongue deep into her throat, imitating the thrusting motion of his hips as his cock tore through her virginity. She moaned as he rotated his hips and sank deeper and deeper inside her.

The pain was sharper than Tonya had expected but as Eric pulled backwards and thrust inside her again, the friction created a small spark. As he did it over and over again the sparks ignited into a flame that heated her body and finally sent her up in smoke.

Eric groaned as she came, the walls of her hot pussy gripping him unbelievably tighter. He couldn't help the orgasm that ripped through his body seconds later.

He kissed her tightly closed eyelids softly and she

reluctantly opened them.

"Are you okay?"

She nodded but he could see the faint glimmer of tears in her eyes and he kissed her again. His penis jerked as it hardened within her tender insides. She moaned and dug her fingers into him. He pulled himself free slowly and they both looked down instinctively. There were streaks of red on the condom. He kissed her again before quickly going to the bathroom to discard it.

Grabbing a washcloth, he dampened it with tepid water and returned to the bedroom. Tonya was still lying where he'd left her, legs tightly clenched together. She opened them at his urging and he wiped the traces of blood from her swollen pussy. She winched in pain as the water stung her torn flesh but let him continue cleaning her off.

After taking the washcloth back to the bathroom, Eric knelt at the side of the bed and pulled her closer to him. Tonya tensed as he covered her sore pussy with his lips but he ate her gently, running his tongue repeatedly over her clit and around her still tender entrance. It soothed one ache and started another. Minutes later she was cumming against his mouth.

As he climbed onto the bed she pulled his head down and kissed him. Lazily, he reached over her to check the time on his mobile phone. It was only just after eleven thirty! So much fucking had taken place since Tonya had walked through the front door he had assumed that it was much later. He pulled her back against him, cupped one of her breasts and idly stroked her nipple. Gradually, they gave into their sexual exhaustion.

They woke up just before one thirty. Eric ordered a large pizza which they fed to each other until it was finished. Afterwards, they went back to his bedroom and sipped cans of chilled beer while they watched The Simpsons on Eric's widescreen television set. He sat behind her fondling her breasts, rubbing his hands repeatedly over her nipples until they looked ready to burst. At the beginning of the commercial break she turned and pulled his head down to the tight peaks. As soon as he started sucking on her flesh his cock became rigid again.

Every time his lips tugged on her nipple Tonya felt a corresponding tug in her womb. The moisture gathered in her pussy until it streamed out and ran between the cheeks of her ass.

"I think you need to be fucked one more time before you go home," Eric remarked as he ran his fingers over her pussy. "You are absolutely dripping."

"Do you want my pussy or my ass?"

Either prospect thrilled Eric.

"Your sweet, tight pussy first—if it is not too sore, and then I want another piece of your lovely ass."

He reached for another condom, expertly rolled it in place and then lay on top of her, sucking on her breasts while deliberately moving his hard cock over her clitoris until she reached down impatiently and put the head against her opening. Her passage was tight and a little sore but he slowly moved his hips from side to side and backwards and forwards in such an arousing manner it obliterated the pain as she matched his rhythm and eagerly met his thrusts. He pressed his pelvis against hers when their hairs met at each forward stroke, gently brushing against her clit. Soon she was sinking her fingers into his shoulders as intense pleasure built inside her, wave after wave, finally cresting in a muscle-clenching release.

The clutching motion of her tight pussy as she came threatened his control, but the thought of plunging into her ass again made Eric bear the almost abrasive action until it subsided.

"Now it's time for a little ass-fucking," he whispered as he turned her over on to her front. She raised her ass and pushed it back at him. He looked at the two choice options of entry she presented to him and his cock pulsed. Was it only two short weeks ago she was an untouched virgin? His patience had been rewarded a hundredfold—now he had unlimited access to a sweet pussy and a beautiful ass. He had to be the luckiest young man alive!

The condom was covered in her juices. Spreading her cheeks, he pressed the end of his cock against her asshole. She relaxed completely and let the head slip past the rim. He reached down to fondle her clit as he slid the rest of his cock inside her. He worked on her clit until he felt her relax further before he started thrusting the full length smoothly in and out of her. As he quickened the motion he remembered her earlier comment about her pussy feeling empty when she came as he fucked her ass, so he tried to get two fingers inside her pussy but it was awkward. She had to open her legs for him to get his fingers inside her but his longer legs were already on the outside of hers, moving them further apart decreased his range of thrust.

Inventively, he held her against him and swung around, sitting on the edge of the bed. With both pairs of feet on the floor, hers wide open over his—it was easy for him to plunge two fingers in her pussy as he rubbed his thumb against her clit, while she thrust her ass up and down his cock. He still had one hand free and he brought it up to roll her nipple as she rammed her ass harder into him. Within minutes they both erupted.

"I enjoyed that!" His chest heaved as he tried to steady his breathing.

"Me too!" she agreed. "It was wonderful—my pussy wasn't as sore as the first time and when I came I almost passed out!"

Eric's mobile phone alarmed just then—it was time for Tonya to go home.

"I can't wait until next Friday," he whispered as he kissed her goodbye at the door.

"Me neither," she whispered back and reluctantly moved out of his embrace.

I'm not going for any frigging medical examination this year, she thought defiantly as she covered the short distance between the two houses. *I'll do as you do, father dearest, and not as you say.*

Maybe next Friday she would sneak in the house and take a picture of him fucking Karen. If he got nasty she would show it to her mother. And if he *really* pissed her off, she'd make copies and hand them out to his patients. He was such a hypocritical bastard!

Now that she had discovered the joys of sex she wanted it often. She might even try skipping the family evening meal and go over to Eric's every night instead. Her mother wouldn't have any objections and Tonya scarcely gave a toss what her father thought. She was looking forward to the upcoming Easter holidays, Eric's parents would still be away so she would go over to his house every day and be fucked every which way.

Eric was a sweetheart and his cock was big, though she was no judge of penis size. She wondered just how good he was. She enjoyed the way he fucked her at the moment so she would let him fuck her for a while longer. *If* sex became boring, she'd let a few of the other neighbourhood boys fuck her before she finally settled down. Either way she intended to have lots of sex. Most girls at her school had been having cocks stuck into them since they were much younger—she had a lot of ground to make up and she intended to do so.

***

A virgin having anal sex may seem a bit far-fetched but for years many young women, especially those brought up by strict, devout Christian or Muslim parents have used anal sex as a means of preserving their virginities for marriage while still enjoying some of the pleasures of sex.

*Originally, I had planned to just explore this phenomenon in **Do As I Say** but then I decided that since **Tonya** had lost all respect for her father, there was no reason for her not to go all the way.*

*****

THE NIGHT BEFORE

*S*uzette James turned over and snuggled up to her sleeping partner, her eyes still closed. She flung her arm out, encountered warm flesh and let her hand wander over a flat stomach and upward to a mound of soft flesh. She moulded it in her hand and felt the distinct hardening of a nipple.

A nipple! For a crazy moment she thought that she was touching her own breast then she realized that *she* would have felt her touch. Her eyes snapped open. She closed and re-opened them quickly to see if the woman asleep on the pillow next to her would disappear.

She didn't.

Then Suzette remembered *the night before!*

Mackenzie!

The company Suzette worked for Latham & Parson had lost their place as market leader in the London antiques business and was keen to win it back. The director had decided on a number of customer-focussed training courses to better equip staff to serve the needs of its one and a half million customers. It was just Suzette's luck that her course was held on a Friday. The stupidly conscientious co-ordinator had been intent on giving a full day's lectures with scant regard to the fact that it was Friday—and for Suzette the start of the weekend, which she usually celebrated at lunchtime with two glasses of wine.

At seven the previous evening Suzette had been the first person out the meeting room as the training day had finally drawn to a close. She'd walked to the nearest pub, sat on a stool at the beautifully lacquered bar and ordered a pint of lager. Thirstily, she'd gulped a quarter of the contents of the glass and her parched throat had felt instantly better. The two glasses of freshly squeezed orange juice she'd drunk while on the course hadn't quenched her raging thirst and the only other liquid they had supplied was water—she never drank the stuff straight.

A man came over and sat on the stool next to hers. She glanced at him fleetingly before looking away. He wasn't her type he was short and had a bit of a belly.

He obviously has a gym-phobia, she thought uncharitably.

"Can I buy you a drink?" he asked in a surprisingly feminine voice.

Was he blind? Couldn't he see that she had an almost full glass in front of her?

"I'm fine thank you," Suzette responded politely.

"I'm Denise, what's your name?" The man held out a small hand.

"*Denise?* What kind of name is that for a—?" Suzette didn't finish the question as she turned and got a good look at him.

He was a woman! Slowly she looked around the bar and laughed softly in amusement. It could only happen to *her*! She had been so desperate for a drink—she had walked straight into a lesbian bar.

"I'm Suzette," she responded. "And I'm only here for a quick drink—I've had a very rough day!"

Denise shrugged, got off the stool and walked away. Five minutes later another woman jumped up onto the stool. Suzette got a whiff of her light perfume but didn't turn her head. Instead she downed the rest of her drink and made to get off her stool.

"Let me buy you another one."

These lesbians were fucking persistent!

Suzette turned to politely refuse. Her eyes met a pair of dark, thick-lashed eyes set in an oval face the colour of walnut shells.

"Hi! I'm Mackenzie." The woman held out a slim hand and Suzette took it in hers. "Please don't go and leave me here all alone, they'll ravish my helpless body."

"I'm Suzette and though I am very pleased to meet you, I'm afraid I really must go."

"Come on, stay for another drink. It's Friday!"

Suzette had only been going to find another pub to throw back a few more pints alone anyway. Lloyd, her current man would be playing happy families with his wife and three point zero children tonight. And Mackenzie seemed like she was a whole lot of fun.

"Okay, I'll stay for just one more."

Six pints later she staggered back to Mackenzie's flat with her. When they got indoors Mackenzie asked if she was hungry. Suzette replied she was starving. She'd avoided the platter of cold cuts served at the meeting like it was the plague. She'd had a mild case of food poisoning at another meeting when she had first joined the company, a *very* unpleasant experience.

Mackenzie served her a big plate of split-peas cook-up rice with a succulent piece of baked chicken and crisp green lettuce on the side. Suzette finished the tasty meal and even cracked one of the bones between her teeth before she remembered that she wasn't in the privacy of her own home.

"What were you doing in a lesbian bar?" Mackenzie asked as they retired to her spacious living room, drinks in hand.

"I could ask you the same question!" Suzette shot back.

"I'm a lesbian and it's my local. I hang out there most weekends," Mackenzie responded candidly.

"Oh!" Mackenzie's comment about being 'ravished' had made Suzette assumed that, like her, Mackenzie had just been there to get drunk.

"Don't worry, I'm not going to jump on you!" Mackenzie reassured her.

Suzette looked at Mackenzie and laughed out loud. If the petite woman jumped on her she could brush her off like a piece of lint.

"Do I look worried?" Suzette countered.

"I may be small but I'm strong!" The other woman pulled her sleeve back and flexed her right bicep and Suzette laughed again. It was the size of a lemon—Suzette's was easily twice as big.

"You haven't answered my question," Mackenzie persisted.

"I desperately needed a drink after the day from hell and it was the first bar I came across."

"Have you ever slept with another woman?" Mackenzie obviously didn't believe in wasting time.

"No."

"Did you ever want to?"

"Why all these questions?" Suzette taunted. "Do *you* want to sleep with me?"

"Yes." Mackenzie didn't pause to think.

"What are you waiting for then?" Suzette was feeling a little drunk and a lot daring. Mackenzie was a neat little package, if she was finally going to see what sleeping with another woman was like, *she* was a perfect place to start.

Mackenzie unfolded her slim legs and lifted herself gracefully out of the armchair she'd been sitting in. She walked over and stood in front of Suzette's chair. Suzette could see that she was trying to decipher if it was a bluff or not. She pulled Mackenzie's head down and covered Mackenzie's soft lips with hers.

Mackenzie quickly pushed her tongue deeply into Suzette's mouth and pressed her back against the sofa. As they kissed Suzette slipped her hand under Mackenzie's top and touched her right breast. Mackenzie's small nipple tightened instantly and Suzette pushed the material aside, pulled Mackenzie upwards and tongued the tight nipple before she pulled it into her mouth. Mackenzie moaned as she ran her hands through Suzette's short, straightened hair. Suzette sucked harder, surprised how much the slim woman's moans turned her on.

"Let's go to the bedroom," Mackenzie whispered as she wriggled free and held out her hand. Suzette grabbed it and was led to the bedroom.

They stripped and jumped into bed. Mackenzie climbed on top of her, kissing her again as she cupped her larger breasts. Suzette was surprised how good Mackenzie's soft hands felt against her flesh. She sat up and continued where she left off, sucking on Mackenzie's tight little button nipples.

When Mackenzie urged Suzette back onto the bed and covered one of her swollen nipples with her lips, Suzette reached down and found Mackenzie's clit. She was wet and without hesitation Suzette rammed a finger inside her pussy. Mackenzie was exceptionally tight! Suzette applied gentle pressure to Mackenzie's clit as she thrust her finger deeper. Mackenzie gasped and drove her pussy furiously against

Suzette's hand. Before you could say Bab's your aunty, Mackenzie shuddered, stiffened and then relaxed against Suzette.

But a minute later she was sliding down Suzette's 5'10" body, licking, kissing and sucking as she made her way down to her pussy. Suzette opened her legs wide as she felt Mackenzie's tongue on her clit. She flicked at it softly, repeatedly, maddeningly until Suzette had to reach down and grab hold of her long hair. Mackenzie quickly pushed three slim fingers inside Suzette as she sucked on her clit in earnest. Suzette lasted all of…twenty seconds.

Mackenzie slid upwards and kissed her, Suzette wrapped her arms around her and held her. Mackenzie felt light and soft against her. When her erect nipples brushed Suzette's an electric shock raced through her.

"Let me get a dildo." Mackenzie murmured as she slid off her, walked to the built-in wardrobe and opened the door.

All Suzette owned was a Rampant Rabbit vibrator that she'd bought when a work colleague had hosted an Ann Summers' night. Mackenzie looked as if she had hosted a similar night and had bought one of every item! It was all neatly arranged by size and classification—anal plugs, dildos, vibrators, nipple suckers, nipple and clit clamps, balls and a number of leather outfits. In a corner stood a weird looking machine that consisted of two padded seats and a handle. Mackenzie informed her that it was a 'Fuck Machine'. Suzette had never heard of such a thing!

Mackenzie selected a long flexible 14" double-headed dildo and they jumped back into the bed. She bent it into an L-shape and inserted one end into Suzette's pussy and then climbed onto the other, easing herself down on it, *slowly*. She lowered her breasts unto Suzette's and the dildo bent into a

U-shape. Mackenzie manoeuvred herself until her clit was right on top of Suzette', then started to softly grind their clits together. Suzette raised Mackenzie's head and plunged her tongue into her mouth. Mackenzie's hands grasped her breasts and gently rolled her nipples, while Suzette slid hers over Mackenzie's slim hips and grabbed hold of the piece of the dildo that remained outside and pushed it against them. It inched further inside her and Mackenzie's gasp told her that it had penetrated her a bit more deeply as well. Suzette pulled and pushed it for a little while, imitating a thrusting motion but her hand soon ached from keeping up the awkward movement. She pushed it back in to the maximum and then cupped Mackenzie's firm butt.

The skin on Mackenzie's ass felt like silk, Suzette ran her hands over her small cheeks and found the even softer skin of her crack. She circled the smaller woman's asshole with a finger, letting the tip just breach the rim, teasing her erogenous zones. Mackenzie's tight asshole resisted when she tried to push her finger a little further, so she continued to tease the tight rim. Mackenzie went wild and started a clit grinding that had them both gasping before they came simultaneously. Then she pulled the dildo out and snuggled up to Suzette.

***

Suzette lay back against the pillows and watched Mackenzie as she slept.

Why hadn't she done this before?

It had been one of her most intense sexual experiences and the *weird* thing was that it didn't feel weird at all.

Even waking up in bed with a strange woman didn't feel odd, unlike the time she'd had too many glasses of red wine and had woken up next to a handsome guy she had vaguely remembered introducing himself as Robert the previous night in the pub. She had opened her eyes at dawn, still dressed in her clothes and wondered how she could have slept in the man's dirty bed. Then she'd followed her nose to the smell of ripe food and pin-pointed its source as a half-eaten slice of pizza under the bed. She had high-tailed it out of the flat before he had woken up. Her only comfort was that she had used a condom—she had been too drunk to smell but thankfully not drunk enough to forget protection. For months afterwards she'd expected to break out into some horrible rash after her exposure to his disgusting living conditions but thankfully six years later she was still rash-free.

Mackenzie's bedroom smelled heavenly fresh. The fine texture of the pillowcase caressed Suzette's skin as she laid her head back against the soft pillow and closed her eyes.

She must have dropped off again because the next thing she felt was a soft mouth brush her breast and then a tongue on her nipple. She opened her eyes and Mackenzie was standing by the side of the bed wearing a bath robe, leaning down to tease her breast.

Suzette stretched lazily and Mackenzie raised her head. "Good morning. Did you sleep well?"

"Never better," Suzette replied truthfully. The comfortable bed and snuggling up against Mackenzie's soft body had given her the best night's sleep in a long while.

"What would you like for breakfast?"

"Let me grab a quick shower and we'll make it together." Suzette started up and then remembered that she didn't have a change of underwear or clothing. "Shit, I haven't even got a pair of clean knickers."

"I've got some new thongs that should fit you." Mackenzie opened her underwear drawer and pulled out two size-eight Agent Provocateur thongs—one black, one red.

"Do you expect me to sew the two of them together?" Suzette asked with a laugh.

"They are an American eight. They'll fit you, trust me."

Suzette laughed disbelievingly as she headed for the en suite bathroom. Mackenzie had left a large peach towelling bathrobe and a new toothbrush out for her.

That's so sweet of her, Suzette thought as she stepped into the cubicle.

After her quick shower, she looked around the bathroom as she dried the moisture from her body. Like the rest of the flat it was simply but beautifully designed. Last night Mackenzie had told her that she was an interior designer. If she had done the work on the flat herself, she was very talented.

Suzette walked back into the bedroom, picked up the black thong and slipped it over her hips. It only fit her because it was a little more than a piece of string and a gusset. The material cut into her pussy like a little clit teaser—she'd be dripping within the hour.

"I told you it would fit you," Mackenzie remarked as she walked into the room.

"You call *this* fitting?" Suzette turned around and pointed to the sides of her pussy the skimpy material didn't cover.

Mackenzie folded over with laughter. Suzette grabbed her playfully, pushed her onto the bed and trapped her under her body. Laugher faded as they stared at each other. Suzette had wondered if the beers she'd drunk had made her want Mackenzie but as she leaned down to kiss her, she realized she hadn't been acting under the influence of alcohol. She opened Mackenzie's bath robe and looked at her freshly-showered, naked brown body. Mackenzie was naturally slender, her skin smooth and soft. Her small breasts were perfectly round and as Suzette admired them she saw the nipples hardened. Remembering how sensitive they were, she dipped her head and wrapped her lips around one taut bud. Mackenzie moaned and arched her back, pressing herself against Suzette's mouth as she circled the hard peak with her tongue. Suzette slipped her hand under Mackenzie's thong, found her clit and stroked it, slowly increasing the firmness of her fingers until Mackenzie was gasping. Mackenzie's hands came up to cup Suzette's breasts and tease her nipples as Suzette opened her mouth and pulled hard on her nipple. Suzette slid two fingers inside Mackenzie's slick pussy and Mackenzie immediately trapped Suzette's hand between her thighs and writhed against her fingers until she came.

Suddenly, the phone rang. With obvious reluctance, Mackenzie checked the caller-ID, then sighed and reached over to answer it. Suzette got off the bed, pulled on the peach robe and went to the kitchen to give Mackenzie some privacy.

When Mackenzie walked in five minutes later, Suzette had already poured percolated coffee into two jugs and slotted four slices of wholemeal bread into the toaster.

"Sorry, I *had* to take that call. It was one of my major clients," Mackenzie apologized as she slipped her arms around Suzette, resting her head against her breasts. "I'll make it up to you after breakfast."

"I'll hold you to that promise."

"Please do." Mackenzie pushed the robe aside and covered Suzette's nipple with her mouth just as the toaster pinged.

Mackenzie ignored the sound and when Suzette tried to pull herself away, Mackenzie hung on to her nipple. Suzette swatted her backside. "Breakfast first—sex later!"

"I'm having breakfast." Mackenzie gave Suzette's nipple

one last tug before she pulled the robe back in place.

After breakfast Mackenzie kept her promise with the help of a few handy tools from the closet. And during the course of the day Suzette tried a few more. The nipple suckers were sublime—she definitely had to get herself a pair of those, but her personal favourite was the Fuck Machine. She definitely wouldn't be getting one of those, because if she did, she would never leave the house! She tried it late Saturday evening and rode herself to two explosive orgasms before she stumbled off it weakly. She just loved the way she could control the speed of thrust herself. Mackenzie preferred the slim 6" dildo attachment but Suzette loved the feel of the mega 8" as it ploughed its way into her.

Being an early riser, she was on it again early Sunday morning before Mackenzie had even awakened. It was very addictive!

Late that evening Mackenzie gave Suzette a lift to her flat in Bromley. They kissed long and lingeringly in the darkened Mini before Suzette went up to her second floor flat, alone. She didn't dare invite Mackenzie inside because she knew that they would end up in her bed, and they both needed rest.

The next morning Suzette showered, dressed and caught the tube to Oxford Circus. Ten minutes after exiting the Tube station she punched a six-digit combination into a panel at the side entrance of a large building and waited until the green light indicated that the lock had disengaged before she pushed the door open and entered the antiques store.

The West End branch was the busiest of the company's four shops and by the close of business she was yawning. As she joined the queue of passengers trying to fight their way on to the tube later that day, she realized that not once in her eight-hour work day had she used the new skills she'd been taught during Friday's training course. She had been just too fucking tired!

Her sugar daddy, Lloyd, came over on Wednesday, as usual. His daughter had piano lessons on Mondays; his two boys had football on Tuesdays and Thursdays; Fridays and the weekends were family days. Wednesdays were the only days he could fit fucking Suzette into his busy schedule.

As usual he brought her a huge box of Thornton's chocolate, some money and another bottle of expensive wine that he seemed to love; *she* preferred the cheap shit and lots of it.

And as usual he got right down to business as soon as he walked in the door. He barely took off his clothes before he had her on her kitchen worktop, pushed into the space between two units. They had never made love in her bed. She suspected that their bed was the only place his wife let him make love to her, so when he was with Suzette he got a chance to get his freak on.

When Suzette had first started seeing him three years ago she had been about a stone lighter. He used to like to fuck her standing up, supporting her weight as she bounced on his cock, her legs wrapped around his waist. A hundred and fifty or so boxes of luxury chocolates later, he couldn't lift her for long enough.

He seemed to be in a bigger hurry than ever. He kissed her as he tried to dry finger-fuck her. When that didn't work he changed strategy. Moving down to her breasts, he pushed them painfully together and sucked on both nipples at the same time. He pushed his finger into her pussy again. It didn't seem as wet as he wanted it to be, so he knelt on her cold linoleum kitchen floor and sucked on her clit. A couple of minutes later he straightened, plunged his cock inside her and kept thrusting until he came. He didn't seem to notice that she *didn't*. He leaned against her until his deflated cock slipped out of her, leaving the condom still stuck inside her, the end peeping out of her pussy like an exotic flower.

He went into her bathroom to wipe himself off, then came out and struggled back into his clothes.

"I've got to go, honey. See you next week." He kissed her, rubbing his stubble against her face and then left.

Five minutes after his departure her face still felt raw but her breasts and her inner thighs had stopped smarting—the brother's beard was like a wire brush! She'd never realized what a selfish fucker he was until now. She was usually as hot as he was when he came over on Wednesdays; even before he walked in the door she would be wet and waiting. But the countless orgasms she'd had during the crazy weekend with Mackenzie had left her mellow. Lloyd had only performed the perfunctory foreplay so that she would be wet enough for him to get his cock inside her. ...*see you next week.* She didn't think so! She wouldn't be staying in next Wednesday for another slam-bam-fuck-you-ma'am from him! She would be at Mackenzie's, sipping the fine bottle of wine and eating the luxury chocolates *he* had supplied.

***

Thursday dragged its feet but finally it was Friday—Mackenzieday!

She threw a few things in an overnight bag before she left her flat in the morning and after work she went straight to Mackenzie's plush pad in Kensington.

Mackenzie opened the door in a sexy, barely-there outfit. Before Suzette had a chance to put her bag down properly Mackenzie jumped up on her, wrapped her legs around her and was kissing her like she'd just returned home from a six-month trek up Mount Everest. Suzette turned, pushed

Mackenzie against the wall and plunged her tongue into her mouth. As they kissed Mackenzie undid the buttons on Suzette's shirt, pulled her left breast out of her bra, slid down the wall and sucked on it eagerly.

"I need a shower," Suzette protested.

"I want to taste *you*...not shower gel," Mackenzie mouthed between sucks.

Well, Suzette conceded, it wasn't as if she hadn't taken a shower before she'd left for work. And, the week before, she hadn't even given showering a thought when they had stumbled into Mackenzie's bedroom.

She reached down and tweaked Mackenzie's nipples until she started moaning. Pushing her back against the wall, Suzette bared them both and sucked on one and then the other. Mackenzie grabbed a handful of her hair but the pain only made Suzette pull harder on her nipples. She nudged Mackenzie's legs apart with her knee and stroked her clit as her ragged moans grew louder. When she felt the tremors start to run through Mackenzie's slim body, she pushed two fingers inside her. Mackenzie almost collapsed as an explosive orgasm racked her body.

By the time they got to the bedroom they were both naked. They tumbled onto the bed for an earth-shattering 69.

Next she tied Mackenzie's hands together with a chiffon scarf, using a slip knot so Mackenzie could untie herself if she wanted to. She pushed a nipple sucker onto Mackenzie's left nipple, pressed the ball at the end of it and watched the suction pull her nipple into the transparent cup, then did the same to her right. Personally, Suzette loved to squeeze the balls about four times on her own nipples—the powerful suction would elongate her nipples to almost an inch and the sensation! But Mackenzie usually only pressed the ball once when she put the suckers on whenever she rode the Fuck Machine. Suzette pressed both balls again, simultaneously. Mackenzie groaned as she writhed restlessly on the bed, arching her pelvis up.

"Come on Suzie baby, eat my pussy," she begged. "Tongue my clit, honey."

Mackenzie's nipples looked twice their size and so incredibly beautiful that Suzette was almost tempted to press the balls one more time. Instead she resisted the urge and lowered her head to lave Mackenzie's clit. Mackenzie groaned appreciatively and Suzette pushed her tongue deep inside her pussy. Mackenzie instantly came all over it.

***

Suzette loved to hear the soft sounds Mackenzie made when she was aroused. She responded to the slightest caress and all Suzette wanted to do was make her cum and cum again. A finger in Mackenzie's ass, not too deep, sent her almost to the point of madness.

When Mackenzie had confessed that Suzette was her first lover in nineteen months she hadn't believed her—the petite woman was far too beautiful to be left on her own that long, lesbian or straight. Until Mackenzie admitted that her last relationship had ended very badly. The woman had ignored a restraining order and continued to harass Mackenzie. It had taken the threats of a male cousin who worked as a bouncer to finally rid Mackenzie of the sadist she had dated for three *long* months.

The woman had moved into Mackenzie's flat within a week of them meeting in an S & M club in Islington. She had totally abused Mackenzie's sweet nature. She had started by purchasing sex toys over the internet using Mackenzie's credit card. When Mackenzie refused to get her nipples pierced so that she could hang small weights from them, the woman had bought weighted nipple clamps and used them instead. Her idea of fun was holding Mackenzie immobile and pressing a lubricated anal plug into her ass before she fucked her with the largest dildo in the house. There had been no *safe word*—she was the one who decided how much pain Mackenzie could take. She had loved to see Mackenzie cry and beg her—she had gotten off on it, until Mackenzie had learned to keep her tears for the bathroom, afterwards.

The last thing she'd ordered on Mackenzie's credit card was the rather expensive Fuck Machine from America through a UK sex shop. It had arrived a week after the woman had finally stopped coming around. Mackenzie had left it in the box unopened for months, imagining some kind of medieval torture device. When she had finally opened it to see if she could somehow break it down to fit it into her rubbish bin, she was surprised to see the benign-looking machine. Cautiously, she had tried the smaller attachment and loved it from the first ride. She could have slapped herself for the wasted time—it was the perfect partner! She still hated many of the toys in the closet but kept them there as a reminder to never get drawn into another abusive relationship.

Mackenzie couldn't stand too much pain. The double-headed dildo they had used the first night was long but slender. Realizing that Suzette liked a fuller penetration, Mackenzie had bought another two dildos: one tapering from a small head on one end to an eye-popping bulbous head on the other; the next, Mackenzie's favourite, had a clitoral stimulator in the middle, a 5½" attachment on one end and an 8" on the other.

Suzette had demanded lots of personal space in all five of her previous relationships, always moving to her side of the bed once she and her male partners had finished making love and it was time to sleep. Now, she loved to have Mackenzie snuggled up to her when they finally went to sleep. She loved the feel of her small, soft, smooth body against hers. She loved the way she smelled, the way she snored softly and breathed through her slightly open mouth. She loved everything about her!

***

Mackenzie started working on her first celebrity home a month later. The Eastenders' star dismissed the interior designer he had originally commissioned after the woman had presented him with a revised bill that was almost twice the agreed estimate. Then a close friend of his had recommended Mackenzie. The schedule was insanely tight but Mackenzie was hoping to have the house ready for him when he returned from honeymoon with his new bride in a few short weeks. The actor wasn't optimistic about her getting it done, which made Mackenzie determined to surprise him.

She was totally exhausted when Suzette arrived on Friday. They had a shower together, crawled into bed and just slept, snuggled up to each other. Early the next morning Mackenzie kissed her goodbye and went off to work. Suzette had offered to lend a hand but after careful consideration they'd both decided it might not be such a good idea—the soap star had a sinfully decadent Jacuzzi which they would have probably found themselves luxuriating in rather than decorating his house.

Suzette, naturally, occupied herself with the Fuck Machine in Mackenzie's absence, only resting it periodically, worried that she would somehow damage it.

She made ox-tail soup for Mackenzie, knowing intuitively that she wouldn't want anything heavy to eat when she came home as she would probably go almost immediately to bed.

Mackenzie's flat was spotless. With nothing to occupy her time, Suzette used a special cleaning fluid to sterilize a few more of the toys in the closet before trying them for size and pleasurability.

Mackenzie came home late evening, tired and grimy. While she hungrily downed a bowl of soup, Suzette filled the bathtub. They got in the water together and Suzette scrubbed the dirt and fatigue from Mackenzie's tired limbs. Then she gently patted her dry and laid her against the covers. Draping Mackenzie's slim legs over her shoulders, Suzette reached up to tease her nipples as she covered her clit with her lips. Mackenzie shuddered to a release in less than two minutes. She reached to touch Suzette's breast but Suzette shook her head and smiled. "Believe me, I'm *fine*."

Suzette didn't know how many times a person could cum in one day but she had definitely reached her maximum. Sunday evening she took the Tube home rather than let an exhausted Mackenzie give her a lift. The next week she got her period, three days later Mackenzie got hers too. Mackenzie was still working frantically to finish the soap star's house, so Suzette stayed home for the first weekend since they'd been seeing each other and gave her flat a thorough cleaning.

In bed early Sunday night she reflected on the times she'd spent with Mackenzie and smiled. She had deliberately gone over to Mackenzie's place on two consecutive Wednesdays but Lloyd had still turned up at her flat on the third. He had accepted her decision to end the relationship but had begged her to let him fuck her one last time. She had done so, for old times' sake. He'd sat her on the edge of her writing desk, and perversely seemed to want to make it last forever as he'd pounded his cock into her for ages. Finally he came and went.

Thankfully, she hadn't heard from him since—he was probably fucking his wife in their bed on Wednesdays instead. Whatever! Suzette was having too much fun to care. She didn't have to put the toilet seat down or to look at boring football matches when Manchester United was playing and she didn't have to worry about stubble burns on her tender parts after they'd made love. Could she go back to being fucked by a man when being with a woman was so much more pleasurable?

***

The next Friday, Mackenzie greeted Suzette in a sexy little bunny outfit to show that she was bright-eyed and bushy-tailed. She had finished the actor's house and he had been very impressed. He'd even invited them to the housewarming party he planned to give in a month's time. He wanted everyone to meet his brilliant designer.

Suzette and Mackenzie spent all Friday night making up for the two weekends they'd lost. Saturday night they went to an amateur evening at the local lesbian bar. Suzette had been practising a few tricks since she had picked up the flyer on an earlier visit but only planned to do her routine if the competition wasn't too stiff.

The first three performers were unimpressive. By the time the fourth came on to the stage, Suzette had decided that she would do her routine.

"I'll be back," she whispered to Mackenzie as she slipped out of her chair.

Mackenzie had no idea what Suzette was up to. Her planned performance was as much a surprise treat for Mackenzie as it was a chance for Suzette to play exhibitionist.

There was only one more performer before Suzette had to go on stage. She slipped off her little black dress and waited, dressed only in her zebra-striped half-cup bra and matching thong.

Earlier, she had asked the DJ to play Soca music to accompany her, starting with Kevin Little's *Turn Me On*. As soon as she heard the intro she walked confidently on to the stage. She danced to the music for about half a minute before turning around and flexing the cheeks of her ample ass in time with the music. The crowd loved it.

Then she left the stage and walked over to Mackenzie, who still looked shocked. Slipping her thong off, she draped it over Mackenzie's head before she bent over in front of her, revealing the tiny bit of chiffon sticking out of her pussy. Mackenzie's face creased with laughter. She held on to the end of the scarf as Suzette walked slowly back to the stage. The crowd oohed and aahed each time a different, tightly knotted chiffon scarf came out of Suzette's pussy. When she reached the stage, there were still one more scarf left inside her. She motioned Mackenzie to get up and walk towards the back of the room. Just as the other end was about to slip out of her, Suzette caught it deftly.

Dramatically she held up one end as Mackenzie held up the other. The small crowd gave her a standing ovation. Suzette indicated that she was going to gather the scarves and Mackenzie moved forward to meet her, also gathering as she went along. Just before they met in the middle, a woman reached out, grabbed a length of chiffon and ran it past her nostrils, inhaling deeply like she was doing a line of premium-grade cocaine. The crowd erupted with laughter.

For her *pièce de résistance* Suzette dampened the suction end of an 8" dildo and stuck it to the floor with a loud bang. Then she did the splits over it, using her hands to support her weight as she slowly lowered herself until the dildo was buried inside her. She unsnapped her bra and waved it over her head like a flag as she once again flexed her butt cheeks until the music ended. The crowd gave her another standing ovation.

Women grabbed her and hugged her or shook her hand as she made her way back to Mackenzie. Minutes later, the owner of the bar walked over to their table with her prize, a bottle of Hennessey and a £100 Patta Cake gift voucher. Patta Cake was an exclusive line by a Guyanese lesbian whose leather and fetish clothing were internationally famous. Mackenzie owned several of the designer's sexy leather outfits.

The owner of the bar asked Suzette if she would consider performing at the club on the weekends. The pay she offered was only slightly less than what Suzette earned at the moment and Suzette was more than tempted to give up her job in the antiques business but she told the woman that she would think about it and get back to her. She and Mackenzie enjoyed free drinks the entire evening; every time they finished a round another table sent them a re-fill—Suzette's little routine had been a definite hit.

When they got back to the flat Suzette gave the vouchers to Mackenzie and the two of them sipped the brandy from fat tumblers, lying naked by the fire on several of Mackenzie's plush rugs.

Suzette considered the tempting job offer all the next week. She'd already thought of adding another nifty little trick to her repertoire—pulling a condom over one of Mackenzie's small hands or slender feet and fucking herself with it.

It would be wonderful to work only on the weekends and have free time during the week to hunt second-hand stores and car booth sales for good antique jewellery. Suzette knew many valuable pieces still lay undiscovered all around the

UK. People were constantly bringing items into the shop where she worked for evaluation totally unaware of their true value. But later, perhaps—right now she needed the discipline of her forty-hour a week job so that she didn't spend any more time at Mackenzie's. They were both as insatiable as each other and at the moment they were still at it like rabbits, if she had any more spare time on her hand the two of them would probably fuck each other to death!

***

The next Saturday after they'd shared a shower, Mackenzie told Suzette they were going to her favourite S & M club, then pulled a gift-wrapped box from under her bed and handed it to Suzette. Mackenzie had avoided the club since her break-up with her ex-lover but she decided that it was time she had some fun again. She also knew that the woman would think twice about harassing her if Suzette was around.

Suzette tore the wrapping paper off and opened the box. Nestled in tissue paper was a supple black leather skirt and matching halter, both with the discreet Patta Cake logo. She threw Mackenzie onto the bed and kissed her to show her appreciation before slipping the outfit on. It moulded to her curves like a second skin and when Mackenzie slipped on an identical outfit in red, and like Suzette wore nothing under the soft leather, they looked set for a racy night on the town. Full-length leather coats completed their ensembles as they caught a passing a taxi and were on their way.

Mackenzie instructed the driver to pull over outside a wine bar in the heart of Islington. As she paid the driver, Suzette looked around to see if there was another club in the vicinity—the people in the wine bar were all decently dressed.

"Come on." Mackenzie grabbed her hand and led the

way down a staircase and into an underground vault beneath the wine bar. Suzette looked around in surprise. Red light illuminated every corner but cast a soft, sensual haze over the large room.

The hundred and fifty or so women in the room were mostly Black. Suzette had never imagined that they were so many Black lesbians in the UK, much less London.

Free condoms were everywhere. The club had one rule: condoms must be used whenever there was penetration. Small bins were placed strategically for their disposal after use.

"I'll see you later," Mackenzie whispered to Suzette after she'd had a quick look around and noted the absence of her ex-lover. She wandered in the direction of a woman using the end of a tasselled whip to penetrate another who was hanging from some chains.

Left to her own devices Suzette moved over to a tall woman standing impassively in a corner wearing a replica of The Changing of the Guard uniform—red tunic, bearskin and all, but the large dildo strapped in the harness round her hips wasn't standard issue for the Queen's Guards. Suzette tore open a condom, rolled it onto the dildo and backed herself onto it. The woman remained impassive as Suzette rode herself to a nail-biting orgasm.

Suzette pulled the condom off the dildo, dropped it into a nearby bin and moved on.

She passed a large woman in a bouncing contraption that consisted of a seat with a round hole cut out in the middle and a pressurized unit from which a wicked looking dildo rose stiffly. A woman of average weight would get about 6" of the projection inside her but the overweight woman was heavy enough to force the seat right down to the base of the unit and get the full 8" penetration.

It's good to see that there are some things in life which favour the overweight, Suzette thought as she watched the enjoyment on the woman's face. She made a mental note to give the machine a try later, *if* she could get on it—there was a line of women eagerly waiting to try it themselves.

Next were four long, opulently-upholstered benches where women reclined, making themselves as comfortable as possible while they waited to be penetrated by anyone who had the urge to do so. Each of the four sections had a maximum penetration length starting at 5" at the first section to a jaw-dropping 9" at the last. An array of dildos was laid out at the side of each section. Two burly female bouncers were on standby to ensure that no one used the wrong dildo or forgot to put a condom on it before use.

There was a separate bench for women who wanted double penetration. Suzette giggled as she looked at the assortment of freaky-looking dildos for use on that section. She was definitely going to pass on that one!

Moving on, she picked up a cane and playfully struck it several times against the ample cheeks of another woman.

Then, in a lone corner stood the tallest woman Suzette had ever seen—she was about 6'5"! At first Suzette thought she was a transsexual but as she got closer Suzette confirmed that the woman had definitely been born female. Her dark skin gleamed in the light. Both of her heavy breasts were pierced and had metal spikes through them. The black dildo she'd strapped on was like the woman herself, the biggest in the room—it stuck out in front of her like a club. Overhead the word *The Amazon* flashed in neon lights.

Suzette debated for only a second before she reached for a condom and ripped it open. It was fluorescent green and as she rolled it in place with both hands she wondered if she had made the right decision. The dildo seemed larger as the bright condom showed it to full effect. The Amazon put her hand around the dildo and shook it menacingly.

Suzette climbed on to the first rung of the three step platform that had been placed in front of the woman to cater for all heights. Then she grasped hold of the foam-covered metal rings that were suspended from the ceiling, closed her eyes and nodded her readiness.

The Amazon's large hand landed on her left ass cheek. Suzette jerked in shock but before she had time to recover the woman landed a blow on the right. The woman slapped the cheeks of her ass soundly for a full minute or so, spacing the blows rhythmically as if listening to a drum and Suzette felt the heat of the blows literally open up her vaginal walls.

As soon as she'd landed the last blow the woman leaned forward, grasped Suzette's hips and forced the dildo past her entrance. She lifted Suzette's right foot onto the second rung of the platform and used her large hands to tilt her ass up as she forced the rest of the dildo into her, inch by inch.

When Mackenzie came forward and kissed Suzette, she opened her eyes and realized in shock that a group of spectators had gathered to watch.

It was always a treat for the regulars when anyone was brave *or* foolish enough to take on The Amazon!

Mackenzie moved lower to suck on Suzette's nipples. Suzette groaned as the woman forced yet another half inch inside her. Mackenzie immediately moved down and tongued Suzette's clit.

Finally Suzette felt The Amazon's huge thighs touch hers. She breathed a faint sigh of relief but the woman rotated her hips and managed to work another tenth of an inch inside her. Then, grasping Suzette's hips firmly, the Amazon treated her to a series of forward and backward thrusts that intensified as the cheering of the crowd reached frenzy.

Suzette met her stroke for stroke, her orgasms coming so fast they were like one endless pleasure-filled burst of bright light.

Holding on to the rings tighter, Suzette pulled her legs upwards and wrapped them snugly around the tall woman's hips, then she backed herself up against the larger woman and rotated her hips until she heard a harsh cry as The Amazon ground herself against her and exploded.

Satisfied, Suzette let go of the rings and collapsed weakly against Mackenzie as the crowd cheered. Suzette was only the seventh woman in three years to take the full length of The Amazon's special friend *Black Mamba* and the first to make the great woman cum while doing so!

The Amazon gave Suzette a crown and a huge bottle of champagne. Then she dipped Suzette low and gave her a deep kiss. The Amazon's tongue, like everything on her, was giant sized and it filled Suzette's mouth. Dazed, she wondered how the woman's tongue would feel on her clit.

"I forgot to warn you about The Amazon!" Mackenzie shouted to her over the noise of the cheering crowd.

"*Now* you tell me!" Suzette laughed as she bowed to the crowd once more before they slowly dispersed in various directions. She knew if Mackenzie had forewarned her about The Amazon she would have made a beeline for her as soon as she'd entered the club—there was nothing she liked more than a good challenge!

Now there was fire in her veins—enough of being fucked, she wanted to fuck someone! She went back to the line of women waiting to have something stuck in them. She ignored the first three sections. She had conquered The Amazon—she wanted to swing a big dick!

She chose the fattest dildo on the rack, strapped up and pulled a condom onto it. Three women were bent over the padded bench. Suzette chose the slim, light-skinned woman with an incredible pair of long legs. The woman had been very popular, and as Suzette had walked over to the section she had seen another woman pull out of her. She grasped the woman's slim hips and the big dildo slid smoothly into her well-fucked pussy. Suzette rode her to a quick orgasm.

But still the fire coursed through her veins, she needed to do some more shafting. A short plump woman reclined next to the other leggy woman, even in heels her feet barely made contact with the ground. Since Suzette had been in the club she'd only seen the plump woman fucked twice and both times the two slimmer women on the bench were being fucked already. Always one to root for the underdog, Suzette pulled the used condom off the dildo and quickly slipped a fresh one on.

She had to bend her knees slightly to slide its large head into the woman. The woman's pussy was very tight—she should have perhaps been in one of the other sections, but like Suzette *she* probably relished a challenge. Suzette urged her off the bench slightly and reached around her fat stomach to finger her clit as she slowly eased the dildo into her. It inched inside her, resisting all the way, pressing the other end back on Suzette's clit.

Finally Suzette got the full length in and started thrusting back and forth. The harder Suzette thrust forward, the more the friction of the woman's clinging walls pressed the other end of the dildo against her. It felt like the dildo was an extension of herself, part of her body—like her own cock!

When the woman came, she thrust herself backwards as she wriggled her dimpled butt. The sudden increase of pressure on Suzette's clit was too much; she tightened her grip on the woman's large backside and rode the orgasm with her.

When she got her breath back, Suzette leaned down and kissed the back of the woman's neck. It had been an unbelievable ride!

Suzette had never realized how powerful it felt to fuck someone. She and Mackenzie both liked being fucked and they had shared many spine-chilling orgasms using the new double-headed dildos. They also both loved to jump on the Fuck Machine regularly and ride themselves to oblivion but she had never thought to strap on a dildo and fuck Mackenzie. It had somehow never entered her head. It wasn't at all like Suzette to be slow on the uptake but Mackenzie's tight little pussy had her too mesmerized to think straight! Even when Mackenzie was wet Suzette couldn't comfortably get more than two fingers inside her. Suzette couldn't imagine how that brutal woman could have fucked Mackenzie with a thick 8" dildo—she could barely take a slim 6" one. That was beyond cruelty; that was pure torture! As for the woman forcing an anal plug in Mackenzie's tight little asshole when Suzette had a job just getting her *finger* inside her. Heaven help the bitch if Suzette got her in a corner—she would kick the shit out of her!

Suzette wished she'd had a ringside seat when the woman had come around for the last time, banging on the door like she paid the mortgage. Mackenzie's cousin had answered the door shirtless, looking as though he had just woken up after a round of fantastic sex. He had, in fact, been napping on the couch waiting for her to come and make a nuisance of herself again. The foolish 5'3" woman hadn't turned and walked away. No! She had demanded, from a man who could have been separated at birth from The Amazon, that Mackenzie come out and talk to her! So he had called Mackenzie out and possessively draped his arm around her before lying to the woman, telling her that Mackenzie was *his* woman now and he would personally fuck her up if she didn't leave Mackenzie alone. Finally she had gotten the message.

Suzette didn't plan on being as nice as Mackenzie's cousin had been. If the woman stepped up to Mackenzie any time she was around it would be fucking war! Hell, if Mackenzie *just* pointed the woman out to her, Suzette would be all over her like a fucking itchy rash. It would take an army to get Suzette's foot out of her ass!

Mackenzie had told her that the woman was so 'butch' she didn't acknowledge she had a clit! *That's* when Suzette knew that the woman couldn't be right in the head—a lot of men would pay good money to have a clit, gay and straight ones, and the woman had hers going to waste! Sacrilege!

Suzette wasn't concerned with all the femme-femme or butch-femme business, she and Mackenzie were doing what came naturally and so far it had been incredible. Since they had begun dating they'd only had one bit of bother—once they had gone to a bar another woman had started chatting up Mackenzie, who had politely informed the woman that she was there with Suzette. The woman had looked at Suzette, almost in horror, and asked, 'Aren't you femme too?'

Suzette had replied, 'So?'

The woman had stormed off, looking seriously annoyed, as if they had broken some cardinal rule of lesbianism.

***

Primed for a night of passion, Suzette went looking for Mackenzie. She found her watching the heavy woman using the bouncing contraption, again. Suzette had forgotten her promise to try it herself—maybe the next time she visited, the woman didn't look as though she was going to get off it any time soon.

She slipped her arms around Mackenzie and whispered in her ear, "I have a special treat for you. Are you ready to go?"

Mackenzie leaned backed against her and nodded.

They collected their jackets and left the club. Five minutes later they were sitting in the back of a taxi heading home, the crown and the outsized bottle of champagne on the seat next to them, Mackenzie's head against Suzette's shoulder.

After her experience with her last partner Mackenzie was still wary of putting herself in any kind of vulnerable position. Unlike Suzette, she had spent the entire night just looking on, having a good time watching others enjoy themselves.

Her slim, sexy legs poked through the opening of her leather coat. As Suzette admired their firm smoothness she noticed that Mackenzie was rubbing them together restlessly. She covered Mackenzie's tightly-pressed together knees with her hand. Mackenzie sighed and parted her legs. Trailing her hand up Mackenzie's soft inner thigh, Suzette touched her bare pussy and found it dripping wet!

She immediately pushed two fingers into her woman's moist heat. Mackenzie bit Suzette's shoulder to stifle her moans, tilting her hips up slightly to give Suzette fuller access. Thrusting her fingers deeper in gradual increments, Suzette finger-fucked Mackenzie slowly, enjoying the soft friction of warm, wet flesh against her fingers. Mackenzie's nipples were standing firmly erect through the soft leather of her skimpy top and Suzette wished desperately that she could bare them and tongue them both. In less than a minute she felt Mackenzie shudder as she came, her mouth opening soundlessly against Suzette's shoulder as she tried to bite back her moans of pleasure.

Suzette couldn't wait to get her home—Mackenzie would

definitely not need the Fuck Machine tonight! She was going to strap on a nice slender dildo, lay Mackenzie back, gently ease it inside her and make her cum and cum again! Mackenzie wouldn't need those impersonal nipple suckers she used when she rode the Fuck Machine because Suzette's lips would see to those sensitive nipples of hers as she fucked her.

From now on *she* would be Mackenzie's personal Fuck Machine.

***

I was surprised how easy it was for me to write **The Night Before***. It's more about two women giving each other pleasure than about lesbianism although I think Suzette has the making of a good butch. I got the idea for the story when a friend asked me if I had ever considered sleeping with another woman. My answer was and still is, 'I've never met one who made me want to.'*

Years ago I spent time hanging out with a group of lesbian friends and had a lot of fun. I was surprised to find that most relationships were butch-femme—I had thought there would be more femme-femme couples. I was also shocked at the level of infidelity—I'd assumed women would be more faithful to each other. Many of the women told me I didn't know what I was missing but honestly the only time I was ever slightly aroused was watching two femmes kiss—that was hot!

*****

SLEEPING HER WAY TO THE BOTTOM

"**Y**ou're next for the office slut—I've seen the horny bitch eying up your butt every time you walk past her office," a high-pitched feminine voice warned.

"Not me!" a deep, masculine voice denied. "I wouldn't touch her with a barge pole!"

"They all say that and before you know it she's got them licking her pussy like affectionate little puppies!"

"Well, that's them! I will *not* be licking her pussy—I never mix business with pleasure."

"I'll give her another month before she's got you by the balls, *too*."

Thirty-nine-year-old Darleen Smith smiled as she listened to the exchange between Shane, the ugliest gay man she'd ever met and Carl, her newest member of staff. She knew they were talking about her—she was the only female in the building. *And* she had made it her mission to sleep with all the men she hired.

Shane's just fucking jealous, she thought. *Pissed off because I get more cock than he does! Ugly bitch!*

Shane was her 'token' employee. Fourteen months ago

she'd hired him when he'd applied for the job of post room attendant in response to her advert. She had planned to go through the motions of interviewing him and then informing him politely by mail that he'd been unsuccessful, *until* he'd sashayed into the room.

Perfect! she'd thought and hired him immediately. The bastards from the Equality Board had been on her back for years about the fact that she only hired straight, Black men. In one inspired move she had satisfied all three of their demands—he was gay, White and a woman of sorts! But from the first day he'd started the job she wished that she ignored the threats from the nosy fuckers and run her business as she'd seen fit. The man was the world's worst gossip and seemed hell-bent on warning all new employees about their predatory boss. It really pissed her off! She knew that he must be sexually frustrated, the only way he probably had sex was to pay for it and she paid him a mere pittance. He chain-smoked, drank like a fish and if his size was anything to go by, ate like a horse. So, unless he was independently wealthy, she doubted that he would have enough money to rent a man to fuck him. She understood sexual frustration, she herself tried to avoid it like the plague. Hell, she wouldn't think twice about strapping on a dildo and fucking his ass herself, if he wasn't so damned ugly!

Carl, on the other hand, was a fine-looking specimen of Black manhood and she would make him eat his words—just before she made him eat her pussy.

"Excuse me guys, are you finished with the photocopier?" she asked, deliberately keeping her voice level.

They both spun around in surprise.

Shane, the cow, rolled his eyes and acted like he didn't give a shit whether or not she'd overheard their conversation. He picked up his file and walked away, rolling his fat hips like he was some plus-sized supermodel on a runway. He had a fierce walk, probably attracting hundreds of men from the back until they took one look at his face and ran for cover. Talk about looking good from behind but not from in front!

Poor Carl looked as though he wanted the floor to open up and swallow him whole. She could clearly see the embarrassment on his handsome face.

"Y-es, Ms Smith. Y-ou can use it now." He avoided her eyes as he stammered the words and she felt just a little sorry for him. He bent slightly to gather his papers and she got a brief glimpse of his tight butt through the material of his trousers. Her mouth watered at the prospect of having those buns in her hands as he forced his young, hopefully large, virile cock into her pussy.

"Thank you, Carl." She smiled as she whispered the words huskily to him.

The utility room was tiny but she deliberately pushed her breasts out further as he went past her. His arm brushed across their firm peaks and she gave a soft, throaty moan.

"I'm so sorry, Ms Smith!" Carl apologized, even more flustered than before.

"There's *nothing* to be sorry about, Carl." She smiled up at him before turning to the photocopier and laying the first sheet against the glass, her nipples tingling in her sheer bra.

He was going to be so easy to seduce.

As she walked back to her private office, she looked around the small open-plan, stylish space her employees occupied and a sliver of pride ran through her. Four years ago she had attained her ultimate goal—being her own boss. Her weekly newspaper *Black Forum* still had a long way to go to rival the better-selling UK Black newspapers but she already had a small, loyal, well-informed, growing readership which included many top professionals. She refused to follow the tabloid-style reporting that made many of her rivals successful. She wanted a serious newspaper that educated the Black population on business and social matters. She had won a top magazine's Business Woman of the Year Award last year and it had done her profile and the newspaper the world of good. She had a high turnover of staff but she didn't mind, she deliberately kept the wages low to attract only young graduates looking for some work experience. She cleverly worded her adverts so that the jobs didn't appeal to young women, the few that still applied she found a way of filtering out during the shortlisting stage. Her young male employees usually left after a year or two to work for the more mainstream newspapers, but not before she'd taught them a bit about journalism, and the various ways of pleasuring a mature woman.

Many women slept their way to the top—she was already there—the *bottom* was the only way to go.

Relaxing back onto her comfy, black executive chair, Darleen thought of her first victim Lawrence Gibbs, an over-confident young man from Harlesden.

***

During the interview he had flirted shamelessly with her and she had known that it would only be a matter of time before she would fuck the very good-looking cocky upstart. It was obvious that he had slept with loads of young women his own age—Darleen had shown him the difference between mere girls and a sexually-liberated, older woman.

She dressed extra provocatively during his first weeks of employment and called him into her office ten minutes before the end of business one Friday. From his interview she knew that he liked to talk about himself. If she had let him, they would have been in her office for at least an hour talking about the mighty Mr Gibbs.

She had turned the air-conditioning off, giving her an excuse to undo the top two buttons of her cream silk shirt. As he entered her office she said apologetically, "I hope that you won't find it too hot. The AC was giving me a slight headache, so I turned it off."

"No problem, Ms Smith," he replied, his eyes going straight to her exposed cleavage.

She opted to sit in the armchairs in her office rather than at her massive oak desk. She crossed her long legs and began the meeting, deliberately keeping her words professional, sending him a clear message that though he might find her sexy, she wasn't into office liaisons.

"Lawrence, the reason for this informal chat is to find out how you're settling in. In the past we've had a rather high turnover of staff and I have decided to find out what is causing staff to look elsewhere for employment after we have invested valuable time and substantial amounts of money training them. I have noted that you are a brilliant writer and would certainly like to have you with us for an indefinite period."

"Ms Smith…may I call you Darleen?"

"Call me Darleen, please!"

"Darleen, I am very grateful for the opportunity to work for a small, closely-knit newspaper like *Black Forum*. I like the fact that the assignments are varied so each journalist gets all-round experience on a variety of subject matters," he paused to take a quick breath. "I'm enjoying the job immensely."

"That's wonderful to hear, Lawrence. Tell me a little about yourself. I'm asking only because I occasionally take members of staff with me to cover important stories all over the UK. These trips may include overnight stays in hotels and working closely all hours of the night. You would have to be available at very short notice. I need to know if that would be a problem for you. If you have commitments, it just simply means that I would have to limit your assignments mainly to the London area."

"Darleen, I am a free agent. I can be available at the shortest of notices."

"That's good to know."

She stood up, walked to her desk and leaned right over to grab her diary—giving him a tantalizing view of her firm legs.

"I just need to make a note of that. I'll pencil you in for another meeting in two weeks' time." She sat back down, crossed her legs and made a quick entry. She looked up and noticed the faint sheen of perspiration on his forehead and the tell-tale glitter in his light eyes. She uncrossed her legs, got up and extended her hand. "I think it would be beneficial to meet regularly for the first three months or so to nipple…sorry nip any problems in the bud. Don't you?"

His amber eyes had lit up when she'd deliberately thrown the word 'nipple' into the formal conversation.

"I totally agree, Darleen." He pronounced her name as though he was saying the word 'darling'.

"Lawrence, I enjoyed our little chat but I hadn't meant to keep you so long. I hope I haven't messed up your plans for the evening."

"I'm just meeting some friends for a drink, nothing special."

"Maybe I'll join you one Friday for a quick drink."

"You're welcome to come today if you like." He was very eager.

"No, I wouldn't want to gate-crash a boys' night out, but thank you anyway."

"You wouldn't be gate-crashing."

"It's very sweet of you but I have a lot to do before I leave today. You have fun."

She walked over to her imposing desk and sat behind it.

"Good night, Darleen." His voice was so wistful she almost gave in.

"Good night, Lawrence."

The next Friday he popped into her office as he was about to leave to ask her if she wanted to go for a drink. She refused, but suggested that they had their next meeting over drinks.

The evening of their meeting she pretended to be running a little late. She asked him to take a seat as she tidied the files on her desk, deliberately standing so that she had to lean over to pick them up, giving him a good peep down her low-cut blouse.

They took a taxi to one of her favourite wine bars only two blocks away from her spacious flat in Fulham. She started off the meeting as professionally as she'd done previously but after a glass of red wine she pretended to be a little tipsy. Lawrence promptly ordered her another and by the time she had a third glass of wine she confessed that she was totally inebriated. He put a strong supporting arm around her and followed her directions to her flat.

She turned and thanked him for bringing her home at the front door but he insisted on staying to make sure that she was alright. She started to undress saying that she needed a shower. Through her half-closed eyes she watched his eyes devour her curves. She took all her clothes off and left them in a pile on her living room carpet before turning to walk to the bathroom. After a quick shower, she came back to the living room dressed in a fluffy bathrobe and a pair of killer bedroom slippers. Right away she noticed that her panties weren't where she'd left them. She'd known that he couldn't have resisted a sniff or two! He stood up and watched her as she walked over to him unsteadily. When she was about a foot away from him she pretended to catch her heel in the thick carpeting and automatically he reached out to break her fall.

Drunkenly she leaned against him, pressing her body into his shamelessly. He kissed her, plunging his tongue deep into her freshly brushed mouth, then carried her over to the sofa. Her loosely tied robe came undone, exposing her firm breasts and he reached over to fondle them. She acted totally out of it as he took a nipple into his mouth. He ran his hand up her inner thigh and rubbed it over her pussy, groaning appreciatively when her juices wet his fingers.

As he started fumbling with his zip, she opened her eyes and he quickly jumped to his feet. She looked down at her breasts—her nipples were standing firmly erect, and there was a visible outline on the left one where he'd clamped his mouth.

"I must have been masturbating," she murmured, as though unaware that he was in the room. She pulled on her nipples making them even more erect and heard him catch his breath. She slid three fingers in her pussy and fucked herself with them, moaning and groaning for her captivated audience of one.

"I need Sambo." She got up and staggered to her bedroom, Lawrence following a couple of steps behind.

Opening her top drawer, she pulled out four dildos of varying lengths and a handful of condoms. She ripped open a condom and rolled it onto the largest of the four dildos— her 8½" best friend Sambo. She climbed up onto her four-poster bed and opened her legs wide, giving Lawrence a full view of her shaved pussy.

She tried to ram Rambo inside her, knowing full well that she couldn't. It took a lot of preparation to get his bulbous head pass her entrance. She was doing it *only* for Lawrence's benefit.

"Sambo, you will rip my little pussy. Let me try Rambo instead." She sat up and grabbed another dildo. 8" Rambo was one of those realistic-looking dildos: he had a small head, which tapered to quite a thick base; balls and a tuft of curly black hair. She quickly slipped a condom on him and tried again. She got his head and about half of his length inside her. "Rambo you are too fat, you will split me apart. I wish Lawrence hadn't left, I am sure his cock would have been just the right size."

"I'm right here, Darleen," Lawrence said eagerly.

She pretended not to hear him, closing her eyes and sighing as she pushed her fingers deep inside her slick opening again. "Lawrence's cock would have fit my pussy just right."

She heard the rustling sound of him taking off his clothes and then the ripping of foil paper. He climbed onto the bed and gently eased her fingers out. She let her hand brush across his cock to ensure that he was wearing a condom.

When she felt the head of his cock against her opening she asked drunkenly, "Is that you, Rambo?"

"Yes." His voice was breathless.

"Fuck me baby, I want to feel your big balls slapping against my ass."

"Rambo's going to fuck your pussy good!" He spread her legs further apart and worked his cock inside her. She had suspected that he would be well-hung; he was over six foot and had large hands and feet. She was right—his cock filled her pussy beautifully, with just the right amount of discomfort to let her know she was being fucked.

"Rambo is going to fuck you hard now."

True to his word he rode her hard and fast, and as soon as he came he climbed off her. Picking up his discarded clothes, he walked out of the bedroom. A few minutes later she heard her front door closing. She lay back on her bed and laughed hysterically before reaching for Sambo. She was primed and needed to put out the fire Lawrence had lit but not extinguished.

The next Monday she walked into the office as though she had no recollection of what had taken place Friday evening, greeting her staff with a sunny, Good morning, and a bright smile.

Lawrence came to her office later the same morning, looking a bit hesitant as he asked her if she'd been okay after he'd left. She smiled and said that she had been fine. He relaxed more as the week went by and she still behaved as though she was totally unaware that he'd fucked her. For their next meeting she took Lawrence to the wine bar once again.

"Lawrence, you must stop me from drinking if you notice me getting drunk. The last time all I remember is you getting me home and then waking up in the morning."

She had brought along two of his published articles and they discussed them at length. By the time they'd finished the discussion she had consumed two glasses of red wine.

"I really shouldn't have another but this burgundy is so delicious," she remarked as she downed the third.

"Another won't kill you, Darleen."

"Just promise you'll ensure that I get home safely if I get tipsy."

"I will look after you, Darleen. Don't worry about a thing."

She downed her fourth glass before he had finished half

of his third.

Then they had gone through the same routine as before, except when she had showered she went straight to her bed, lay across it naked and closed her eyes. Within minutes he climbed onto the bed with her. He went straight for her breasts. She let him enjoy himself for a few minutes, watching him move from one breast to the next, his hand occasionally reaching down to stroke his hard cock. Suddenly he looked up, saw her eyes were opened and froze.

"What are you doing, Lawrence?" She asked, as if she'd just awoken from a deep sleep.

"I-I…"

"You've been a naughty boy Lawrence. I am going to *punish* you." She flipped him over unto his back with surprising strength and sat on him. She reached into the drawer and pulled out four pairs of handcuffs. He didn't resist as she attached his hands to the corners of the headboard and then moved off the bed to handcuff his feet, it wasn't the first time a woman had held him captive.

She then stood naked at the side of the bed and looked down at him. "This time, Rambo, *I'm* going to fuck you good." His eyes widened as he realized that she'd been faking the first time.

She left him there for a few minutes while she went to her spare room to get dressed in a black leather outfit. The cut-outs of the bra left her nipples and most of her breasts exposed, the panties were designed to be worn during penetration.

She walked back into the room and his penis jerked as he took in her outfit. Then she leaned over and took his cock deep into her mouth, letting her throat close over the head. She blew him, swallowed, then crawled onto the bed and leaned over him. Pushing her breast against his mouth she commanded, "Suck it."

He opened his mouth wide and took the whole tip of her 34F breast into his mouth. She watched his cock quickly harden.

He was such a breast man.

"Enough." She pulled her breast away and reached into her top drawer for a condom. Using her mouth, she rolled it onto his cock and then climbed onto it. She leaned back so that he could raise his head and watch his cock sink into her pussy. She used her strong thigh muscles to raise herself almost to the tip of his cock and then drop quickly down to the base. She only had to do it ten times before he came again.

Again she gave him her breast for a few sucks and again he was hard in minutes.

"Do you want to fuck my asshole?"

He nodded eagerly.

She pulled a medium sized dildo from the drawer and lay on his chest with her legs on either side of his head. She pushed it into her soaking pussy as he watched, then she turned over and pushed it slowly into her asshole and slowly back out again, and again. Then pulling it out completely, she positioned herself over his upright cock and sank onto it. She moaned and groaned as it slid inside her. When the whole length buried deep, she gyrated her hips until he came again.

"Did you enjoy that?" She knew he had, the way he had raised his hips off the bed for deeper penetration had told her so.

"Yes," he confirmed. "You've got a nice tight asshole, Darleen."

"I am *so* glad you liked it because now that you have fucked my ass, *I* am going to fuck yours."

Immediately he started to struggle against the handcuffs.

"Relax, honey. The more resistance you put up, the more it will hurt."

She drizzled a little lubricant on to her forefinger and probed his asshole. He kept his cheeks tightly clenched but she still managed to work her finger inside him and his cock stirred again.

"See, you like it." She pointed at his hardening cock. "Now be a good boy and open up for me."

He relaxed and gave up the fight, letting her work her finger in and out of him for a while. When she pulled her finger out and reached for an anal plug, he started to struggle again but this time she noticed that it was more for effect than anything else. She used the fingers of her left hand to separate his cheeks and her right to bury the slim 5" anal plug inside him. His erection was the most magnificent of the evening. She left the plug tightly wedged in him, climbed onto his cock and rode him until they both came.

Then she took off the handcuffs, gently held him against her and let him suck on her breasts for a while—she thought he deserved a treat for being such a good boy.

After that he came to her house every Friday evening and they would fuck for hours. Needless to say by the time she'd moved on to her next victim six months later, she'd had Lawrence taking the full length of Rambo up his ass and liking it *very* much. Some men just needed to be taught what they liked.

Recently she'd watched a documentary about the new craze in America where women were strapping on dildos and fucking their men's asses and how much the men were enjoying it. She'd thought, *Damn! I probably invented that shit. If I'd bought the patent I'd be a filthy-rich bitch now.*

***

After she graduated with BA in English from Cambridge University, Darleen had worked for *The London Chronicle* newspapers. Seven years later she had still been waiting for her big break. She'd numerous stories published and had even written a few articles that had made the front page but she kept being passed over for promotion. Then her editor gave assignments to four other journalists to go to the carnivals in Rio and Trinidad. He had known her parents were Trinidadian and that she went to the Island regularly but he had completely ignored that fact. When the journalists returned and she'd read their wishy-washy articles she had thought, *fuck this!* She would have done a far better job and she would have been able to give a grassroots point-of-view.

She decided there and then to look for a way of earning extra money to start her own newspaper. She had always been a good dancer and when she saw an advert for non-Caucasian strippers she went along for an audition. The club, Exotic Dreams, catered for wealthy businessmen with a leaning for foreign women. She was staggered at the impressive pay they were offering.

When the female owner of the club had asked to see her naked, Darleen hadn't even hesitated. The woman had nodded in appreciation as Darleen stood unashamedly in front of her. Darleen was blessed with a superb body: she had inherited her large, firm breasts from her father's side of the family and her long legs from her mother's. Within a week of her audition she was *Carnival Queen* and the second most popular act at the club. A nineteen-year-old Jamaican girl with her energetic, no-bones-in-her-body Dancehall Queen routine was the men's favourite dancer.

Darleen, always competitive, immediately started working on her fitness and to tighten her already firm body. She bought a Pilates machine with part of her first week's wages after another stripper attributed her own fantastic figure to the machine. Within two weeks Darleen felt the benefits. She practised her floor routine at home for hours and even started going to the club when it was closed to perfect her pole-dancing skills. The first time she unveiled her new move—flicking on to the pole in a handstand, she knew she had just moved up a notch in the popularity stakes. But the Jamaican girl didn't take her defeat lying down, she too invented a new routine and then so did Darleen. The competition between the two of them raised the standard of all the other dancers' performances and the club had become even more popular.

Darleen had worked Friday, Saturday and Sunday nights at the club and had earned ten times as much as she did at *The Chronicle*. She'd never slept with any of the customers, though once she'd been sorely tempted. A wealthy Arab had taken a particular shine to her and had come to see her dance whenever he was in the UK on business. He'd thought nothing of paying her an extra five thousand pounds for a private lap dance and once he had slipped her a note promising to pay her fifty thousand pounds if she came to sleep with him at The Savoy. She'd actually been on her way to the Strand when images of a room full of Arab men waiting in line to ravish her body filled her head and she'd panicked. It had taken her a while to stop kicking herself over the large sum of money she turned down because she had suddenly gotten cold feet.

Eighteen months later she'd had enough saved to leave *The Chronicle* and start her own newspaper. She'd stopped stripping as soon as she'd begun to make a decent profit from her newspaper but she still used her Pilates machine for an hour each morning. It kept her body in top shape; no one looking at her naked would believe her true age.

***

Darleen had hired Carl three weeks ago and had done so because he had been the best looking, the tallest and the youngest of the three men she'd shortlisted for interviews. He had been quietly confident during the interview but she'd sensed an innate shyness that she'd found rather sweet.

She had already had her first one-to-one with him and the other was due at the end of the week. He would need a different approach from the one she'd used on Lawrence— he didn't seem the type to take advantage of a drunken woman.

She wasn't worried about claims for sexual harassment. When she was finished with the young men they were totally pussy-whipped. She had only buggered Lawrence because she had rightly sensed that he was freaky enough to enjoy it, but too much of a macho man to let a younger woman do it to him. The rest of the young men had enjoyed the full use of her pussy, grateful for the knowledge she imparted to use on younger women who were usually very impressed by their sexual expertise. If Darleen snapped her fingers now any one of them would come running, like that!

On Friday she wore her shortest skirt for her meeting with Carl. She'd had her legs waxed only the day before and they shone like polished glass. Before he came into the room she took off her bra and massaged her nipples into mini bullets. She sat on the armchair opposite his and instead of crossing her legs she opened them ever so slightly, *Basic Instinct* style, so that he got a glimpse of her smooth upper thighs and the occasional flash of her sheer panties.

Fifteen minutes into the meeting he still seemed embarrassed about the comment that he'd made earlier in the week but rather than relieve his discomfort she decided to use it to her advantage.

"Carl, were you serious when you said that you wouldn't touch me with a barge pole?"

"No, Ms Smith," he replied regretfully. "I was just annoyed with Shane for teasing me. I didn't really mean it."

"I was extremely hurt by your comment," she pouted for a second. "But just to show you that I don't bear a grudge, let me buy you a drink at my favourite wine bar."

She grabbed her jacket and her small handbag and preceded him out of her office. She hailed a passing taxi and in less than fifteen minutes they were at the wine bar. She held his arm as they walked into the bar, surprised that in her 3" heels she only came up to just past his shoulder. He must be about 6'6" tall!

She led the way to a quiet corner and ordered a red wine for herself and a double Remy Martin for him. She could see other women checking him out and she felt good that she was the one with him. There were men looking at her as well, in particular a good-looking man sitting four tables to their left. He was with a petite blonde woman but he couldn't keep his eyes off her unbound breasts.

Suddenly Darleen had a brilliant idea.

"Oh no!" The distress in her voice was worthy of an Oscar nomination.

"What's the matter, Ms Smith?" Carl asked concerned.

"That guy over there—the one with the blonde—used to be my ex-boyfriend. I can't believe he would bring the hussy he left me for, here to my favourite drinking spot."

Carl looked over at the well-dressed Black man who was still staring across at their table. "Do you want to leave?"

"No. I can't give him the satisfaction." She fluttered her eyelids hoping that Carl would fall for her damsel-in-distress routine. "Do you mind pretending we're a couple?"

"I don't mind at all." Carl pulled his chair closer to hers and put his arm around her shoulders, his hand inches away from her left breast. She itched to slump her shoulder and let his fingertips brush her nipple, but it would be too obvious.

"It's no use—he will know we are just friends," she sighed dramatically.

"Not if I do this." Carl bent his head and kissed her, his lips surprisingly firm and thorough against hers. She arched her neck when they left hers to trail across the column of her throat and downwards to the slope of her breast. A few millimetres and they would cover her....

"They're leaving." Carl suddenly sat back in his chair and finished his drink.

She looked over at the now empty table. The couple had pulled on their jackets and were heading for the door.

Damn! So much for that plan!

When she turned back to their table Carl was on his feet, buttoning the jacket of his suit.

"Ms Smith, I'm afraid I have to go—I have plans for the evening. Thanks for the drink." He bent to kiss her cheek and left.

Where the hell did he learn to kiss like that? she wondered, thinking about the way his earlier kiss had almost made her forget her name. She ordered a bottle of red wine but she was still fairly sober when she entered her flat at eleven forty-five that evening.

Thank God for Rambo and Sambo.

An hour and a half later as she lay naked on her back, pushing Sambo frantically in and out of her clutching pussy to achieve her second orgasm she screamed, "Rip my pussy with your big cock, Carl. Yes, tear this fucking pussy up!"

***

The next Monday she stopped at Carl's desk to check the progress of an article he was working on. He assured her that he was ahead of schedule. She gave him one of her sexiest smiles as she moved away from his desk.

At 6.30 that evening she came out of her office to get a coffee. The outer office was deserted except for Carl. She grabbed him a drink—black no sugar, and walked over to his desk. He smiled and covered her hand with his as he took the mug from her.

"What are you still doing here?" she asked, as he took a sip of the dark liquid.

"I'm just finishing the article."

"But it's due on *Wednesday*!"

He was a bit enthusiastic!

"I'm just trying to stay on top."

"Good. Keep it up." She walked back to her office but as she got to the door she turned and said, "Come and say goodbye before you leave."

"I will." He smiled at her, then bent his head once more as his fingers flew over the keyboard.

Today was the day she would make her move. She wasn't making fast enough progress with him and she was beginning to lose patience; he should have been so easy to seduce! When she finally got her hands on him she would punish him, give him an extra pussy-whipping for giving her so much trouble.

As administrator of the network she was aware the minute he logged off. She quickly perched on the end of her desk, opened her legs wide and waited for him to come to her office. It took him less than a minute to pop his head around her door.

"I'm leaving now, Ms Smith." His voice was casual as if he *hadn't* noticed her erect nipples poking through her unbuttoned blouse or her naked pussy staring out at him.

"*Carl*, do you find me attractive?"

"You are a very beautiful woman, Ms Smith," he replied with calm detachment.

Why was he so fucking cool? Was he gay?

"Do you want to fuck me?"

"Yes."

Oh, thank God!

"Okay, but if you want to stick me you have to lick me. Can you do that for me?"

"I'd *love* to do that for you." He moistened his lips in anticipation.

"Okay, I want you to come over here to me, on your knees."

Carl crawled over on his hands and knees and she spread the lips of her pussy in readiness. When he got to her desk he pushed her back against it and buried his nose in her pussy like he was sniffing a rose. Then he spread the lips and ate her like she was his first meal of the day and he was ravenous; like he'd forgotten to have breakfast, missed lunch and couldn't wait for dinner. Occasionally he plunged his long tongue inside her as far as it would go before he went back to feasting on her clit. She pulled her skirt up further, gripped the edge of her desk and opened her legs to give him fuller access. His cunnilingus technique was phenomenal! She moaned his name out loud, without embarrassment. The only other person who had ever sucked her pussy with this kind of expertise was the second man she'd slept with; an older St Lucian called Justice. He hadn't been very big in the penile department but the first time he'd put his mouth on her clit she had cum within minutes.

How could someone so young eat a pussy with such expertise, she wondered as she approached her climax. But just as the first spasm gripped her insides, Carl pulled his lips away and stood up.

Startled, she looked up to see what was wrong. He was standing there looking down at her, his eyes cool and unconcerned, as though seconds ago his face hadn't been buried in her pussy.

"Carl, *please!*" she begged when she realized that he meant to leave her hanging.

"Are you sorry that you've been teasing me, sending me insane for the past month?"

"Yes. Please finish me off." She couldn't wait until she got home to use Sambo or Rambo—she needed to cum now!

"Okay, I'll make you cum but I need a reward."

"Anything—just come back here and eat my pussy *now!*" She said the words with a bit more authority hoping he would remember that she was still his boss.

"I'll hold you to that." He put his hand under her hips and lifted her to meet his lips, his arms taking most of her weight as she held on to the end of the desk. Her body formed a handstand. She knew if he dropped her suddenly she would probably fall on her head or break her neck, but she didn't care. He used his hands on her hips to work her pussy back and forth off his tongue. Less than a minute after he resumed his titillation she came violently against his mouth. He let her sink slowly back onto the surface of the desk and then let go. She had to pull her legs together and curl up on her desk to get her equilibrium back. Fuck!

When she sat up Carl was sitting in one of her armchairs, watching her coolly.

"Do you want to come to my place for a quick drink?" She *needed* that tongue on her clit again.

"No. But I'll come for a *slow* fuck."

She couldn't believe it was her shy Carl saying words that make her clit throb. She grabbed her keys, locked up the office in record time and in minutes they were in a taxi heading to her flat.

As soon as she closed the front door behind them, she started ripping her clothes off but Carl took his time. She watched him slip his shirt off his shoulders and her mouth opened in astonishment—his suits had disguised the unbelievable breadth of his shoulders and his incredible six-pack stomach. But she was a bit disappointed when she looked down at his crotch and noticed that though he looked as large as she'd hoped, he wasn't erect. Shit!

He kept his boxers on, picked her up in his arms and strode to the bedroom.

"I have some condoms in the top drawer." She liked sex but not enough to die for it. She never rode bareback.

He opened the drawer and rummaged through it, but instead of condoms he pulled out a pair of battery-operated nipple clamps. He took her slim hands in his and wrapped them around the wooden slats of her headboard.

"Keep them there, and I don't want to hear a word out of you. If you disobey me I'll use the handcuffs and I am sure there is duck tape somewhere in this flat."

He sounded serious, but she loved it. She always gave them a chance to do their thing first round because second round was hers and when she flipped the script it was hell to pay! The more masterful he was now the more she would make him whimper later. He didn't seem to be a freak like Lawrence and he was a bit big for her to hold down but if she managed to get the handcuffs on him she was definitely going to serve him a bit of Rambo for leaving her hanging at the office. It had been far too long since she'd strapped on her big-balled friend and given some young man a good 'seeing' to. Carl was quickly shaping up to be the one to break her dry spell.

He gave her nipples a few firm tugs, rolling and elongating them into erect peaks with his fingers, almost like a doctor doing an experiment to see how erect they could get. She couldn't read what was going on in his head but his cock was still soft.

When her nipples were rolled to his satisfaction he attached the clamps to them and pressed the switch on the small box that contained the batteries. Instantly Darleen's nipples responded and were pebble hard within seconds. Slowly he turned the knob towards the maximum setting.

"It's too high," she moaned.

The biting teeth sent waves of pleasure running into her pussy. Moisture oozed out of her and soaked her Egyptian cotton sheets, but the sensation was too much. She reached for the switch but he held it away from her.

"Do I have to get the handcuffs?" he asked. She shook her head. "I want you nice and wet—I want you to beg for my cock. Do you want me to eat your pussy again?"

Weakly she nodded and he spread her legs. Once again his nimble tongue pulled an orgasm out of her that started deep inside her womb.

He turned the knob down slightly, decreasing the charge and the clamps sent a gentler, but still intense electric charge through her nipples.

He got off the bed and she raised her head to admire his firm butt as he walked out the door. He returned immediately with a pack of Zulu condoms.

"I've got my own condoms—yours won't fit me." He said the words as if he was accustomed to saying them.

Zulu my ass!

Darleen gave a little snort of disbelief; men always

overestimated the size of their cocks.

Then he dropped his boxers and a monster, that made Sambo look tiny, reared up and smacked his taut belly. Her eyes almost popped out of her head as she shook it to clear it. She must be seeing double!

He ripped the packet, pulled out a black condom and slid it onto his massive length, then stood there and watched her coolly as he stroked himself.

"What are you waiting for—bring that big cock and stick it inside me," she commanded.

She was impatient to feel it inside her. She'd never seen anything like it before! She couldn't wait for him to slip that massive head through her pussy lips and up inside her. It didn't even matter that he seemed to be taking control; for once she was happy to relinquish it.

He continued to stroke his rigid cock as he watched her hips lift off the bed in response to the nipple clamps and the anticipation of his cock. "Women usually pay a lot of money for the pleasure but I'll make an exception this time—since you are my boss, I'll fuck you for free."

How could she have possibly known that Carl and his three older brothers ran an ultra exclusive male prostitution service for mature Black women? They had realized in their teens that they had been a bit more blessed in the appendage area than the average male but had just enjoyed the adulation of their girlfriends without giving it much thought. But as they grew older they decided to start their business *Hung*, when it seemed like every woman they slept with commented on their size. They had regular meetings, exchanged new ideas or techniques and any other matters pertaining to the business. They all had regular jobs to avoid suspicion; their service was strictly cash only—the tax man didn't get his cut.

Carl, the youngest and the tallest of the brothers was the *most* blessed. Their very successful business was run on a referral basis and they were solidly booked for the next six months. *Hung* was the by-word on the lips of discerning professional Black women who were either too busy for relationships or just needed to be properly fucked.

Opening up a birthday card to find a *Hung* invitation inside was the ultimate gift for many women. For those celebrating their fortieth birthdays Carl had an all-night specialty that no woman could forget once she'd experienced. He was planning to give it to Darleen tonight.

"By the way, Darleen, I won't be at work tomorrow—I'll be spending the day in bed sleeping after staying up all night fucking you."

"How dare—" She stopped as the words registered. *All night?*

"No more talking now. I e-mailed my finished article to you just before I logged off so you have no cause for complaint. I told you that I liked to stay on top. In a minute I'll be on top of you." He laughed at his own corny joke but she didn't join in, she just wanted him to hurry up and give her some of that incredible cock. "You didn't realize the significance of me finishing it a day in advance did you? No, you just thought I was trying to impress you, didn't you? You were thinking poor sucker Carl, he would do anything for me, including crawl on his knees and eat my pussy. Well, it is pay back time and I think I should warn you that I practise Tantric Sex. I really can go *all* night. Now, enough talk—time for some action."

He climbed onto the bed, knelt between her legs and pushed two fingers inside her. He thrust them in and out a few times before pulling them out and smearing her pussy juice all over her entrance and swollen lips.

"You need to be *very* wet." She still couldn't get over the change in him, it was as if they were having a conversation about the weather, and yet his calm manner aroused her more than if he spoke dirtily to her.

He sat back on his heels, pulled her hips onto his thighs, put the head of his cock against her dripping entrance and slowly pulled her onto his rigid length. Darleen had been so mesmerized by the length she'd missed the impressive girth!

Nothing, not even Sambo had prepared her for the way it filled every nock and cranny of her fanny. His control was awe-inspiring as he slowly pushed his cock into her, using his large hands to move her hips backwards and forwards. Surprisingly she didn't feel sore but the fullness of his penetration stimulated all the nerve endings in her vaginal passage. She tried to inch up the bed to escape as the sensations threatened to make her scream out loud.

Carl tightened his grip on her ass and quickly forced a full inch inside her, just to punish her. "I said *don't* move a muscle. I'm the one in control here, you move *only* when I tell you to do so. Do I make myself clear? Or am I going to need those handcuffs?"

She tossed her head from side to side—her open mouth couldn't even form the words, the pleasure was so unbelievably intense. Moments passed as Carl patiently worked himself inside her. She was amazed that even when she felt she didn't have room for another quarter inch, he managed to get another full inch inside her. There was only a dull ache as he filled her, slowly letting her stretch before going deeper.

Carefully, he pulled her further up on to his cock. As he waited he raised his head and looked into her pleasure-overloaded eyes. He looked nothing like the shy young man she'd taunted at the office. He gave her a supremely confident smile and winked at her as he tightened his hands to pull her upwards again.

"Darleen, I have a feeling that I'll be the last young male employee you will mess with for a while. Today I'll be the perfect gentleman and give my cock to you slowly, but if you ever tease me again I'll ram you so hard and fast you won't be able to sit down for weeks. And if you are really, really naughty I'll fuck your ass as well!"

Darleen couldn't respond as he buried another eighth of an inch into her. She had slept with dozens of men and by the time she was twenty-five years old she had realized that men were easy to pussy-whip. She had taken great pleasure in giving them her pussy and making them want more, but she had never completely misread a man like she had done Carl. It wasn't only that his cock had her completely sprung, but his awesome control was making her lose hers!

"Almost there."

He opened her legs wider and did a quick flip with his legs as he pushed hers up so that he was now lying above her, his knees on the bed. The muscles in his arms stood out as he balanced himself a few inches over her body. He looked into her eyes and for the first time she saw how aroused he was as he leaned down and kissed her. Then he raised his head, arched his neck and groaned as he slipped her another bit of his cock.

Surely, there can't be any more, she thought.

She raised her head and looked down; there was still about another inch and a half to go and generous soul that he was—Carl seemed bent on giving it *all* to her.

***

I wrote **Sleeping Her Way to the Bottom** *because I liked the idea of an intelligent, successful Black woman taking what she wanted, whenever she wanted. The fact that she may have met her* *match serves as a note of caution to the women out there who may choose to follow in her illustrious footsteps.*

*****

FRUITS AND VEGETABLES

*E*lizabeth Parker's clitoris was unusually large and sensitive. She discovered it quite by accident while bathing at the age of sixteen. Her mother had always insisted that she wash herself properly and she'd been using her flannel to thoroughly cleanse herself when the cloth slipped and her bare fingers had accidentally brushed against something that had sent a shiver through her entire body. Innocently she had done it once more and again the same sensation had raced through her. So she had done it again, and again, until she had cried out as a spasm of pleasure seized her body. Instinctively, she'd squeezed her legs together, trapping her hand against the ultra sensitive nub of flesh.

Her mother had heard her loud moan and had come running to the bathroom. Before Elizabeth had had time to pull her hand from between her legs and straighten, her mother had been standing in front of her with a look of contempt on her face. Later that day she had warned Elizabeth that she would go blind if she kept touching herself like that. Since Elizabeth already needed thick glasses she vowed never to do it again; she was always terrified whenever she lost her spectacles and had to blindly hunt for them. The idea of not seeing at all terrified her. But her clitoris refused to remain hidden once she'd discovered it, even when she walked the top of her legs brushed against it and she sometimes had to stop for a minute, or try to walk more slowly, or with her legs slightly apart to avoid cumming in the middle of a busy street or a school corridor. She even started to wear seam-free panties because even the ridge of a gusset gave her intense multiple orgasms.

For years she had ridden her favourite horse bareback but the day after she discovered her clitoris she found that the gentle motion of the powerful beast as he trotted around the enclosure created a delicate friction against it. Less than ten minutes into the ride she'd had an orgasm and another before her mother had called her in for afternoon tea. Reluctantly she'd dismounted and left the horse to graze.

After that, she rode him in the early evening, just before dinner, when her mother was busy in the kitchen and she could ride undisturbed. Every day she would wrap her arms around the chestnut's neck, lay her head against him and in an hour's ride she would have four or five orgasms before she slid weakly off his back and led him to the paddock for the night. If the weather was too bad for riding, later in bed she would pull a blanket or towel back and forth between her legs and cum a couple of times before she slept.

She started wearing baggy clothes when her mother told her that her big ass was common and put her on a strict diet. But even when Elizabeth starved herself and lost over a stone her behind had become no smaller—in fact it looked more prominent on her smaller frame—so she had given up dieting and tried to cover it up instead.

When she was thirteen a reckless hairdresser had taken one look at her thick hair, imagined that she needed a super strength relaxer and had then left the cream on for too long.

Within a week her hair had broken off in clumps and the hairdresser, fearing a lawsuit, had told Elizabeth that she must be allergic to some chemical in the relaxer and advised her never to straighten her hair again.

Her height, glasses and her thick natural Afro made her a bit of a geek in secondary school. No one ever asked her on a date. Growing up with a glamorous mother made her feel ugly in comparison, she had inherited her father's looks and his brain. He loved his only child and told her constantly that men would see her beauty as she got older.

When she left for London to attend university, she was sad to leave the father she loved, glad to finally get away from her overbearing mother and heartbroken at leaving her horse. Her first night in London was very lonely and the orgasms she gave herself with her towel couldn't compare to the powerful ones she would have had riding her beloved horse and she had cried herself to sleep.

She wasn't like the average university student, she was painfully shy and avoided contact as much as possible. Her weird looks put off even the usually horny university students, but a fifty-two-year-old Nigerian professor who taught her Programming Fundamentals noticed the shy young woman and made his move. The short, fat, balding man had a history of preying on naïve young women and as soon as he saw Elizabeth he knew he'd found a potential victim. He lured her into his office late one Friday evening, on the pretext of discussing an assignment she'd handed in. He discreetly adjusted the shutters on the double windows, dimmed the lights and locked the door as he asked her to take a seat.

He expertly steered the conversation to personal matters and before she knew it, she was confessing that she didn't have a boyfriend and was still a virgin. He told her that she was pretty and begged her never to change her style, knowing that he couldn't compete with the young men who would flock around her if she ever had a decent makeover. When he saw that she was blushing, he told her to bring her chair around the desk and sit beside him. He put his hand under her skirt and inched his fingers slowly upwards until they touched her panties. Honing in on her fat clitoris, he moulded it through the soft material and she came within a few minutes. He kept moulding and she kept cumming, shuddering and gasping, completely unaware of her surroundings. The professor was amazed at how easy it was to control her. He had sensed that she was lonely and that it wouldn't take much to get her into bed but he had never imagined he would be able to manipulate her so effortlessly. Before she left his office he kissed her lightly and told her to take her bra and panties off before she came to see him the next Friday evening, promising her even more pleasure.

She left his office as happy as any woman experiencing her first crush. He was older than her father but finally she had found a boyfriend. When she got home that evening she was tempted to finger herself like he had done but she remembered her mother's warning. It was okay for him to touch her and go blind, but she wouldn't risk it. Instead, she rubbed a towel between her legs until she came once more and then fell asleep.

As he had instructed, the next Friday she took off her underwear before going to his office. He sat her on his desk and stood in front of her as he unbuttoned her shirt and bared her breasts. He pulled her large, virgin nipples into tight peaks with his fingers, realizing they had never been touched by another person when she almost fell off the desk at his first caress. When they were fully erect he circled them with his tongue as she clutched his shoulders and moaned loudly. Heady with the power he wielded over her, he nibbled and pulled on them firmly, occasionally nipping them with his teeth. She got more and more aroused as he carried on and by the time he slipped his hand under her skirt she'd cum twice already. He pushed a finger into her tight pussy and finger-fucked her until she came again.

No sooner had the professor discovered her nipples, they *too* started giving her trouble. She suddenly found the lacy material of her bras too abrasive to wear in public because they rubbed against her nipples and made them stick out. People stared at her whenever this happened and she soon resorted to putting round cotton wool pads inside the cups of her bras to reduce the friction and conceal her nipples.

Thankfully, every Friday the professor sucked on them, giving her a temporary ease from the sweet torment before finger-fucking her dripping pussy. He gradually increased the number of fingers as he sensed her need. He had never met a woman who was so open to being pleasured. His only regret was that he was no longer a man in his prime—she would have been an ideal fuck.

Every week he popped a Viagra tablet down his gullet before she came to his office but his cock never so much as stirred until late one Friday evening about four months into their affair. Sitting comfortably on his chair, while she lay back on his desk, he was using one hand to hold her pussy lips open while he buried three short, fat fingers into her pussy, when he felt something he hadn't in years—blood pounding through his old dick. He quickly freed it and pushed it up inside her. He must have popped her hymen during one of his extreme finger-fucking sessions because he encountered no barrier. The excitement of actually fucking again quickly overtook him and he came within minutes.

That night Elizabeth re-lived the feeling of his smooth

length inside her, it hadn't hurt and had felt so much better than his fingers but he had stopped before she'd had a chance to really enjoy it.

The next time he bent her over his desk as soon as he felt his old dick rouse but he couldn't get the semi-hard erection he achieved past her tight entrance. But his wily mind had thought of a contingency plan. Pulling a small dildo from his desk drawer, he had used that instead, sinking it deeply and giving her several orgasms before he was through with her.

Knowing that he was unlikely to get another firm enough erection and realizing that Elizabeth needed deeper penetration, the professor bought a slightly larger dildo for her next visit. And gradually, he increased the length and girth of the dildos, hardly giving her time to outgrow one before buying another larger, thicker one. Within a couple of months he had an enviable selection of dildos, the cost inconsequential to the immense pleasure he derived from watching her eager, tight pussy stretch a little more to accommodate each new one.

Shyly, one Friday she asked him why he'd never used his penis again. He explained that he didn't want to risk her getting pregnant but promised he would get some condoms for her next visit. Not wanting to lose face or the chance to continue fucking her, the professor sought some advice from the shop assistant in the sex shop where he frequently went to buy dildos. Just before Elizabeth arrived the next week, he took a fat 8" black dildo and a harness from his briefcase, carefully loaded his flaccid cock and old balls into the hollow at the base and strapped the harness around his waist. He then pulled his clothes back on and waited, the expensive, flesh-like dildo protruding out of his fly. As soon as Elizabeth entered the room, he instructed her to climb up onto his desk. As she spread her legs he saw the moisture already glistening between the fat folds of her pussy—as usual she had spent the day in a sensual haze, absentmindedly taking notes during her lectures while thinking of the professor.

"I bought some condoms so I'm going to fuck you today." Turning to the side, he nonchalantly ripped open a condom and rolled it onto the hard length. He hadn't been able to resist buying a nice, meaty dildo—she'd been so delirious with pleasure the only time he had fucked her he doubted she would recall the size of his dick. Positioning himself, he pushed slowly inside her, sucking hard on one of the nipples she had bared herself. He pulled back intermittently to increase his forward thrust but the dildo gradually slid all the way inside, bit by bit, and soon he was thrusting in and out of her smoothly.

The professor suddenly felt like a young, virile man again. He had been quite the 'fuckman' in Nigeria. His father had been an eminent politician and as a young man the professor had lived a life of sexual excess, screwing countless women before being forced to flee to the UK when it was discovered that his father had misused government funds. The British diet, and very occasional fuck from a wife who had realized only after marrying him that he had brought none of his wealth when he'd come to the UK, were responsible for his weight gain and the diabetes he developed in his early forties. Arrogantly, he had ignored the doctor's diet suggestions and the diabetes had worsened, leading to near impotence by his fiftieth birthday.

After he made Elizabeth cum twice, he turned her over and fucked her from behind as she bent obediently over his desk. He had fucked thousands of women in his youth, but never had he met one like Elizabeth—completely led by her clitoris and nipples. He watched her big ass bounce firmly each time he thrust to the hilt inside her. He wasn't into anal sex but she was so obedient to his will, and since he wasn't using his own cock, he didn't see why he shouldn't sample her tight ass. Vowing to fuck it the next time she came to his office, he held on to the end of the desk and watched the big dildo slide in and out of her pussy, again and again. It gave him such a thrill that he kept up the motion for long minutes, enjoying the sight, her moans of pleasure and the feeling of youth. Reluctantly, just before ten o'clock, he stopped. And *only* because the cleaners were due.

For Elizabeth it was the most fantastic time they'd ever had. His penis was bigger than any of the dildos he had used. And good heavens! The way it had stretched her pussy! The way he had thrust it in and out!

The next Monday the department sent an email to all the students informing them that the professor had had a mild stroke on his way home late Friday evening and wouldn't be lecturing for some time. The 'fuckman' had fucked too much—poetic justice for the old horny bastard most would say! But Elizabeth cried her eyes out at the news. He was the only person, other than her father, who had ever told her she was pretty. He had made her cum every time they were together—with his cock, fingers, dildo or just by sucking her nipples. She knew that people would say he had taken advantage of her but she had enjoyed every minute of it. She waited patiently for his return but he never did. Another stroke paralysed his entire right side and his doctor advised him that the stress of travelling to work every day would probably trigger another stroke or even kill him.

For the next month or so Elizabeth lay in her cramped room at night and rubbed herself with a towel, thinking of the pleasure he had given her. But as time went by she concentrated more on her studies and less on sex. By the time she graduated university she had managed to control her wayward clit and nipples and had stopped masturbating.

***

Monday evening, three weeks before Christmas, twenty-six-year-old Elizabeth came home from work, made herself a tuna and sweet corn salad and ate it at the small dining table in her kitchen as she read a Dan Brown novel.

After washing the dishes and tidying the kitchen, she went to her bedroom, stripped quickly and walked to her small bathroom. She brushed her teeth and was just about to step into the shower when she heard a tap on her front door. She couldn't think who it could be. She had never spoken to any of the tenants in the other three flats in the building and had no friends who visited her. Quickly pulling on her dressing gown over her naked body, she walked to the door and peered through the peephole. She didn't recognize the young man standing outside, but even distorted through the lens he was quite good looking. Nervously, she opened the door a fraction and peered through the crack. Only one side of his body was visible through the small opening.

"May I help you?" Her voice sounded as nervous as she felt but she couldn't help it, she wasn't used to dealing with people face-to-face regularly.

"Sorry to trouble you. My name is Jonathan Weeks. I just moved in next door and I was wondering if I could borrow your vacuum cleaner." He moved so that she could see his face more clearly and she almost gasped. He wasn't merely good looking—he was breathtaking! His neat, jet-black dreadlocks were pulled back into a ponytail. At 6'4" he was about 5" taller than she was and though he was slim, she could see the muscles of his toned body under his T-shirt. His toffee complexion was smooth and flawless, his lips full and almost feminine. Somehow they only added to his sex appeal.

He smiled at her and she almost fainted dead away! Her clitoris, which had behaved itself for years and years, suddenly started throbbing. She had to squeeze her legs together to silence it.

"Sure. I'll get it for you." She removed the night chain and opened the door more fully before she turned and walked to her tiny kitchen cupboard.

Jonathan had been a little surprised when the tall, timid woman with the wild Afro had opened the door and peered at him myopically for a second before she had shyly looked away. As she walked away from him he noticed her small waist and the full cheeks of her behind and felt a stirring in his groin. Her breasts bounced as she walked back towards him holding a compact vacuum cleaner. Her big nipples poked through the thin material and he found his eyes drawn to them. As she came closer, he realized that she was naked under the thin dressing gown.

"There you go," she said, handing him the appliance.

"Thank you very much." He deliberately covered her hand with his as he took it from her. He saw the blush that quickly spread over her cheeks as she pulled her hand away, but pretended he hadn't noticed.

"You're welcome." She sounded breathless, as though she had run for miles.

"I thought I had brought everything I needed but I completely forgot about a vacuum cleaner and the carpet is rather dusty."

"It's okay," she assured him and started to close the door.

His mind whirled as he tried to think of a reason for delaying her so that he could enjoy looking at her nipples for a while longer. "Let me tidy up and you can come around for coffee later."

"I have some work to do, but thanks for the offer."

"Come on. It's my first night in a new flat, take pity on me." He smiled so disarmingly she couldn't refuse.

"OK," she agreed. "I'll come for a quick cup of coffee at about eight o'clock."

"It's a date." He gave her another smile as he turned to go into his flat.

She closed the door and leaned against it, weak with longing. She glanced downwards and was surprised to see her nipples showing themselves clearly through her pink bathrobe. She hoped Jonathan hadn't noticed them or she would die of embarrassment. She had never been this affected by a man before, not even the professor had made her feel this achy sexual need. She wanted him desperately but knew he was far too handsome to want her back. She ran her hands over her nipples to soothe them but the discomfort intensified. Soon she was tugging urgently on the erect peaks and with each pull there was an answering throb in her groin. She continued until her stomach clenched as an orgasm ripped through her.

Minutes later she stood under the shower and let the water cool her flushed, heated body. Her nipples were still erect and now her clitoris was *raging*. She had to obey its call. She touched her pussy tentatively with her hand, still apprehensive about her mother's warning that fingering herself would lead to blindness. She always tried to use anything but her fingers but the need was too great! She felt compelled to run her bare hand over the curly hair that covered her pussy again and again. As she pressed harder and harder against the mound of her clitoris, she discovered the pleasure that went through her when she touched it just *so*. She spread her legs and touched it repeatedly until she had another orgasm. She leaned against the shower cubicle as she swam in a sea of pleasure.

Slowly she surfaced from the sensual fog and remembered Jonathan. She quickly washed herself and turned off the shower. Dressing hurriedly, she rushed out of her front door, already a few minutes late.

Jonathan opened the door at five past eight and was surprised to find her in a very baggy top and a long skirt, wearing a pair of plain, unflattering black rimmed glasses. He didn't comment as he ushered her inside.

Sipping his coffee as he sat opposite her, he noticed that her eyes were glassy and dazed. He wondered if she had a dark side. Maybe she'd smoked some pot before she'd come over to his place. The thought made his cock throb. He loved the idea that there was a wild woman under those baggy clothes, ugly glasses and bad hair—he definitely had to get to know her better.

Every time she parted her lips to sip her coffee his eyes followed the movement. Her Naomi-type full lips were shaped into a perfect Cupid bow. It was her best feature, although with the thick, tinted lens in her glasses he couldn't really see her eyes properly. Earlier when she'd answered the door she hadn't looked directly at him for more than a few seconds. And when she had brought the vacuum cleaner back, he'd been too busy looking at her nipples to notice her eyes.

She seemed keen to get back to her flat and perversely, it made him keener to keep her in his. As she sipped the last of her coffee, he tried to think of a common interest they might share.

Books! With her studious looks she would probably like reading.

"Have you read *The Da Vinci Code*?" The bestseller was on everyone's lips, even non-readers had read it, so there was a very good chance that she would have done.

"Yes." Her whole face lit up as she smiled. "I have also read *Angels & Demons* and *Deception Point*. I'm finishing *Digital Fortress* at the moment."

"I read them all in less than two weeks." He smiled. "I am an electronic engineer so I love the gadgetry. Which one's your favourite?"

"I read *Angels & Demons* first and loved it so much I bought the others. I guess that's my favourite. Which one's yours?"

"*The Da Vinci Code*," he replied without hesitation. "I read that first...maybe that's why it's my favourite."

She smiled at him and he smiled back. Instantly her clitoris throbbed. She suddenly jumped up and said, "I really must go *now*."

She had reached the door and had opened it before he got there, but he still managed to brush a kiss across her cheek before she squeezed through it. "Thanks again for the loan of the vacuum cleaner, I'll return it tomorrow."

She nodded, quickly opened her door and went into her flat. He smiled as he closed his door, while they had discussed the Dan Brown books she had forgotten to be shy. In those moments he had glimpsed the woman she could become with the right stimulation. All he needed was to find things that interested her and pull her out of her shell.

He reached down, grabbed his cock through his jeans and shifted it to a more comfortable position. He had just split up with his girlfriend Anne who had complained that he liked sex too much. She'd said that there must be something seriously wrong with him for wanting sex so often. She thought sex once or twice a week was too much, every night was perverse. Plus, she complained, he always made her sore. He'd tried to convince her that she only got sore because they didn't have sex often enough but she wasn't swayed. She'd thought once they had gotten over the initial stage of the relationship that he would want to screw less but it seemed as if he wanted sex more often, not less. She was right, at twenty-four he felt hornier than at eighteen.

He had met Anne at a friend's party a year ago. Watching her dance had given him an instant hard-on and when he plucked up the courage to ask her for a dance, she had held him tight and let him grind his erection against her. They had slept together that same night and two weeks later he moved into her flat, thinking that it would mean sex on a regular basis; instead she'd started to ration the pussy. She always got sore when they had sex, and wouldn't be convinced that it was because they didn't do it often enough. It had all come to a head when he had tried to get some pussy while she was fast asleep a week ago. She had been sprawled on her back, legs apart, wearing no knickers as she always did at night. The temptation had been too great for him to resist. When he had fingered her she sleepily enjoyed it, becoming moist enough for him to attempt intercourse, but as soon as he had slipped inside her, she had woken up. He had pretended that he had been unaware of his actions —trying to convince her that he was a 'sleepfucker' who unconsciously fucked in his sleep, the same way a sleepwalker walked in his. She hadn't bought it, giving him a week to find somewhere else to live. Luckily, the estate agent had found him this flat in less than a day.

The building had previously been one large house. Some enterprising property developer had converted it into four small flats and hence, the interior walls weren't as soundproof as they should be. Loud noises could be heard through the connecting walls.

Just after Elizabeth left, Jonathan grabbed the monthly

engineering magazine he had bought earlier in the day and lay on his bed to see what was new in the world of electronics. Engrossed in the magazine he missed the first faint moans coming from Elizabeth's flat but eventually the sound permeated his consciousness. He closed his eyes and concentrated for a moment. She was definitely moaning. He pressed his ear against the wall and listened more carefully.

"Kiss me Jonathan. Yes, suck my breast, *please*." A series of loud moans followed by, "Play with my clit and make me cum."

She gave another loud groan and then there was silence.

She called out his name! Jonathan was elated—he had been due his weekly fuck when Anne had kicked him out. He was dying for some pussy.

The next evening he rapped on Elizabeth's door at seven but she wasn't home from work yet. At quarter to eight he heard sounds coming from her flat and immediately rapped on her door again. She came to the door wearing a mud-coloured trouser business suit. She smiled shyly at him and moved back to let him inside.

"You worked late today," he commented, mesmerized by her lips.

"Yes, my colleague and I are writing the programme for a new procedure. We had a problem with a few lines of code."

"Have you had dinner yet?" he asked, knowing very well she hadn't.

"I was just going to cook myself something."

"I've cooked some pasta, you are welcome to come and share it with me," he invited.

"I couldn't impose." She flushed with embarrassment.

"Come on, there is enough for the two of us."

"Okay."

She smiled and once again he thought, *under that hair and glasses there's a beautiful woman just waiting to get out.*

"Go and change your suit. You don't want to get pasta sauce all over it."

As soon as she went into the bedroom he stuck the small electronic device, which he had kept concealed from her, against the wall. He stood back and looked at it critically—it was completely concealed by the abstract motif of the wallpaper. Next he rushed to the bathroom, stuck another one on the wall there and hurried back to the living room.

Five minutes later she came out of her bedroom wearing an oversized T-shirt and the same skirt she'd worn the previous day.

When they sat down at his kitchen table, he poured her a glass of wine as she helped herself to a small portion of the pasta. He promptly piled some more onto her plate.

"I need to lose weight," she protested.

"Why are women always dieting? A lot of men like women who look like women and not little girls. I love women with curves, like you."

She didn't say anything but he saw her blush and quickly take a forkful of pasta to avoid responding to his words. He took pity on her and changed the subject, asking her about programming. He listened as she spoke with enthusiasm about her job and was more determined to get her out of her protective shell.

She left just after nine and as soon as she walked into her flat the motion sensor in the device he had stuck on her living room wall came on. He watched as she double bolted the door and then went straight into her bedroom. He lost her for a few moments—he was going to have to find a way of getting one of his devices into her bedroom—then she came out completely naked! He stared at the monitor unable to believe his eyes. She had small breasts, with big pouting nipples, that would fit his hands perfectly. Her trim waist flared into wide hips and heavy thighs. He got a fleeting glimpse of her behind before he lost her again as she walked into the bathroom. The sensor in the bathroom came to life as it picked her up and he got a good look at her magnificent ass as she was about to step into the shower. The girl from the block, whatever she was calling herself these days, had nothing on Elizabeth!

Minutes later she re-emerged and walked back to the bedroom. And then she was at it again! He put his head against the wall and listened.

"Oh Jonathan, put your finger in my pussy. Oh that is nice, I like it. Yes, put another in, I like two fingers in my wet pussy. Stick them inside me, stick them deep. Oh yes!"

She moaned and groaned until once again there was silence.

The next day he waited until she'd left for work before picking the simple door lock and slipping into her flat. He put in a device in the bedroom, carefully choosing the location to achieve maximum coverage. Then he placed one in her kitchen but decided against putting yet another in the shower cubicle. The steam would fog the lens and the humidity render it unusable in less than a week. And it was quite costly to make each miniature device.

At six o'clock that evening, Elizabeth walked through the door carrying a Sainsbury's carrier bag in each hand. He switched the multi-view screen to single view as she entered the kitchen. She pulled a frozen meal box from one of the carrier bags, took off the sleeve and read the cooking instruction on the reverse. Then she pierced the plastic film covering with a fork and popped the meal into her microwave. She pressed a few buttons and the light in the microwave lit up as the turntable started slowly spinning. She emptied the carriers and put away the rest of the shopping while she waited for the meal to cook.

His heart clenched at the lonely picture she made, eating the meal at the small table in her kitchen as she quickly scanned the pages of a woman's magazine. He imagined the two of them cooking meals together, then making love as soon as they'd consumed the food.

Give me a chance and you'll never be lonely again, he vowed.

She went straight to the bathroom when she'd finished eating, brushed her teeth, stripped and stepped into the shower.

He had deliberately placed the device in the bathroom a little lower than the others. He saw her stroke herself through the bottom of the glass shower cubicle; the top had completely steamed up. When she stepped out to grab her towel and dry herself off, her large nipples were pointing forwards like two mini prunes.

She went into the kitchen, opened the refrigerator and pulled out a bag of carrots. She chose one, made a circle with one hand and first pushed her finger, then the carrot through it. She shook her head and tried another one. She smiled and left it on the counter as she re-sealed the bag and put it back in the refrigerator.

As she walked back to the bedroom, carrot in hand, Jonathan knew that she didn't plan to munch on it. She pulled out a packet of condoms and put one on the carrot. Then she lay back, opened her legs and pressed the condom-covered carrot against her pussy. He quickly zoomed in and got a tight shot of just her pussy. The carrot was fat and she had some difficulty working it inside her.

Damn, she looked so tight!

The devices didn't record sound but he pressed his ears

against the wall to hear the words she was repeating, "Fuck me Jonathan. Oh yes, please, fuck me with your big, hard cock."

He pulled his cock from his jeans and wanked himself as he pressed his ears against the wall, awkwardly rotating his eyes to the sides to catch the footage on the surveillance monitor. The way her tight pussy clung to the carrot made him wank himself harder and harder, imagining that it was his cock inside her and not the lucky carrot. He shot his load onto his bedroom carpet as he watched her cum.

The next day as soon as she came home, she went to the fridge and got another carrot. She quickly slipped a condom on it, pulled off her panties and lay on the bed her skirt raised to her waist. She must have been thinking about the carrot-fucking all day because she was already wet. She pushed it deep inside her but pulled it out after about two minutes and walked back into the kitchen. She looked into the bag that contained the carrots but didn't seem to find what she wanted. She closed the fridge and stood looking around the kitchen for a moment before she walked over to the fruit bowl, selected a banana and took it back to the bedroom. She put a condom on it, lay back and inserted it into her wet pussy, biting her bottom lip as she forced the large, half-ripe fruit inside her. Her pussy walls squeezed it and Jonathan imagined his cock being given the same treatment. Just the thought of it made him cum.

God, he was dying to sink his cock into her!

As she pulled the battered looking fruit out and plunged it back in as deep as she could get it, Elizabeth smiled. When she had left home her mother had instructed her to have her five portions of fruit and vegetables daily. She may not be eating five portions every day but at least today she was *getting* two large ones! And bearing her mother's advice in mind, when she pulled the banana out after two orgasms, she peeled it and made a milkshake.

On her way home from the tube station the next day she noticed stout, firm-looking green bananas for sale in an African food shop. She had walked past the shop every day after work for the last three years and hadn't noticed the bananas before. Now just the sight of them made her clitoris swell. She peered into the dimly-lit shop and sighed in disappointment—the shopkeeper was a young man. She felt too embarrassed to pick out a few of the bananas and take them to him at the counter, she would probably blush and he would suspect the reason for her purchase.

So instead, she went past her flat to the supermarket again and bought a bunch of bananas, this time carefully choosing a hand of four long, straight green ones which would probably not ripen well enough for eating but would be perfect for what she had in mind.

As soon as she got home she pulled one from the hand and rushed into the bedroom. She didn't even bother taking her panties off; she just slipped the gusset aside, put the condom-covered banana against her wet pussy. It was larger and firmer than the one the day before and she had to relax her muscles to get it inside her entrance but gradually it slid inside. She forced about half of it inside her, and then started working it back and forth, building a nice smooth rhythm as her juices moistened the condom.

Jonathan groaned and quickened the motion of his stroking hand along his hard shaft when he heard her scream, "Yes, Jonathan fuck me with your big cock. Fuck me, please!"

He was so willing to do all she asked! He would pick her lock and be inside her in a flash if he didn't think he would frighten her witless. He had to find a way of breaking the ice.

The banana filled Elizabeth so satisfyingly she forgot to have dinner. After three orgasms she pulled it out, curled up and went to sleep, still in her work clothes.

The next day she washed her hair before she fingered herself, collapsing weakly against the shower cubicle as an orgasm raced through her. She came out of the shower, wrapped a towel around her head as she dried her body and applied cocoa-butter lotion to her skin. Then she vigorously towel-dried her hair and used an Afro comb to tease it out.

By lunchtime she was pacing her small living room restlessly, looking like a caged tigress. Suddenly she pulled on a jacket and left the house. Fifteen minutes later she came back clutching a carrier bag. She closed the door, grabbed something long and green from the bag and rushed into the bedroom.

She stripped, lay on the bed and quickly put a condom on the cucumber. It was much fatter than the bananas and Jonathan watched her struggle to get the end of it inside her. Every time she pushed or pulled on the cucumber he could see the folds of her pussy cling to the condom. She patiently worked about 3" of the cucumber inside her, all the while repeating, "Fuck me, Jonathan. Yes, fuck my tight pussy with your big, hard cock!"

She came twice, placed the cucumber on her bedside table and she lay back against her pillow with a smile.

Jonathan decided enough was enough! She was going to send him crazy! She obviously needed to be fucked, she was calling his name, he wanted to fuck her—perfect! He rushed over and rapped loudly on her door.

She opened it, still tying the sash on her bathrobe. Her eyes had that same dazed, glassy look they'd had the first day she'd come over for coffee. He could smell the tantalizing heat of her pussy. "Can I come in?"

"Sure." She didn't really want him in her flat right now. She was still buzzing from her last orgasm but she was too shy to refuse him entry. Plus she suddenly became aware that she smelled a little odd.

"Were you busy?" he asked casually.

"No. I was just lying down."

"Good. I have decided to give you a makeover." He pulled a brand-new comb from the back pocket of his jeans.

"What?"

"You heard me. You are a young woman and you should look like one."

"I'm a hopeless case."

"No, you're not. I think you've been deliberately hiding behind all that hair and those glasses so that men can't see you."

"I'm near-sighted and I'm allergic to relaxers—there is nothing you can do about either."

"There's plenty I can do with that beautiful, thick hair on your head."

"Like what?"

"I can plait it, twist it or cornrow it."

"You?" She laughed as she tried to imagine him plaiting her hair.

"Yes, I used to work part-time at my uncle's barber shop when I was at university. His wife's salon was on the other side of the shop and when we weren't busy she taught me a few things."

"My hair is really thick, are you sure you can handle it?"

"Come here." He grabbed her and pushed her down onto one of her dining chairs.

Carefully parting her hair into sections, he sprayed her scalp with the light olive oil moisturizer she used and gave her a firm head massage. She had to bite her lip to stop herself from vocalizing her pleasure as his fingertips moved over her scalp in a caressing, arousing manner. Her clit started throbbing like mad!

Her wild hair was softer than it looked and in less than two hours he'd transformed it into an elegant Goddess style which had been very popular years ago. Most women had loved it because if done correctly it suited every shape of face and flattered even unattractive women. Jonathan had seen another woman with the style as recently as a few months ago and it hadn't looked outdated. From time to time, as he moved around her to position himself to cornrow a section of hair, he got glimpses of her breasts. Her nipples seemed to grow harder before his very eyes.

When he was finished he grabbed her hand, led her to the bathroom mirror and took off her glasses. "Look how beautiful you are! Even if you don't like contact lens you should buy a trendy pair of glasses."

She looked at herself and was amazed to discover that she'd inherited her mother's luscious lips. For years she'd only looked in the mirror to make sure her face was clean. It was almost like looking at a stranger.

Jonathan looked at her as well and confirmed what he had suspected all along—she *was* quite good looking. His cock hardened appreciatively.

"I have another pair of glasses but I don't wear them," she said, almost unconsciously, still not believing that the woman in the mirror was really *her*.

The young assistant at the opticians had chosen a pair of designer frames she had thought suited Elizabeth perfectly. Though she had disagreed, Elizabeth had been too shy to say so, but as soon as she had left the opticians she had switched it for the free pair and hadn't worn the designer pair since.

"Bring them and let me see," Jonathan urged, convinced without seeing them that they had to be more flattering than the pair she currently wore.

She retrieved them from her handbag which she had dropped onto the small table by the door in her haste to use the cucumber. The narrow black-rimmed spectacles had thinner lens and were much lighter than the other pair. He stood behind her as she put them on.

"They are perfect for you," he complimented. "I don't want to see you wearing those other ones again."

She nodded in agreement and he put his arms around her, and pulled her body against his. His cock hardened even more as her voluptuous ass brushed against it. "The next time I'm going to twist your hair. I want you to see the real beauty of it. Many women would kill to have a full head of hair like yours."

"Actually I like your dreadlocks," she admitted, looking at his neat locks in the mirror.

"That's even better—I could hook you up some nice thin locks." Her abundant hair would be perfect for it.

He tightened his arms and pressed himself against her.

"Okay, makeover out of the way, let's get down to some serious business. Last night I heard you moaning and calling my name. I thought you were ill at first and almost came to check on you but after a while you stopped and I figured you were okay. Why were you calling my name? Was there something you wanted from me?"

She nodded weakly. She knew that *he* knew exactly what she wanted from him.

"Something like this?" He cupped her breasts through the robe and a bolt of pleasure shot through her.

"Yes." Her voice was barely a whisper as he rolled the plump nipples between his fingers. When he pushed the material aside and covered them with his hands she leaned back against him and closed her eyes.

"Open your eyes and look in the mirror, I want you to see my hands on your body."

She opened her eyes and at first she avoided meeting his eyes in the mirror but as he tweaked her nipples more and more firmly, her half-closed eyes met his.

"Beautiful. Just beautiful." She didn't know if he was referring to her or her breasts but it sent another shiver through her.

Together they watched his hands play with her nipples. Then he kissed the side of her neck and pressed his erection between the cheeks of her voluptuous behind. The feel of his throbbing cock against her made her clitoris ache and she rubbed it between her upper thighs, her hips moving sensuously against him. Sensing her need, he opened the robe and exposed the naked glory of her body. She sighed as he reached his hand down and found her clitoris.

He'd thought that it was the angle of the lens that made her clit appear large on the monitor but as he fondled its fullness he realized that hers was the most prominent he'd ever come across. He brought his other hand down and pushed a long finger up inside her pussy as he continued to rub her outsized clit. She came instantly against his hand.

"Let's go to the bedroom. I want to fuck you on the bed. I want to push my big, hard cock into your tight pussy." He deliberately used the words he'd heard her utter through the walls and her knees nearly buckled at the sound. Weak with desire, she leaned back against him as they made their way slowly, a little awkwardly to the bedroom, his cock pressed up against her ass, his finger buried inside her, his thumb stroking her clit.

When they got to the bed he turned her around and

pushed her onto it. Suddenly she remembered what she'd been doing before he'd come over. Her eyes flew to the top of her dresser—the condom-covered cucumber was there in plain sight. His eyes followed hers. Shaking his head in disapproval he leaned over and picked it up.

"Why would you use this when I was right next door?"

Her eyes slid away from his. "I didn't know if you wanted me."

"I wanted you from the first time I saw you."

She smiled up at him in surprised disbelief.

"Honestly," he assured her and bent to kiss her. "Have you ever been fucked before?"

She nodded.

"I mean by a man *not* a fruit or vegetable."

"Yes."

Not quite believing her, and remembering the trouble she had with the first carrot, he asked, "How long ago was that?"

"About six years ago."

"And you haven't been fucked since?"

"No," she replied quietly, suddenly feeling unloved, too tall and too ugly again.

"I'm so glad you *saved* yourself for me," he murmured against her lips before he kissed her softly.

The words instantly made her feel better.

He pushed her back against the bed, eager to see her clit with his naked eye. Her pussy was glorious! It was quite hairy and not only was her clit prominent so were her inner lips. They were darker than the surrounding genital area and like her nipples had a shiny appearance, similar to black grapes.

Eagerly, he pushed her legs back, spread her pussy and tongued her fat clit. The smooth texture even felt like grapes and he let his mouth explore the whole area. Then he pushed his tongue inside her and tongue-fucked her until she relaxed totally and opened up for him, ready for some cock.

He sat up and quickly slipped out of his clothes. Her eyes widened in appreciation as his erect cock bobbed with every movement he made. He reached for the packet of condoms on her bedside table and extracted one. He rolled it on, his cock jerking as he climbed onto the bed and kissed her.

She didn't suck on his tongue when he pushed it into her mouth—it was as if she had never been French-kissed!

"You have to suck on my tongue. Put yours in my mouth and I'll show you."

He pulled her tongue into his mouth and sucked on it. When he slipped his into her mouth again she sucked on it greedily—she was a quick study.

He rolled her nipples between his fingers as he kissed her. She groaned and he increased the pressure. Breaking the kiss, he covered her left nipple with his lips. She moaned his name and started to move her hips under his as he moved to her other breast. Like her clit, her nipples were the biggest he'd ever sucked on. He loved their firm, smooth texture.

"Jonathan, I need your cock inside me, now. I've waited so long, I can't wait any more." Her eyes met his pleadingly, her hand on her clit rubbing furiously. "Fuck me now, please!"

"Okay baby, spread your sweet pussy for me."

He reached down and positioned himself against her as she held her fat pussy lips open. His cock was thicker than the cucumber but with a few shimmies of his hips he got the head past her entrance. He kissed her as he sank deeper into her warm depths. She got tighter as he went deeper but he used his hips like a corkscrew, working his cock slowly but surely into her. Several minutes later his rigid cock was buried to the hilt.

"As I move backwards and forwards I want you to move your hips from side to side," he instructed. He withdrew and sank slowly back inside her a few times and she obediently gyrated her hips as she met his thrusts eagerly.

"Am I doing it right?" she asked as he paused for a moment.

"You're a natural," he complimented encouragingly. "I was going to wait until the next time to put some sideways motion into my thrust but I think you can handle everything I have to give right now."

He kissed her deeply as he increased the speed, depth and the range of his movements. She climaxed within minutes, digging her nails into his butt. He slowed his thrusts but didn't withdraw, knowing from his voyeuristic ventures that she would usually continue to fuck herself with whatever fruit or vegetable she was using from one orgasm to the next with scarcely a pause. He measured his strokes carefully and made her cum another time before he took her with him again as he came. He pulled his cock out of her slowly, her greedy pussy walls trying to hold on to him.

"I don't want you to use another fruit or vegetable again. Do you hear me?"

"Yes, Jonathan."

"Just let me know whenever you need fucking."

"Yes, Jonathan."

For the first time she looked directly into his eyes without shyness. Her eyes were an unusual shade of dark brown, just lighter than Cadbury's milk chocolate. She smiled and he leaned down to kiss her full mouth.

They lay together on the small bed for about half an hour, kissing and caressing. He played with her clit, occasionally squeezing a long finger inside her. She stroked him, running her hand up and down his rigid length and gently cupping his balls. He desperately wanted to fuck her again but suspected her pussy would be too sore, if the way it was gripping his finger was any indication. He'd had to really force his cock into her once he had gotten the head past her entrance. He would have to satisfy himself with masturbating as he watched the re-run.

"Jonathan?"

"Yes?" He raised his head and she smiled up at him.

"I need fucking."

Needing no further encouragement, he pulled her into a kneeling position and placed himself behind her as soon as the words left her lips. Her tight pussy resisted his first two thrusts but on the third she pushed back hard as he thrust forward and his cock forced its way into her slick folds. He quickly built the tempo and soon her ass was bouncing as he slammed himself against her with quick, hard strokes.

"Yes, fuck me hard, Jonathan!" She grabbed the headboard and pushed herself back at him.

He still couldn't believe he had his cock buried so deeply inside his timid neighbour's pussy. She turned out to be the best fuck of his life. Her sweet, grasping pussy was pure heaven. He grabbed her fleshy hips, tilted them up slightly and drove his cock forward. She moaned and lowered her torso even more, making him go even deeper inside her. He reached down and fingered her clitoris and she came immediately.

He fucked her another two times before he went back over to his flat early the next morning. They both had single beds but they had already made plans to buy a larger bed for her flat the next day. He would give up the lease on his flat and move in with her—he wanted to be there to fuck her anytime she felt the need. All indications showed that she would need fucking as often as he needed to fuck her. It was a win fucking win situation but he couldn't become complacent. He didn't want to have to murder some innocent fruit or vegetable because it had fucked his woman.

After he left, Elizabeth stretched lazily and smiled. Finally she had a man to fuck her again. Jonathan's wonderful, thick, throbbing penis had felt so much better than the professor's. He had easily put the older man in the shade. Good grief! The way he kissed her deeply, sucked firmly on her nipples, expertly sucked on her clitoris and fucked her with his tongue!

No more fruit and no more vegetables.

Just Jonathan!

She smiled as she nodded off to sleep, imagining him on his narrow bed on the other side of the thin wall thinking of her as she was thinking of him.

***

Phallic-shaped **fruits & vegetables** *have implicit sexual connotations. Though dildos are widely available, many women and men are too shy to purchase them so instead they use things that are easily available. No one looks twice at anyone buying fruits or vegetables in a supermarket...unless the shopper is selecting a cucumber with far too much attention paid to its length or girth!*

*****

OXFORD BLUE

*E*mma Boateng laughed as the quiz contestant got the answer wrong. She hadn't liked the arrogant older man from the start of the show and didn't want him to win, although she acknowledged he was the better of the two vying to win the mid-week edition of Countdown.

Her telephone started ringing. She looked across at it angrily, willing it to stop. It didn't. She got up, marched over to it and snatched the receiver off its cradle.

"Hello?" She knew her voice didn't disguise her displeasure but if it was another call from the bank trying to give her advice about what to do with the twenty-five thousand pounds it had taken most of her working life to save, she wasn't even going to try and be polite this time.

"Mrs Boateng?" The deep male voice was unfamiliar and sounded unsure.

"Yes," she literally barked into the telephone, hoping whoever he was, he would quickly tell her what he wanted from her.

"It's Samuel Bekoe, I was Andrew's friend when we were boys...I don't know if you remember me."

"Samuel! Of course, I remember you!" she reassured him

before quickly apologizing, "I'm so sorry I was rude but the bank keeps calling me about investment options even though I've told them repeatedly I'm not interested. It's very annoying."

"I understand perfectly, Mrs Boateng. The reason I am calling is that I am back in London for two weeks before I go up to Oxford. I wanted to see Andrew before I leave, is he home?"

"He went out with some friends just after lunch but he should be home for dinner. Would you like to join us around eight o'clock?"

"I would love to," he replied enthusiastically. "My parents have moved back to Ghana and I am just renting a room until I go up to university. I had to make my own lunch today and I'm afraid I made quite a mess of it. Thank you very much for inviting me."

"You're welcome and while you are here, feel free to come over and eat with us any time. If you'd like, I can even show you how to make yourself some simple meals."

"Mrs Boateng, I would appreciate that very much. I'll see you at eight, goodbye for now."

"Goodbye, Samuel."

She caught the last five minutes of the quiz show and was quite pleased when the teenaged boy managed to guess the conundrum within ten seconds and beat the older man by a single point. She flicked through the channels to see if there was anything else to watch but nothing piqued her interest. She switched the television set off, closed her eyes and relaxed against the supple leather chair.

The last time she had seen Samuel he'd been fourteen years old and very tall for his age. She had liked him the most of her son's many friends. He had always been polite and well mannered. Whenever she came home with any shopping and he was visiting Andrew, he'd rush to help her with her bags. The Christmas before he had left for Ghana he had given her a beautiful scarf two days before the holidays. She had kissed his still-hairless cheek, pleasantly surprised at his thoughtfulness. She had always bought him Easter eggs, birthday and Christmas gifts but she had never expected one in return. Months later, when she had worn the scarf to work a female colleague had commented that it was an exclusive item from a top designer. Emma had been stunned. Knowing Samuel would have been offended if she had given it back, she'd fervently hoped he had bought it in a sale and not spent an exorbitant sum on her.

The following summer he and Andrew had gone to the cinema and on their way back they'd been attacked by a group of three White boys. The boys had shouted racial abuse at her son and his friend, but they'd both ignored them. The three boys had continued to follow them for about ten minutes, calling them names and making monkey sounds. Then one of them had punched the shorter, smaller-framed Andrew on the back of his head and he'd fallen to the ground. Samuel had turned and floored the boy who had hit Andrew with a single punch. The other two boys had attacked Samuel but he'd beaten them both down.

When the police had arrived they had arrested Samuel and Andrew, and taken them to the police station, although they had tried to explain that they hadn't been the ones to initiate the fight. Emma always tried to convince herself that they had taken one look at Samuel's height and the already impressive breadth of his shoulders and assumed he was much too old to be fighting the younger boys. But deep down she knew the decision had more likely been racially motivated. She and her husband had arrived at the station just before Samuel's parents and had demanded that the boys be immediately removed from the filthy holding cells. They had waited for Samuel's parents to arrive and then they had all left together, furious that their well-behaved teenaged sons had been put through that kind of unnecessary trauma.

A week later Andrew told her that Samuel's parents were sending him to a boarding school in Ghana. They had gone to the airport to see him off. It was the last time Emma had seen her son cry, even Samuel had shed some tears as he'd hugged her goodbye.

***

At precisely eight o'clock the doorbell rang and Emma went to open the door. She didn't check before unlocking it and almost screamed as a giant of a man filled the doorframe. Then he smiled and she relaxed—Samuel still had the slight gap between his front teeth but he had grown much taller and broader than she had ever imagined he would. And so much more devastatingly handsome!

"Samuel?"

"Yes, Mrs Boateng, it's me."

She held her arms out in welcome. He bent and wrapped her in a tight embrace.

"Samuel honey, come in, please."

He handed her a bottle of wine and a bunch of roses before taking off his jacket and hanging it on the coat rack near the door.

"I'm afraid Andrew isn't home yet, neither is my husband but we will start dinner without them."

"I don't mind waiting," Samuel lied. He was quite hungry but he didn't want her to feel that she had to stick to the set time just because of him.

"No. I baked a lovely fresh salmon and it will dry out if we wait. They know that I have dinner on the table at eight each evening, if they can't be here on time it's their loss."

"Okay. Where can I wash up?"

"Right through there." She pointed to the door just beyond the entrance of the utility room that housed their smaller second bathroom.

By the time he re-emerged a few minutes later she had set the table and the stuffed salmon was giving off a delectable aroma. She sliced a large portion of the tail for him, expertly leaving all the bones behind. Then he helped himself to the lightly steamed vegetables.

"Don't be shy Samuel, eat as much as you like," she encouraged. "Andrew is probably having fish and chips with his friends anyway and my husband is most likely at his *second* home."

Samuel looked at her in surprise but she just sadly shook her head and he refrained from asking the obvious question.

They discussed the events that had occurred in each other's lives since they had parted at the airport. Samuel seemed so much more mature than her son who was only five months younger. His manner and mannerisms were those of a much older man. She wondered if they had done the right thing by keeping Andrew with them instead of sending him away from the UK.

Samuel did full justice to her carefully prepared meal and it warmed her heart to see her efforts appreciated. Andrew loved fish and chips and her husband hardly ate dinner at home, often the food she prepared ended up in the bin.

She hugged Samuel again as he left just after ten thirty. Neither Andrew nor his father had come home and Samuel decided that he would come around early the next day to see his friend.

***

An hour later, Samuel lay on his back on the uncomfortable bed in his cramped rented room and stroked his stiff aching penis. He hadn't masturbated in years but a cold shower had done nothing to ease the throbbing in his groin.

As a fourteen-year-old boy he'd had the biggest crush on Emma Boateng and now almost six years later she still had exactly the same effect on him. She had been a legal secretary then and whenever she came home dressed in one of her smart suits and her high heels, his heart had leapt painfully in his chest. She was about 5'7" but had weighed about a hundred and twenty five pounds, most of it on her lower half. She'd had a real African woman's behind—high and round. Her breasts had been small and firm looking. Even as a teenager he had imagined that he could span her slim waist with his hands. She had laughed a lot and seemed so much younger than his parents and all other parents he knew, it had been hard to imagine she was old enough to be anyone's mother.

He remembered how he had cried when he had hugged her goodbye at the airport, his poor teenage heart breaking at the thought of never seeing her again.

She had gained a little weight since he had last seen her but it only made her more feminine and even more appealing to him. When she had reached out to hug him in greeting he'd felt his penis harden—that's why he'd asked to use the bathroom. Later, after her second hug, he had walked to the tube station with a massive hard-on.

She was the reason he had come to the UK two weeks early; he had been desperate to see her again. He couldn't believe that Andrew's father would be stupid enough to have an affair when he had such a beautiful wife. *He* couldn't imagine any woman more good looking or sexier than Emma Boateng. And he'd had many since the age of sixteen.

***

Emma had met her husband-to-be Thomas Boateng when he had returned to Ghana after studying for his CIMA in the UK. It had taken him two years longer than he'd planned to achieve the accounting qualification. The girl he'd had been in love with at the time had grown tired of waiting and had married someone else *just* before he had returned to marry her. A month later, on the rebound, he had asked Emma's parents for her hand in marriage. She hadn't hesitated, although at the time she'd only been sixteen years old, twelve years younger than him. She had always dreamed of going abroad to the UK or the US and had been grateful for the opportunity.

They were married before he had returned to the UK and she had joined him six months later already pregnant with his son. He was her first and only lover. When she had given birth to his son he'd seemed as happy as she was. She had continued the secretarial courses she had begun in Ghana and as soon as Andrew had started primary school she started working full-time. They'd had a decent marriage until three and a half years ago when Thomas had abruptly stopped fucking her.

As soon as Emma noticed her husband's lack of interest she had gone out and bought sexy lingerie to try and add some spice to their sex life. But when she had walked into their bedroom, fresh from the shower wearing a sheer negligee, he had turned his back on her and gone to sleep without a word.

She had thought that maybe he was having erectile problems until she noticed, when he slept only in his boxer shorts as the weather improved, that he still woke up hard in the mornings.

His first love had also moved to the UK with her husband. And as soon as the man died following a massive heart attack, Thomas had started an affair with his widow. It had taken Emma a few months to connect his lack of interest to the death of the woman's husband and when she did, it had really hurt her. It angered her that he had no pride whatsoever—the woman had rejected him for another man, yet he was willing to give up the love Emma had offered him over the years to chase a dream he'd been denied.

Emma would have shared him with the other woman if he had wanted her to, but he made it quite plain that he wasn't interested in her body anymore. Depressed, Emma had begun to comfort-eat and the weight had piled on. But soon she'd realized that she was jeopardizing her health and cut back on the sweets and biscuits. Instead she had thrown herself into her work, doing a lot of extra hours and saving her money, knowing that any day Thomas could ask her for a divorce. The speed which had made her one of the top legal secretaries in London backfired, last year she'd developed Repetitive Strain Injury (RSI) in both wrist and was ordered to rest for at least a year if she ever hoped to return to work again.

***

The next morning Samuel arrived at eight thirty, dressed in a white polo shirt and blue jeans. He and Andrew had a brief chat as they shared breakfast and it became quickly obvious that they had very little in common—Samuel had no idea what the latest computer game was; Andrew paid scant notice to world events. When he left for his part-time summer job Andrew didn't make any arrangements to see his friend again before he himself went up to Nottingham to attend university.

At eleven Emma invited Samuel into the kitchen to start the cookery lessons.

"Did you bring extra clothing?" she asked.

He shook his head, looking puzzled.

"Cooking can be a messy business," she explained. "I don't think that either Andrew's or my husband's clothing would fit you, so you'll have to wear an apron."

He laughed as he bent forward for her to slip a red and white striped apron over his head. She moved to tie it for him but he took the ends and tied it himself.

She showed him how to make a few easy dishes like lasagne and spaghetti bolognaise using the same basic tomato sauce recipe with minced beef. When they finished they set the dishes out on the dining table and she watched him scoop large portions of each dish and pile them onto his plate.

"You'll get fat!" she warned as she watched him tuck into the food with barely concealed relish.

"I'll be rowing for Oxford, I'll burn off the extra calories."

The exclusive boarding school he'd attended in Ghana had an amazing rowing tradition and almost every student who applied to Cambridge or Oxford with a decent academic record was accepted. Samuel had been the captain of the rowing team and last year they had broken the longest standing record in the school's history.

He spent the rest of the day with her and they laughed so much together she felt young and carefree for the first time in years. She forgot her worry about her wrists and the humiliation of her husband's rejection. When they said goodbye at the door she held him to her for a long time, grateful that he had reminded her of the happy person she used to be.

The next day he arrived just before noon and they went straight into the kitchen. She had decided to teach him some traditional Ghanaian dishes and had laid out the appropriate ingredients.

Ten minutes later they were standing side-by-side in the kitchen when she reached over to grab a handful of the onion he had just diced and accidentally brushed against the front of him. The hiss of his indrawn breath was loud in the quiet room. She looked up at him in surprise and her heart almost stopped at the expression in his eyes before he looked away.

They finished cooking in silence but instead of eating the food as he had done the previous day, Samuel said that he would take it home and eat it later.

As he was leaving early, Emma offered him a lift. He accepted graciously enough although he seemed reluctant to spend any more time in her company. Perversely, she wanted to see if what she had seen in his eyes was real or the imagination of a desperate woman. She didn't know what she would do with the information but his look had awakened something inside her. She was as shocked as she was intrigued.

When she pulled up in front of the large house in Whitechapel where he was renting a room, they sat in the car in silence for a few minutes.

"Do you want to come up for a cup of tea?" he asked finally.

"Okay."

Samuel almost died of embarrassment; he had asked _only_ out of politeness. He led the way up the steps to the third floor and though he had already mentioned that the room was substandard he felt that he had to warn her once more as he pushed the door open and let her precede him into the sparse room.

"The room is terrible, but as I only wanted it for two

weeks, I don't mind."

Emma looked around the small room in dismay. She knew his wealthy parents would be worried to death if they found out that their youngest child was staying in a place like this, even if it was only for a short time. She turned and looked up at him, "You should have come and stayed with us."

"I couldn't be in the same house with you twenty-four hours a day and *not* have you—I would have gone insane." This time he held her gaze, his eyes tortured like he was desperately fighting some inner battle.

No one in all of Emma's life had ever looked at her with such longing!

Her heart melted. She held out her arms and he bent to hug her tightly, pressing his body against hers, the bulge of his erection pressing into her yielding softness. She held him silently, thinking that her feelings should be motherly, they weren't.

Samuel's small room was no place for them to make love and she baulked at the thought of using the spare bedroom in her own house. She reached up and kissed him swiftly on the mouth. "I will make some arrangements for tomorrow."

She left quickly before she gave in to the desire curling around her insides.

When she got home she rummaged through her lingerie drawer and pulled out the exquisite pieces she had bought to entice her husband which had lain unworn for years. Some of them were too snug but others looked better on her now that she had filled out slightly. Like all her underwear they were white, the colour her husband had insisted she always wore. She pre-soaked them to revitalize their brightness, then washed and dried them on a delicate cycle. Later she packed them into a small overnight bag with a few toiletries after buffing the nails of her hands and feet to a high shine.

The next morning she went to the bank, made a withdrawal from her personal savings account and booked a room for ten days at an exclusive hotel in the West End. At first, the concierge was sceptical when she insisted on paying cash but his trained eye swiftly identified her discreet designer clothing and accessories, and he accepted the payment without murmur.

She called Samuel on his mobile phone and told him to come over as soon as he could.

She was filled with nervous excitement as she lay in the large bath, a deep-cleansing mask on her face, surrounded by shea-butter suds instead of the designer brand the hotel had supplied.

She had spent the night thinking about the irrevocable step she was about to take and was surprised how much disappointment flowed through her every time she thought of cancelling it. That very first night, before she had recognized Samuel, she had felt a sudden, intense arousal as she looked up at him. Her body had responded to his latent sexual power, but she had pushed it out of her mind as she tried to connect the man he'd become to the young boy she used to know. It was as if fate had brought them together at this time and this place. She knew as surely as she knew her name if she let this moment slip away, it would be the biggest regret of her life. If it had been one-sided she could have ignored her feelings but the hunger in Samuel's eyes matched the yearning that coursed through her body.

After her bath she looked at herself critically in the full length mirror as she applied shea-butter lotion to her skin. She looked surprisingly good for a woman in her mid-thirties but she couldn't compete with the nubile young women Samuel could get just by snapping his fingers. She didn't feel as confident as she slipped into one of her sexy outfits and looked at herself in the mirror. It was the least revealing of all the lingerie she had packed in the bag, although it only came to mid-thigh. The slit in front revealed her stomach, her lace-covered crotch and her firm thighs every time she took a step.

Less than half an hour after she called Samuel she heard a tap on the door. She peered through the peephole and ensured that it was him before she opened the door.

"Emma!" The sound of her name on his lips for the first time went straight to her heart. He closed the door, dropped his rucksack, pulled her into his arms and held her for a long time, his heartbeat thundering in her ears. "I've *prayed* for this moment…I never thought it would come."

The emotion in his voice removed all remaining traces of doubt. He wanted her and she wanted him. That was *all* that mattered.

He released her and started to take his clothes off. She reached out to unzip his jeans as he pulled off his polo shirt. His torso was magnificent—every muscle honed to perfection. The light sprinkling of silky black hair covering his broad chest tapered down the middle of his flat stomach and into his boxers, which were the same dark blue of his jeans. The outline of his erect penis was visible through the soft material but she looked away quickly. If she thought of the difficulty he would have getting it inside her, she'd panic.

He sat on the bed, pulled her onto his lap and kissed her, his tongue gently seeking as it probed her mouth, not demanding as her husband's used to be. She was amazed at the pleasure she got from sucking on his tongue and when she pushed her tongue into his mouth he seemed to enjoy sucking on it just as much. She was surprised, whenever she'd pushed her tongue into her husband's mouth, he'd behaved as if she was trying to take the dominant role and promptly push it back out. They exchanged long kisses and for the first time she realized how erotic kissing could be.

He unhooked the single fastening on the front of her top and she slipped it off her shoulders. She watched as he swallowed convulsively when he saw her breasts for the first time. They were larger than they once were and not as firm as when she was a young girl but the extra weight she had gained had filled them out beautifully. They looked like full, lush, ripe fruit. His hands trembled as he touched them and suddenly she lost all her inhibitions; he was as nervous as she. She took a deep breath and let the air push her stomach out to its slight, natural roundness. She had been trying to keep it sucked in but it didn't seem to make much difference and holding her breath was making her dizzy.

Samuel watched her nipples harden as he stroked them. He had often fantasized about seeing her breasts but he had never imagined that they would be so beautiful. With a groan of pleasure he eagerly took one of her erect nipples in his mouth and sucked on it. Tenderly, she held him against her as wave after wave of sensation washed over her. He moved to the other nipple and gave it the same treatment. She felt a flow of wetness dampen the crotch of her panties and Samuel's thigh beneath. He laid her back against the soft pillows and pulled them over her plump thighs. Then he lay beside her and kissed her as he pushed a long finger inside her to stoke her desire. She was slick with her own juices but her tight walls clung to his finger.

"God, you're so tight!"

He kissed her as he worked another finger inside her entrance and then gently thrust them back and forth a few times. He pulled them out slowly, carried them to his mouth and tasted her nectar. She found the simple action unbearably erotic. She closed her eyes and moaned as another sliver of pleasure raced through her.

Her moan of arousal made Samuel quickly sit up, rip the packet containing the extra sensation condom and roll it onto his erection. He covered her body with his and kissed her softly as he put his condom-encased penis against her entrance. He gently pushed the blunt head against her several times without gaining any ground, trying to gradually widen her entrance without causing her too much pain. Impatiently, she opened her legs a bit more, reached down and pressed it hard against her and finally the head slipped inside her.

He groaned as her vaginal walls held his penis in a tight grip. Even if she had been having regular sex with her husband it probably wouldn't have mattered, he was much bigger than Thomas. Patiently, he worked several inches into her vagina. When he felt her body resist further entry, he withdrew slowly and just as slowly thrust forward, then again, and again. He kissed her lips, her neck and the side of her face. Occasionally, he whispered words of endearment into her ear before he traced her lobe with his tongue. He supported most of his weight on his bent arms that were wrapped around her body, holding her securely against him.

It had been so long since she'd been held. But even when Thomas had held her, he'd never been this tender with her, not even on their wedding night. Emma tried to blink the tears away but they overflowed her eyes and ran down the sides of her face. She buried her head into Samuel's broad shoulder as the sobs started deep in her throat.

"Emma? Am I hurting you?" He cradled her head gently in his hands. The concern in his voice made her cry even harder. "Do you want me to stop?"

"No, Samuel." She pulled away slightly and met his

concerned eyes. "It's wonderful, please don't stop."

She opened her lips and offered him her mouth. He covered it with his and quickened the undulations of his hips. Soon she was sucking on his tongue urgently and rotating her hips as she came. She felt every contraction as he spilled his seed into the condom deep inside her seconds later.

He eased himself out of her still erect, pulled her back against him and held her. There were no words needed as he stroked her nipples into hard peaks again, his penis jerking restlessly against her hip. Then he lifted her thigh, placed it over both of his and inserted his penis into her from behind. Usually it was a position he avoided because it didn't allow full penetration but it was perfect for Emma's tight vagina. His strokes were firmer as he pressed himself against the ample cheeks of her behind, which regulated his forward motion and left almost a third of his penis outside her. It didn't detract from the pleasure of her vaginal walls fiercely gripping his penis. When he felt himself about to lose control again, he reached down and fingered her clitoris gently and she was lost. He joined her within a few strokes.

Afterwards, they had a shower together. Insisting that she rest her hands, he soaped and scrubbed both their bodies but let her do his muscular back.

His goodbye kiss before she caught a taxi home was the sweetest and longest they had shared all day.

Andrew didn't come home until after ten. Her husband sneaked in just before dawn. She couldn't understand why Thomas insisted on coming home every night regardless of the hour. At first she had thought that it was because the hypocritical woman didn't want her neighbours to see him leaving her house so soon after her husband's death but after almost four years there had to be another reason.

She honestly didn't care; she had stopped caring once the

pain of his rejection had lessened. Now that she had Samuel's lovemaking to compare to his, she cared even less. Thomas certainly wasn't Mr Wonderful!

When he had roughly taken her virginity on their wedding night without any foreplay she had assumed that it was the only way—her mother had warned her that her first time would be painful. When he had fucked her another three times the same night she had borne the agony and fought back her tears as he plundered her sore vagina, accepting that it was the way to womanhood.

When she had come to the UK heavily pregnant and he had insisted on fucking her every night, up until the very night her waters broke, she accepted that it was her duty as a wife to meet her husband's needs and suffered the discomfort.

When she had lain in the maternity ward surrounded only by strangers screaming his name as he stood in the waiting room while she gave birth to his son, she hadn't questioned his right as a man not to witness the painful process, understanding that it was a part of a woman's burden.

When he had impatiently demanded sex two and a half months after she had given birth, instead of the three months that her mother had told her was necessary for proper healing, she had not denied him, grateful that he hadn't demanded it any sooner.

Over the years she had learned to accept the selfish way he fucked her and to even derive some pleasure out of it for herself, baffled why people made such a big fuss about sex. But now Samuel has shown her the difference between fucking and lovemaking. Now she realized that her wedding night needn't have been one she still looked back at with a shudder, that sex didn't have to be about satisfying a man's needs but also her own. And *finally* she understood what the fuss was about!

She had come home last night almost as sore as she'd been on her wedding night but just the thought of Samuel's gentle lovemaking soothed the ache in her swollen vagina.

The next morning she served Andrew breakfast, then showered and dressed. Five minutes after he left the house, she did too.

Samuel was in the middle of a full continental breakfast when she tapped on the door. He wrapped his arms around her and gave her a long kiss before pulling her onto his lap. He fed her bits of his all-butter croissant and she literally felt her hips gain another inch. She shook her head when he offered her a cup of coffee. She only drank decaffeinated since she had realized that her beloved five or six cups of strong black coffee each day were responsible for the horrendous breast pain she had experienced each month during her period.

"I missed you *so* much last night." He kissed the side of her neck and cupped her breasts through her clothing.

"I missed you too," she responded and wrapped her arms tightly around him. "I'm going to leave a little bit later today because I was home all by myself until ten o'clock last evening."

"Good. That will give me just about enough time to do all that I want to do to you today." There was no arrogance in his statement, just a solemn vow of promised pleasure.

Her insides turned to liquid as she remembered the gentle way he had filled her the previous day. She excused herself and went into the bathroom to change. She came out wearing an underwired bra and matching panty set made of sheer, finely woven mesh. Her dark nipples and the triangle of her curly bush were clearly visible through the material.

Samuel was just stepping out of his boxers and she had a

good look at his penis for the first time. It wasn't out of proportion with his splendid physique but on an average man it would have been outrageous. She sat on the bed and watched him roll a condom onto its rigid length. Then he slipped two moulded black rings over the condom. She looked up at him in surprise, wondering what they were.

"I bought them in Soho last night," he explained. "They will stop me from going too deep."

He'd had to really concentrate on not hurting her the day before and it had diminished his pleasure just slightly. When he'd been cumming all he had wanted to do was bury himself deep inside her but he had known that he would have caused her too much pain. With the rings in place he could relax and enjoy himself.

His eyes lit up as he took in her sexy outfit. When she raised her leg slightly to reveal that the panties were crotchless his penis jerked in appreciation. He bent his head and sucked on her nipples through the mesh, the slight texture of the material adding to the wonderful sensation his mouth was creating. When he pushed her legs up and spread the lips of her vagina with his hands she assumed that he was going to penetrate her with his penis. She jerked in surprise and delight when he knelt on the carpet and covered her clitoris with his mouth.

"Samuel, darling!" She reached down and tenderly stroked his head.

She had read about this in books but she had never thought it would feel this wonderful! Her pleasure increased when he pushed his tongue into her vagina as far as it would go and continued to stimulate her clitoris with his thumb. Soon she was lifting her hips to meet his stiff tongue as he stabbed it repeatedly inside her. She screamed his name unashamedly as she came against his mouth.

Then he surprised her by picking her up easily although she weighed almost one hundred and fifty pounds. She clasped her hands tightly around his neck as he reached down and positioned his penis against her before he put his hands on her ample hips and pulled her onto him slowly. After a few strokes he marched into the bathroom and placed her on the edge of the bathroom sink.

They were reflected in the mirrored walls and she watched his penis enter the fat lips of her vagina—it was almost as if she was watching someone else make love—and her arousal grew in intensity. She leaned back and opened her legs wider so that he could plunge into her more deeply. His skin was only a shade darker than hers but in the mirrors the slight contrast in colouring of their glistening skin was more pronounced than in actuality and it added to the eroticism. The muscles in his firm butt rippled as he thrust backwards and forward between her wide-open, plump thighs. When he bent his head and took her nipple into his mouth, the sight of it in the mirror sent her over the edge. Her contracting inner muscles took him with her moments later.

Then he bent her over the same basin and she watched avidly as he took her from behind. She looked lush and womanly in contrast to his rock-hard larger body. The sight was beautiful and intensely arousing to her. He had spread his longer legs but she found herself on tip-toes as she tried to deepen the angle of entry of his penis into her vagina. Her eyes met his in the mirror and they exchanged just a few pleasure-filled glances before they both gasped each other's name as he thrust forward and spilled his life-force once again. He relaxed against her for a moment, his groin pressed against her glorious behind.

Minutes later she was up against the bathroom wall,

holding on to two conveniently placed light fittings as he vigorously plunged his penis into her. He supported most of her body weight with his rower's arms but it had no effect on the effortless rhythm of his hips. Soon the delicious friction of his thrusting penis overcame her and once again she sobbed his name in release. Samuel let his body have its way as her clenching inner muscles squeezed him almost painfully.

Finally sated, they returned to the bed and lay in each other's arms. He stroked her soft skin and intermittently dropped light kisses on her face, neck and shoulders as they talked. After some persuasion he accepted that this would be a once in a lifetime occurrence. She wanted him to go to Oxford and enjoy his university experience to the fullest and not worry about her. She would be fine—he had given her a new lease on life.

They had a shower together and then walked the short distance to an exclusive French restaurant for a meal. They sat across from each other feasting on fine cuisine and sipping champagne as they talked. No one seeing them together would have thought that there was a sixteen year age difference between them. Samuel had the presence of a man ten years older and even the extra pounds hadn't detracted from Emma's youthful good looks.

Replete from their sumptuous meal, they lay naked under the covers of the huge bed. Emma confessed to Samuel that he was the first person to pleasure her orally. Immediately, he kissed his way down her body and did it again, this time slipping two of his long fingers inside her as he tongued her clitoris.

"Yes, Samuel! Oh yes, sweetheart, yes! Ye-ee-es!"

She raised her head and watched him move his mouth sensuously over the responsive bud. Pleasure built inside her until it was almost painful. The tempo of his thrusting fingers responded to her movements. As she approached her climax she quickened the motion of her hips; his response sent her tumbling over the edge. She gritted her teeth and held onto the heavy wooden headboard as she wrapped her legs around his head and held him against her.

When he slid up the bed to reach for a condom, his beautiful penis was like a dark chocolate roll that had been left in the fridge to harden. Dark chocolate was Emma's *weakness*. She pushed him back against the bed and lovingly wrapped her lips around the head of his penis and drew it into her mouth. His harsh groan filled the quiet room. She held the thick shaft and guided it along her tongue as far as it could go, keeping her mouth soft but applying a firm suction-like pressure on his smooth flesh. She pursed her full lips and let it slip in and out of her mouth, repeatedly. When she stopped to ask him if she was doing it right, using her hands to continue the caressing motion of her mouth, his inarticulate groan gave her all the answer she needed. Eagerly she resumed, intent on giving him as much pleasure as he'd given her. Within minutes he stiffened and quickly pulled her head away as his jerking penis shot a stream of viscous white fluid in the air that almost touched the high ceiling before it fell back and splattered them both. They laughed helplessly for moments before they used two hand towels to clean each other off.

Soon the towels were abandoned as their hands touched the parts on each other's bodies that they had learned, in only days, were the places where caresses gave the most pleasure.

Just after nine, she kissed him lingeringly one last time before she left the room.

The next day she stayed at home to ensure that Andrew

had packed everything he needed for university and to prepare the food for his small farewell dinner party. On a whim she invited Samuel over for the party and also to spend the night in their spare room. For a change, Thomas came home on time to have dinner with his family and she was pleased for Andrew's sake.

Thomas spent most of the time talking to Samuel. Like Emma, he seemed slightly regretful that he hadn't sent Andrew away with Samuel. But Thomas had vowed never to put his child through the trauma of separation he had felt when his parents had left him in Ghana at the age of eleven after a family holiday from the UK, but Emma had been just as reluctant to send her only child so far away. Thomas had hoped that Andrew would get into Oxford or Cambridge but he had just missed the entry requirements.

She listened to Samuel's respectful answers to her husband's many questions and it confirmed what she had known when she had made the decision to sleep with him— that he would be discretion itself—not once during the entire evening did he, by word or action, reveal anything that could make her husband or son even a little bit suspicious of the two of them.

When his other friends had all left Andrew escorted Samuel up to the guest room as Emma tidied the kitchen. Thomas was fast asleep by the time she joined him on the queen-sized bed. She lay in the dark hoping that Samuel wasn't as restless as she was.

The next morning Samuel accompanied her as she drove Andrew to Nottingham to start the first year of his Mathematics degree. As she kissed her son goodbye she realized that finally he was a grown man, not a little boy who needed her. The moment was infinitely bitter-sweet.

She had worn a formal pleated skirt suit to present the

face of respectability to the other parents she would encounter also dropping off their offspring at the university. On the journey back, Samuel discreetly slipped his hand under the folds of her skirt and fingered her almost to distraction. They arrived back in London after eight o'clock and drove straight to the hotel. Samuel went up to the room first; she followed five minutes later.

He was naked and waiting for her when she got there, already wearing the condom and the rings. She didn't bother undressing—she climbed onto the bed, slipped the gusset of her high-waist panty aside and sank onto his hard-as-granite penis. He came almost immediately. She climbed off him and undressed slowly, folding each item of clothing neatly over the back of the sofa before removing another. Samuel's penis jerked every time she turned around and bent to lay a garment over the chair.

When she was completely naked she walked slowly over to the bed, her breasts bouncing sexily with each step. She slipped one of the rings off his erect penis and climbed on all-fours onto the bed. He slid off the bed and pulled her closer to the edge. Separating the swollen lips of her vagina, he carefully inserted his penis and slowly pressed forward. She moaned softly as she felt the extra length pierce her deep inside but she loved the *sweet* pain of it. His hands reached for her breasts and held them firmly as he bounced himself against her beautiful behind. She tipped herself up and on his next stroke he went almost an inch deeper, they both gasped. She ground herself wantonly back against him, moving her hips to match the driving rhythm of his as their moans of pleasure reached fever pitch. She reached a toe-curling climax that immediately triggered his. Then, almost without pause, he turned her onto her back and buried his still erect penis in her warm depths. He kissed her as he withdrew his penis and plunged it back inside her, again and again.

She left him just after midnight, barely able to concentrate on the quiet roads as the memory of their lovemaking sent delicious shivers through her from time to time. For the first time Thomas didn't bother to come home at all. Finally she realized that he had only been making an effort for his son. Didn't he know that Andrew had been fully aware that he sneaked into the house at the most ridiculous hours of the morning? How stupid could he be?

But *now* she didn't have to pretend either.

She spent the rest of the days and nights with Samuel just going home occasionally to do anything that was necessary and to check for any messages from Andrew, although he had her mobile phone number in case he needed to reach her in an emergency. But it seemed as though her son was having too much fun settling in, he hadn't called her since his first night on campus.

The days and nights spent wrapped in Samuel's muscular arms were the most glorious of her life. They were two people simply enjoying the pleasure of each other's body— the past, the present and the future all forgotten. They made love almost to the point of exhaustion, then slept, ate and made love again.

They shared a long bath together the night before he left, uncaring as the water splashed over unto the pristine white tiles as they frolicked in the shea-butter softened water. Finally when they stepped out of the bath, Samuel pulled on a bathrobe and wrapped a towel around her before picking her up and taking her to the bed. He quickly dried her body before laying a fresh towel across the bed and pushing her gently onto it, turning her onto her stomach. Opening the bottom drawer of the bedside unit, he took out a small carrier from The Body Shop. Her eyes widened as he reached into the bag and pulled out a small bottle of sweet almond oil and an even smaller bottle of pure lavender.

He rubbed his hands together, warming them before he opened the bottles and poured a generous amount of almond oil and a few drops of lavender into his cupped palm. He started to massage her body firmly, his large hands paying special attention to her shoulders and neck. When he turned her over, she pulled his head down and kissed him in gratitude before she let him continue. He started with her feet and worked his way upwards to her thighs, lightly running his hands over her pubic hair before he continued up to her stomach and then her breasts. He tweaked her nipples between his lubricated fingers and she watched in amazement as they hardened and grew larger than she had ever seen them. The sight of them seemed too much for Samuel, he cupped one of her breasts and took an engorged nipple into his mouth and sucked on it greedily.

The massage was abruptly ended. He stood up and quickly pulled on a condom. When he reached for the ring she put her hand over his and stopped him.

"Tonight I want *all* of you inside me." It didn't matter if she was sore tomorrow—she just needed to feel the full length of him buried inside her before they parted.

He threw the towel over one of the richly upholstered dining chairs and sat on it, his erect penis jutting upwards majestically. Slowly she lowered herself onto it, gripping his broad shoulders as his penis filled her and filled her. She threw her head back and moaned his name as he sucked hard on her aroused nipples. She moved urgently against him ignoring the dull ache as his penis pushed through her resisting tissue. Finally their hairs met. She paused for a moment as her body softened around the head of his penis before she started slowly bouncing up and down on him, keeping the movement small so that her nipples were within reach of his eager lips.

For minutes she rode him wordlessly, concentrating on the wonderful feel of his penis as it pushed deep inside her. When she began to tire he put his hands under her thighs, lifted her feet off the floor and held her in place as he penetrated her more fully with small, subtle movements of his hips. She came instantly, powerfully, laying her head against his and gasping his name over and over again.

He lifted her and staggered back to the bed still sheathed inside her. For a moment he lay still above her, his eyes staring deeply into hers. Then he kissed her eyelids, her nose and finally her mouth as he used his strong arms, which were still hooked under her thighs, to gently but inexorably pull her legs up further until they rested a little uncomfortably, but not painfully so, on his broad shoulders. He thrust into her slowly but surely, going as deep as it was possible for him to go. And *finally* she felt the full length as he penetrated her to the maximum. Her lips parted and he captured her soft sigh of awe.

They made tender, passionate love all that night and into the next morning. At 10 o'clock they had a shower together to get dressed so that Samuel could catch the 11.15 train but as they soaped each other's bodies in the glass-fronted cubicle their passion ignited once again and they stumbled back to the bed locked together, for a final, *last* farewell session of lovemaking.

He lay quietly on top of her, his arms wrapped tightly around her, his penis buried to the hilt. He kissed her softly as he made tiny, circular motions with his slim hips, leaving the full length of his penis embedded inside her. Her orgasm when it came was the most powerful she'd had. She sobbed his name as her clenching muscles immediately pulled his out of him. He had tears in his eyes as he leaned down and softly kissed her; she wondered if they were triggered by her own.

When she waved goodbye to him as the 14.15 train pulled out of the station that afternoon, she bravely fought back her tears. Samuel had the makings of a great man. Some day in the future when he had attained the heights for which he was destined, she would look at him with pride knowing that somewhere deep inside him he carried a memory of the ecstasy they had shared.

Thomas finally put in an appearance late one Sunday evening, walking into their house unconcerned, and without a word of greeting. She looked at him and realized in shock that she had never really loved him; that he was just a habit to which she'd become accustomed. Calmly, she asked him for a divorce and was amazed by the shock on his face.

Had he thought that she would have continued to live the celibate life of a wife whose husband was clearly in love with someone else? Samuel had made her realize that she still had a lot of passion left in her. At only thirty-six she'd be a fool to waste the rest of her life without the pleasures of a man's body. She intended to find a man to make her happy and she was going to be very choosy about it. She wanted a man who knew how to love, and make love to, a woman. If he was a bit younger than her, that would be perfect, but not so young that it would cause a scandal, she didn't want to embarrass her son.

Did she feel guilty that she had slept with her son's friend? Just a bit. Did she regret it? No. Would she sleep with him again? Probably not, but in ten blissful, fun-filled, rapture-laden days he had given her more pleasure and taught her more about sex than her husband had in twenty years of marriage. *That* was priceless!

***

My loyalties are divided in **Oxford Blue.** *What would have happened if they had been caught? Her son would have never forgiven her and she would have been branded a scarlet woman for seducing a younger man. But didn't she deserve some pleasure in her life? She was an attractive woman still in her prime and though he was a much younger man, he was an adult in his own right. Was she wrong to take pleasure where she found it?*

*****

TELEPHONE SEX

*T*rue fucking story! So sorry I had to use bad language in the opening line but believe me, when you read on you'll understand why I am still pissed off after almost six months. Women, take my advice—never have telephone sex with a man you haven't slept with. Men, if you are reading this— don't make promises you can't fucking keep!

I met Richard at Night Moves nightclub. When he took me in his arms I thought I'd died and gone to heaven, he smelt and felt so fucking good! He stuck his tongue in my ear and told me to call him Dick. My clit started jumping right away—Black men don't generally use that shortened version of their name, so I knew the man was trying to tell me *something*.

First, give me a few minutes to describe this brother. He was about 6'3" with shoulders so wide he must have to turn sideways to get through a standard door. His stomach was flat and he had an eight pack instead of a six. His buns were high—not 'girly' high, but high in the kind of masculine way all you could think of was him riding you and you holding onto his ass like it's a saddle. Yes, *that* kind of masculine. When he smiled he had dimples in each cheek and perfect, white teeth. He had neat, shoulder-length dreadlocks and the man knew how to wear clothes. Fuck me!

We were dancing hip to hip and my clit was smack bang on what felt to me like the biggest cock in London. I know a big cock when I feel one, I have felt several. I mean the thing was long, and it was fat, and it was hard. By the time we'd finished dancing Lovers' Rock my thong was soaking wet. There might have even been a puddle at my feet but I was too busy reaching up to kiss him to be bothered looking down.

I wanted to fuck him that very night but he was too fine for a one-night stand. If I am horny and just want to be fucked, I'll take a guy home after a party, fuck him and kick him out of my bed when we're done. If I want a relationship, by that I mean two or three or sometimes even four fucks, I'll take his number after I've rubbed up on him all night and then call him before the end of the next week. Then I'd fuck him. The little wait would have made him just that bit keener and hornier. He'd feel as though he'd had to do some work to get my pussy and he'd appreciate it a lot more.

As Dick, I mean Richard, and I danced I pressed my breasts against his broad chest so he could get the full effect of my twin peaks as he cupped my ass and rubbed his big, hard cock against my clit. We danced like this until another guy tapped him on his shoulder and whispered a few words to him. He told me he had to leave, so we exchanged mobile phone numbers and a nice, long goodbye kiss.

After he left I looked around the club, it was only 3 am but all the good men had been taken. There were a few stragglers hanging around but what the hell would I have done with any of them?

Frustrated, I left the club and walked to my Saab 9-3

Convertible, which I'd managed to park only a corner away when another car had pulled out as I'd approached the club. I turned the radio on and listened to Choice FM as I raced out of Shoreditch.

I didn't notice that I had a voicemail until I took my mobile phone and house keys out of my bag when I got to my flat. It was from a secret admirer who said that he wanted to do nasty things to me.

I called Richard right back and asked him if he wanted to come over and do the things he'd threatened to do in his voicemail. That's when he told me he was in a car heading for Birmingham, where he lived! He'd only been in London for his cousin's thirtieth birthday; he had driven down with a friend and they were now taking turns driving back.

"Why didn't you tell me that you don't live in London?" I was pissed off and I didn't hide it. When I am horny, I get that way.

"Well, it was difficult to talk with my tongue in your mouth," he reminded me.

He had a point, I am not usually one for kissing or too much foreplay but the man could kiss! He hadn't drunk any alcohol all night—he had bought a Breezer for me and an orange juice for himself when I had finally let him come up for air. His breath had been minty fresh and I'd kept sucking on his big, fat, agile tongue. It had been like sucking on a juicy spearmint cock and I love spearmint.

"I guess you're right," I laughed. "But if I'd known that you were travelling back to Birmingham so soon I would have taken you back to my place. I only live fifteen minutes away from the club. I could have given you some pussy and had you back in the club before your friend missed you."

"Damn! I wish you'd told me this earlier because I was dying to get my hands on that big ass of yours." I heard him speak to someone and then he said, "I have to go now, let me call you when I get in."

I fell asleep with my mobile phone right next to my pillow. I didn't want to miss that call for anything in the world.

He called just after eight.

"Hey, Honey!" God, even his voice was sexy! "What are you wearing?"

"I'm naked." It was true. I had used the fullest setting on my massage shower to pummel my clit until I came. Afterwards, I was mellow but still horny, so I jumped into bed and played with my toys for a while. Another two orgasms had finally taken the edge off my horniness.

"I'm glad you're naked, it means I can start right away, although I wanted to peel that sexy red dress off you."

"I'll let you do that the next time, sweets," I promised.

"Lie back, I want to kiss you all over," he instructed.

"I am lying back, baby."

"Good. I am running my tongue between each of your sexy toes, along your instep and then your ankle. I am moving up the inside of your leg, kissing the side of your knee and now I am moving up your inner thigh and already I can feel your heat. I look up and I see the moisture glistening between your folds. I can't wait any longer I need to suck on the juicy lips of your fat pussy. You are dripping from all that grinding we were doing earlier. I taste your juice and it's sweeter than nectar. I can't get enough of it. I hear you moaning my name as I open your pussy lips and push two fingers up inside you as I suck on your clit."

"Your tongue feels so good on my clit. Suck me, baby."

"You are begging me to put Dick inside you but I want you to cum in my mouth first."

"Oh please, give me your cock!" I was so caught up in

the shit I was begging for real.

"Be patient, your pussy is so tight I can barely get two fingers inside you. I need to get at least three inside your pussy before I can attempt to put my big cock in you. I don't want your pussy to get sore too quickly because once I get inside I'll be there all night."

"See if you can get another finger inside me now, baby. Yes, that's it. Push it in, I can take it. Aaaah, that's so good."

"Not as good as my cock, baby."

"I think you can try your cock now, sugar."

"I am not so sure. What's the biggest dick you've ever had in your little pussy?"

"I don't know—maybe 7½ or 8 inches."

"I've got 10 inches, baby. And if I am really turned on or your pussy is tight this boy can gain an extra half an inch. When he is eager, he gets longer and fatter. Sometimes he gets so fat I can barely get my hands around him and my hands are big, baby."

"Fuck! You are making me want this cock bad! Give it to me, baby. Give it to me now!"

"Okay. You're taking my three fingers well, so I guess I can give you Dick. Spread your pussy for me."

"I'm spreading it, baby."

"That's right! Hold your lips open for me—let me get this big head inside your pussy. Damn baby, you are still so fucking tight!"

"You're right, your cock is big but my pussy is stretching to fit it. Don't hold back, give it to me, I want all of it—I can handle it."

"I am giving it to you, I am sucking on your nipples and you're rotating your hips and slowly Dick is sinking into your pussy."

"God, he is filling my pussy up."

"You've got all of him inside you now—damn baby your pussy is tight!"

"That's right. Now fuck me hard. I've been a naughty girl, punish me with your big dick."

"I slap your big ass twice and then push your legs up. I am giving you the full length and you are begging for mercy but I keep pounding away."

"Fuck me, baby. Fuck me hard!"

"Suddenly your pussy is gripping me even tighter—I think you're going to cum."

"I'm cumming, baby."

While he'd been talking to me I had my vibrator against my clit. As soon as he said the work 'cum', I came.

"You scream my name as you cum, makes me fucking cum too. Dick is spurting gallons of thick cum right inside your pussy but he is still hard. Are you ready for the next session?"

I was still a bit woozy and I forgot to answer.

"Don't tell me you are too sore because I warned you about the damage Dick can do to a pussy. Now he is rearing to go again, so uncross your damn legs and let him get into that tight hole again."

"I'm ready whenever you are, sugar."

"I am giving you Dick again. Damn girl, this pussy is still tight, when last have you had a cock in this pussy?"

"It's been a long time, so I need you to fuck me good."

"After I cum one more time in your pussy I am going to fuck your ass. Have you ever had a cock up your ass before?"

"No," I lied.

How the fuck was he going to know the difference with his big cock?

"I am sticking a finger in your ass to get the ball rolling.

Damn baby, even your asshole is tight, but if you want to be my woman you'll have to learn to take Dick up your ass. I must warn you—very few women can take Dick up their asses, but it's a test you have to pass. Dick loves pussy but when he is feeling freaky he likes a bit of ass. And right now he's getting that freaky feeling."

"I want Dick to be the first man to fuck my ass, baby."

"Dick loves a big ass and yours is nice and fat. Dick is getting impatient I think he wants to get into that ass right away. I think he wants to pluck that cherry in your ass, baby."

"Your finger feel so good."

"You like that—I'll put another one in."

"Yes, stick two fingers in my ass, baby."

"Now I've got two, no three fingers in your ass. I am pulling Dick out of your pussy. He is slick with your juices. I am spreading the cheeks of your sweet ass and putting his head against your tight asshole."

"I can feel him trying to get into my asshole. Push him harder, baby."

"His head is in, his shoulders…damn, baby you've got half of him inside your ass already."

"Oh yes, I can feel him."

"Damn baby, your ass is nice!"

"It's all yours. Fuck me hard and make me cum."

"You're taking the full length now. Your ass is so fucking tight it makes me want to cum again."

"Cum for me, baby—I want to feel your spunk deep in my ass."

"Aa-aa-ah!" I assumed that was him cumming.

"How was it for you?" I asked a minute later. I like a bit of feedback, even if it's telephone sex. I like to know if there is room for improvement or if I am still on top of my fucking game.

"That was nice!"

"Thanks, baby." When Richard said 'nice' I knew he meant 'fantastic'.

"Honey, you are the kind of woman Dick and I have been looking for. A woman we can fuck both ways. Dick is going to enjoy fucking you often. Boy, we're going to have some serious fun!"

That was the beginning.

He called me every night that week and every time he called it was a different scenario. Whenever he was speaking as Dick he would make his voice deep and sexy. It would turn me on so much I had to put my phone on speaker so that I could have my hands free to use my toys.

By Friday evening I was ready to go to Birmingham but he told me he had to fly to Berlin early the next morning. He was a computer analyst for an international company, and he and a few colleagues had to go to oversee the opening of the new branch in Germany.

By Saturday I was like a match—ready to scratch against anything. The man had me hotter that any man had before. I was almost ready to go up to a complete stranger in the street and beg him to fuck me, please. I was even dreaming about sex in my sleep, waking up in the morning my sheets wet like I'd peed the bed. A grown woman like me, strung out like a horny fucking teenager!

I couldn't pull out my little black book because usually when I break up with men I break up with them rough. I just wake one morning and can't stand the sight of them, so I tell them to get the fuck out of my house. If I do it too nicely they think I'm joking so I have to be brutal. The problem is that now I had an itch none of them would scratch it for me. Hell if I was on fire most of them would throw fuel on me instead of water. If I called any of them they would probably say, 'Honey who?' and then slam the phone down with a 'fuck you!' as soon as they recognized my voice.

Well, all of them except my sweetie, Terry. So I dialled his number.

I don't have to introduce myself or wonder if anyone else would answer the phone, Terry was likely to be sitting there waiting for my call. As the phone was picked up I whispered nastily into it, "My pussy's dripping—she needs you—come over now. And don't forget your big cock."

I know you're thinking, How could a man forget his cock? Trust me, he is so eager to please me he could run out the door and leave his cock. And Terry without his cock is of no use whatsoever to me.

He has just the sweetest cock! It is beautifully tapered, big and nice-looking—no ugly veins and as straight as an arrow. It gets so hard you could use it to hammer nails into wood and talk about staying power—he wears me out, and usually I can go all night. For some strange reason I actually like to suck his cock and I will swallow his cum because it's so tasty. I am not one of those women who *just* love to suck a cock. I only suck guys' cocks to get them to eat my pussy because I love a man's mouth on my clit.

After sex Terry doesn't say shit, but during sex I can't get him to shut the fuck up! He asks me the same dumb questions over and over again. "Whose pussy is this, Honey? Am I fucking you good, Honey? You like my big cock, Honey? This cock sweet, Honey?"

Yes, Honey is my real name. Men tell me it suits me—I tell them *I* know.

If I let him, Terry would suck on my breasts all night. Sometimes I go to bed at night with him sucking on my breast, I wake up in the morning and he still has his lips wrapped around my nipple. Fuck! I am not one of you sisters with sensitive fucking nipples. Sucking on my breasts does nothing but irritate the hell out of me. I'll let a brother suck on them for a while to get his kicks if he wants to, but Terry behaves as though it is his full-time job, instead of self-employed accountant. We're in the cinema watching a movie—he wants a suck, I'm in the kitchen cooking—he wants a suck, I'm vacuuming the carpet—he wants a suck, he's driving the car on the fucking motorway—he wants to pull over onto the hard shoulder just for a suck! Sometimes he makes me feel like a nursing mother, and since I can't stand children, I end up chasing his ass back to his house in Chelsea.

I met him at Moonlighting nightclub. Yes, I know what you are thinking—seems like the only place the bitch can 'pull' a guy is in a club. I admit 99.9% of the guys I've slept with I met in clubs, but what's wrong with that? When you see a man in a club, you can check out his moves when he's dancing. If you like what you see, you can dance with him and get an idea of the kind of luggage he is carrying. After all, I can't very well walk up to a man in the street and rub myself against him, can I?

Most of the men who go clubbing are men who leave their wives or women at home and go out looking for adventure. I give them some and send them back when I'm done. Where's the harm in that? Sometimes I don't want a man who hasn't got a woman to go home to because those are the ones who don't want to leave your bed in the morning.

Anyway, back to the night I met Terry. I was eyeing up this tall, good-looking brother who was standing opposite me. The man was sex on legs—but the bastard wasn't checking me! He knew I wanted him—I had made it quite obvious. Honey is my first name; Comb is my middle name not *subtlety*. When I want a man I let him know. So, he knew that I wanted him and he knew that I knew that he didn't want me. It was fucked up!

He stood there looking at me like his shit didn't stink and mine did. He probably thought I was too big, that if he took me to dinner he'd have to order two portions for me. You can't educate fools—nobody had told him that a woman like me would ride him all night non-stop. Yes, I may eat two portions but he could lay back and I'd do all the hard work in bed because I'd have the energy for it. I am built solid, but hell I don't have any spare tyres. I am voluptuous not fat. His fucking loss! He missed some *good* pussy.

Next thing I know some slim 'ho is whiining on him. He is getting his groove on and looking in my fucking direction as if to say, *yes bitch, this is how I like my women—thin!* Well, I wasn't taking that shit off him. I wasn't going to let him diss me like that!

That night I'd been wearing a padded push-up bra under my low-cut dress. My breasts were like pow! pow! Nipples ready to poke a brother in both eyes! Hell, they were turning *me* on every time I looked down and I am not really a 'breast' woman.

Terry, I found out his name later, had been checking out my breasts since he'd walked into the club about half an hour before, his tongue hanging out of his mouth. He was wearing glasses so I didn't have to worry about my breasts accidentally blinding him. He wasn't bad-looking but he was about 5'10" and his feet looked small so I hadn't even considered giving him any play. I believed that whole theory about men's shoe size and height indicating cock size and until then it had worked for me. I figured that Terry's cock was medium sized, one size too small for me. Personally, I find small and medium sized cocks, like tight shoes—uncomfortable!

But the fine brother had left me looking like a jackass so I smiled at the shorter-than-my-ideal-man Terry and he'd run right over like an obedient puppy—tongue still hanging out but now his tail was wagging as well.

The DJ was playing soca music. Usually I use that kind of music to shake my ass in men's faces but the fine bro and his slim 'ho were all up in each other's arms, so I said *tit for tit* and pulled Terry's head down and laid it on my beauties. He started panting, and knowing him as I do now, I am surprised he hadn't whipped one of my breasts out and sucked the nipple right there on the dance floor!

After just one dance he asked me if I wanted a drink. Now that's a brother with some style. Just for the hell of it, I replied, 'Courvoisier neat.'

He ran to the bar and came back with a treble or a fucking quart of some amber liquid and I smiled to myself. If he thought that he would bring me Three Barrels or some other cheap shit I'd throw it in his face because I know my brandy. I took a sip and it was the real fucking thing!

And he kept buying. I had left my car home that night, so as fast as he was buying I was throwing them back. *I* don't worry about date-rape drugs. Any fool who drugged me and fucked me when I'm out cold, better fuck me again when I come to the next morning, or I'd kick the shit out of him!

After we had danced a session of Soca and then Reggae they played some Soul. I put my arms tightly around him and we started to grind. I was wearing my favourite 4" Pradas and although it made us about equal height our hips didn't fit flush and he kept bending to rub his face across the top of my breasts. Anyway, we were dancing and he was rubbing something hard and long against my thigh which I assumed was his thigh bone. I thought nothing of it and just kept grinding.

And oh, by the way the fine-ass brother who had dissed me earlier? He didn't go to the bar once all night. I saw the slim 'ho go and get herself a drink twice but he never even bought himself a glass of water. Maybe he drank her saliva—he had his tongue deep enough in her throat. Even if he was a Christian and didn't drink, or a Muslim who was fasting for Ramadan, he could have at least paid for her drinks. The stingy bastard! Yes, I watched him all night—the fucker was mean but he was still fine! I wouldn't lie, if he had pushed that slim 'ho off him and called me over, I would have dropped Terry and taken her place against that hard body in a flash. What can I say? I am a sucker for fine men.

Terry hooked up my drinks nicely. I can tell you he spent a tidy bundle at the bar that night. When he asked if I wanted a lift home I said yes, of course. Why wait in the cold to pay for a cab when I could get a ride home for free?

When we got outside the club, sweet man that he is, Terry told me to wait just by the entrance while he went to get the car—he didn't want me walking too far in my high heels. When a shiny, metallic-blue Lexus pulled up to the curb next me I was thinking, *you still got it, you sexy bitch!* Then Terry stuck his head out the window and told me to get in.

Seeing the big ride I suddenly think to myself, *he's been so sweet, he deserves some Honey.* And nothing makes me more willing to share my sweetness than a nice big car.

"Do you want me to come over to your place?" I asked, sensing that he was the kind of guy I'd fuck at night and then sneak out and leave before he woke up in the morning. I sensed that he might be an 'overstayer' so my place was definitely off-limits.

He nodded eagerly and we were on our way. He didn't say three words throughout the whole journey but he was a good driver, so I rested against the plush headrest and had a light snooze to re-charge my batteries.

His semi-detached house was very stylish. He had a plasma television set, serious hi-fi equipment and the biggest CD collection I have ever seen. I could tell his furniture was ultra expensive. He definitely had a bit of dough.

As soon as I got inside I was rearing to go. "Let me suck your cock."

I thought I'd do the decent thing and give him some head rather than let him frustrate me with his cock. A medium-sized cock is okay for sucking but not for fucking.

He dropped his pants and my jaw dropped! Good thing too because I had to open as wide as possible to get his juicy cock into my mouth. Minutes later we were in a 69 and he was sucking on my clit like he was hungry. He got me so hot I couldn't wait for him to stick that cock inside me and when he did, *hmmm*!

I am not saying that I have some kind of tight pussy. I've been taking big cocks since I was sixteen but I had to let Terry ease that jumbo cock into me slowly. If his cock had belonged to any other brother he would have had to register it as a dangerous weapon and get a licence before he discharged it. But Terry was very patient. He took his time and worked that cock into me. It touched places in my pussy I never knew existed and I have *personally* explored my pussy many times.

Then he started to suck my breast real hard, like he was trying to get milk. I thought, *this guy is a freak,* but hey, by then his cock was way up in my pussy and he could have done anything he wanted. Every now and again he raised his head and gave me a little kiss and then went straight back to sucking on my breasts—he seemed to have a problem deciding which one was his favourite—he kept going from one to the other, trying to make up his mind.

We fucked for about two hours solid and then slept. When I got up in the morning I had me some more of that big cock before I had breakfast, which he served me in bed. We literally fucked all day and when he dropped me home late Sunday evening, I was wearing one of his T-shirts, no underwear, nipples and pussy sore like first time.

He would be my man if he wasn't so frigging boring—if he talked less when we are fucking and more when we are not. He has the biggest cock I have ever had—I have seen a few bigger in porn videos, though it may have just been the angle of the camera. He makes a hell of a lot of money, has a nice house and two sweet rides I drive whenever I want. He treats me well and takes me to posh places I could never afford on my rubbish salary. But he loves the missionary fucking position. He likes to have a nipple in his mouth when he's fucking so even when I'm riding him I have to face forward. I prefer to ride him the other way around, so that his cock goes into my pussy at an awkward angle and feels even bigger but after only two minutes like that he always begs me to turn around.

And he likes to ask me for sex. Damn! Throw me down and have your wicked way with me! Drag me by the hair, hit me over the head, anything but ask me for it! Sometimes I'll say no just for the hell of it—even if I am dying for his sweet cock. Bad enough that he asks me for it every time but it is the way he asks that really makes me want to slap him. He always asks, 'Can I sex you?'

Not can I fuck you? Can I screw you? Or can we have sex?

Damn! He knows I hate when people use the word

'sexing' instead of 'having sex'! How can a man be an ACCA and not remember that shit? Unless, he is doing it deliberately to annoy me—maybe, somewhere inside my big pussycat lurks a lion!

Being an accountant he loves figures—he certainly loves mine. So if I need sex or I'm in-between men I call him. He'll come over and give me a nice session and leave when I want him to. A long time ago some woman gave him a bit of a complex about his big cock just because she couldn't handle it. Yes, she was one of you tight-pussy sisters! I sometimes hope that he gets a nice woman who would appreciate him as well as his cock because I am too much of a hardhearted bitch. But I'd really miss his cock if I couldn't get it when I needed it, so maybe not!

I had a bath, dried myself off and worked some Chanel No5 body lotion into my skin. Then I touched my pulse points with the perfume and slipped into a sheer, lacy bodysuit. I was ready for him. Terry always buys me real nice perfume. The last time we went to Blue Water Shopping Centre he had bought me the Chanel No5 set. It has a crazy effect on him. If I wear it when we go out, he'd be hard all night. Sometimes we have to leave early because I get worried that he would do permanent damage to *my* cock being hard for so long. Yes, his cock is mine!

Within an hour and a half he was knocking at my door. I walked slowly over and opened it. His eyes almost popped out of his head when he saw my new bodysuit. *I* was busy checking out the four heavy Marks and Spencer carrier bags he had in his hands. There was easily a week's worth of shopping in them. And the good stuff too. The man knows how to appreciate a woman's curves. He wants some meat to hold on to, not bone. He knows that I didn't get to this size chewing on some fucking celery or carrot sticks.

We quickly put the shopping away and jump into bed. We didn't have to waste too much time with foreplay—he was hard before he walked through the door and Richard had me wet all week.

We started off with a 69, I needed to cum fast and it took too long to get his cock inside me. He hadn't seen me in a couple of weeks so he was ready for a quick draw, aim and fire—*draw* his cock from his boxers, *aim* it at my mouth and *fire* whenever he was ready.

With the warm-up out of the way Terry and I got down to some serious fucking. And as usual, he barely got the head of his cock inside me before he started, "I missed this pussy so much, Honey, did this pussy miss me? Honey, I've been dreaming of fucking this pussy. Oh Honey, this pussy is so sweet—"

He would have gone on but I quickly stuck a nipple in his mouth—that kept him quiet. I missed his cock too, but you don't hear me asking him any questions, do you? I don't mind a man asking me a question or two while he is fucking me but having a whole conversation. Out of fucking order!

Me, I'm a silent fucker. I don't have time to talk while I'm fucking—the only time I open my mouth is to suck the man's cock or issue instructions if the dumb fucker can't get shit right. You know—words like 'right there' to a clueless fucker, 'harder' to a timid fucker or 'faster' to a lazy fucker.

I hoped Richard wasn't planning to bring that conversation shit to bed when I finally got my hands on him. He should know that telephone sex was for the telephone, because I certainly didn't need *another* Terry.

Later Terry and I cooked a nice meal together. That's what I like about the brother; he could handle his business in the kitchen as well as the bedroom. We went back to bed, ate the food off two trays and fucked again before we took the empty dishes back to the kitchen. I like to try and burn the extra calories off before they get a chance to sit on my already-perfect hips and ass.

When Richard called me from Germany that night, Terry was on top of me giving me his big cock, his mouth on my nipple. I knew he wouldn't make a sound, so I didn't even let him stop while I took the call.

Sunday he helped me clean my flat and we had one last missionary fuck before he left at eleven in the evening. And you know the last thing he did at the door? Yes, he had a suck! I kissed him goodbye and the next thing I know he is pushing up my T-shirt for one last suck—he had to say goodbye to the 'nipps' as well. Sucking my breasts is the one thing he never asks permission to do.

Richard came back from Germany on Tuesday and it was telephone sex for the rest of the week. When I asked him if he was coming down on the weekend he started hemming and hawing. I got pissed off. He was pulling my strings, jerking me around like a puppet, playing me like a fucking piano! I started wondering if he had a girlfriend—not that it mattered by then, I just wanted to be fucked! All I wanted were those 10 *fat* inches he promised me. I know some of you bitches with your little tight pussies are thinking what is it with this bloody woman and her big dick obsession? All I can say is that if you've never had a dick inside your pussy that was so big you felt it in your throat, you haven't lived! What's a little pain? Come on—no pain, no gain!

Me, if I had me some money I'd quit my job right now and go on a world tour looking for big cocks. So far I've only had Black cocks but I would jump on a cock of any colour if it was big enough and hard enough.

Hell, watch this space! Reality TV is becoming trashier by the minute; soon some bright spark will think of one involving big-cock men. I'll be the first contestant in line. Don't worry, when you watch the show you will recognize me—I'll be the sexy, voluptuous sister with the fucking permanent smile.

If I want to be tickled I get a feather, when I want to be fucked I get a big cock. Even before I started fucking I made up my mind that I only wanted men with big cocks, I knew no small dick would satisfy me. If a man drops his trousers and I don't like what I see I tell him plain, *hell no!*

Once, I let this brother, who had been hitting on me non-stop at work, take me for a nice dinner at an expensive restaurant and then back to his flat for a bit of nookie. When we got naked he handed me his prick (I can't even call it a cock it was so small) to suck. I asked him, '*Do I have something stuck in my teeth?*' He replied, puzzled, '*No, why did you ask?*' I said, '*Well, I thought that was the reason you handed me this fucking toothpick!*'

I refused to let him stick me with it. Fuck, the tip was so thin it was like a pin, it might have punctured a vital organ inside me and I could have bled to death. I swear my clit was bigger than his cock; I could have fucked him with it and given him more satisfaction than he would have given me with the cock he must have stolen from a spider monkey.

I mean I was grateful for the lovely, expensive dinner but not *that* grateful.

Even though my pussy was wet and I was horny—I work in the same office as the brother so I don't curse and go on bad, like I am fucking dying to! I just climb back into my clothes and ask him to take me home. Then he started grabbing me like he wants to beat me, asking me if I was going to leave him like that? Like what? Was *I* the midwife who delivered him and mistook his penis for the umbilical cord, and snipped most of it off? Fuck no! I pushed him out the way and took the night bus home because I hadn't walked with enough 'vex' money to get a taxi back to my flat. I didn't even worry about some stranger ravishing my sexy body on the way home because I knew that *at least* the man would have a bigger cock than he did.

Didn't he ever look down at himself? How could he not know that he should keep that shit to himself and not go showing it off to other people like he was proud of it? If there was a legal minimum requirement of cock size for an adult male, his ass would have been charged the maximum penalty for being *undersized*. Hell, I would create a law just to keep people like him off the streets, endangering innocent women. I was surprised that his bathroom didn't stink of urine. *Maybe* he sat down to pee.

I would have let the matter lie, he had paid a lot of money for the dinner. If he had come back to work and kept his fucking mouth shut, that would have been the end of that. But *no*, the next week at work he was bragging to the guys how he had given it to me good and all of them were looking at me like I was the biggest 'ho around. Don't get me wrong, I don't mind people thinking I am a 'ho—it's a badge of honour I wear with pride. Hell, if he'd had a big cock *I* would have been the one bragging at work that he had fucked me because I like people to know I'm sexy and that men can't resist me. But he deserved some punishment for putting me through the trauma of looking at his tiny tackle. I mean the thing had given me nightmares for two whole nights after I'd seen it. Had me dreaming that some mysterious disease had killed off all the big-cock men and there were only small-cock men left in the world. *That's* my worst nightmare. Forget falling off tall buildings without a parachute, being eaten by lions or bitten by venomous snakes—those things don't scare me half as much as a small-cock man!

So the next time he was standing with the guys at the coffee machine, puffing out his chest like the *pea*cock he was, I walked right up to him and held up my thumb and index finger just about an inch apart, in his fucking face, for all of them to see the length of the stick he'd apparently beat me with all night.

He called in sick the next day and when he finally came back to work two weeks later, he walked around the office like a neutered dog. Still, it could have been worse, if I'd indicated the girth, or in his case *the mirth*, he would have had to resign. I felt a little bit sorry for him but that's what he got for messing with me. As I said before I am rough on men—if they fuck with me, I fuck them up!

***

Finally I told Richard that I was coming to Birmingham if he didn't come to London, so he agreed to come down but suggested that we had dinner and a chat first.

I took a cab and met him at the restaurant. He looked even better than I had remembered. The restaurant was quiet and we had a corner to ourselves. As we were waiting for appetizer, which *he* ordered, not me, we shared a few kisses. Then a few more as we waited for our main course. I was wearing a skimpy black dress and he slipped me a finger as we kissed. Usually I love food more than sex but the feel of that big finger reminded me of the bigger *finger* he'd promised me, I wanted to say forget the damn food.

Anyway, we finish eating and I thought he'd ask for the bill. Instead he ordered dessert, and took his time eating the large slice of lemon cheesecake. I had to tell him that we'd get coffee at my place before he ordered that too. Delaying fucking time.

We got stuck in traffic and he promptly stuck two fingers

in me as we crawled behind an old Ford Fiesta.

"You're so wet, baby." He used Dick's voice and I almost came, but just as I was about to, he had to put his hand back on the steering wheel to go around a corner.

Finally, we got to my flat and he slipped my little black dress off me. That night I hadn't worn underwear—not wanting anything to get in the way of his big cock and my wet pussy. He bent, took one of my nipples in his mouth and rolled the other with his fingers.

"You got fat nipples, baby," Dick said as he made his way down to my shaved pussy. "Damn girl, look at the way this pussy is pouting its lips like it's angry. Nice!"

I was so glad he liked it because it had taken me the whole day to get over my first and most definitely last Brazilian. The woman who owned the salon must be into some serious S & M—she meant to pluck out every last stray hair from my pussy before I left. I can't believe I actually paid her to enjoy herself. Bitch!

But it was worth it as Richard started giving my pussy a serious tongue lashing. He *ate* my pussy—not tentatively like some men do as if they are scared it would live up to its name and scratch them, but like he was enjoying a banquet. I had known that he would have been good with his tongue from the way he'd been kissing me at the club and the restaurant, he didn't disappoint in the slightest. But that was fore-*fucking*-play, I wanted the fucking! When he pushed his sweet, big tongue up inside my pussy, I couldn't wait another second. I reached for his belt but he held himself away and whispered, "Patience."

I wanted to say, the name's Honey not Patience, but I lay back and let him have his wicked way with me a little longer.

When I reached for his crotch again he pushed my hand away saying, "Not yet."

"Not yet, what?" I asked impatiently. "I want to hold it."

"Let me make you cum first."

That was the worst thing he could have said to me. I faked that shit in no time.

"Now give me my 10 inches." I sat up, impatient to see Dick, to feel Dick, to taste Dick and to have Dick in my pussy. 10 inch dicks are like UFOs, many people claimed to have seen them, but until you see one for yourself, you are a sceptic. Deep down I was a 10-inch-dick believer. I couldn't wait for my first sighting.

He slowly undid his belt. "Actually, I lied about the length, it isn't that long."

What? I almost had a heart attack!

"What about the fucking girth, did you lie about that too?" I asked angrily.

"It's fat but *not* that fat," he replied.

"You know what—just show me the fucking cock." I was beginning to get really pissed off. I had been so looking forward to meeting that *big* boy.

He dropped his trousers and came to lie next to me on the bed, his boxers still on. Of course, I fish the cock out in no time. It was flaccid, that's not a word I can even spell but it jumped right into my head when I saw his piece of dead wood. And I mean dead! I thought maybe it was playing, so I poked it—it didn't move. Thinking it was a recent death I decided to give it CPR. I put Dick in my mouth and blew him till my jaws ached. Nothing! I rubbed Dick between my breasts until I nearly chaffed my skin. Nothing! I put my finger up Richard's butt. You guessed it, nothing!

How could a tall, big-footed, thirty-three-year-old, prime beefsteak have a penis that is not only small but also doesn't work? How is that possible? Even if he was fucking every day of the week since he was twelve he should still have something in reserve. Then he tells me that he had some kind of viral infection the year before and sometimes he can't get an erection.

So I was like, "You had a viral infection *last* fucking year, so what the fuck are you doing here with me *this* year? Getting me all hot and bothered and then you tell me this shit. When we were having dinner or *before* you started sucking on my clit—*that* was the time to reveal your *fucking* infirmity. NOT NOW!"

I swear if he wasn't a big guy I would have punched him in the gut, hard. Thank God he'd paid for the meal because I would have had to hit the non-fucker as big as he was! Then I remembered the nightclub and the big dick he'd been swinging that night.

"How come you got an erection that night we were dancing in the club?" I asked like an idiot—usually I have more sense but I think by that time the no-big-Dick drama had fucked up my brain.

"That night you really turned me on, baby," the bastard lied with a smirk on his face.

Fuck that bullshit! What I felt in his pants that night in the club was massive and even if that matchstick of his did get erect it could never get to those proportions. Trust me— he must have had a dildo or some kind of fake cock down his fucking trousers that night!

If I wasn't a strong sister, the man would have had me undergoing some serious fucking therapy right now. Imagine him trying to make out that his dick was as dead as a doornail because *I* wasn't fucking turning him on! The way his tongue was all up in my pussy drinking my juice like it was fine wine, the way he was sucking on my breasts and running his hands all over my hot body—the fucker couldn't get enough of me! He was turned on like a light bulb—he just couldn't find the switch to turn his cock on too! I don't care that the man was fine, the fact that he couldn't raise to the fucking occasion was nothing to do with my body or my performance. I know I am damn sexy—men tell me so all the fucking time. Shit, sometimes when I catch a glimpse of myself naked in a mirror I have to ask myself, *who is that sexy bitch staring back at me?* I would definitely fuck me if I was a lesbian. I am legendary when it comes to fucking. I leave men when I get fed up of them, not the other way around. Grown men have cried when I've told them I'm not giving them this pussy anymore.

So there we were—me naked, pussy dripping—Richard sitting on the bed in his black silk boxers—Dick hiding in shame.

I just said, "Excuse me, Richard and you too Dick, while I fuck myself since neither of you is up to the job."

I took out my biggest dildo and plugged my tired-of-waiting-for-his-big-cock pussy. The dildo felt nothing like I'd imagined his cock would, though the way I was faking multiple orgasms he didn't know that. He sat on the bed and watched me until I had to tell him not to let the door hit him on the way out.

What could he have possibly been waiting for? Maybe he'd been sitting there praying for a miracle. Didn't the fool know that prayers could only heal a *sick* Dick not a *dead* Dick? What pissed me off is that he came all the way to fucking London to *not* fuck me! All I had was the brother's first name and his mobile number—it wasn't as if I could have found him in a big city like Birmingham. I don't think the name of his cock would have helped narrow the search if I had done a house-to-house, do you? So why would he travel all the way here just to embarrass himself?

Men! If I could find me a nice big dildo that smelt like a

cock, felt like a cock and could squirt like a cock, I would strap it on to a woman and we'd be on! It would last as long as I wanted it to and cum when I wanted it to. I wouldn't need men and their tired-ass dicks.

But in the meanwhile, at least I have sweet Terry!

***

I wrote **Telephone Sex** *because I have found that most men who brag about their sexual expertise never seem able to perform when put to the test. Some boast that they are well-endowed...and they are...when viewed through magnifying lens.*

This story is a prelude to my next book **Bedtime Erotica for Freaks (like me)** *about seven women just like Honey, who follow their sexual destinies and damn everyone else! A book for the open-minded sexual connoisseur.*

*****